TWO SUMMERS OF BILLY MORTON

Two Summers of Billy Morton

Barry Stewart Hunter

First published in 2018 by
Martin Firrell Company Limited, 10 Queen Street Place,
London EC4R 1AG, United Kingdom

ISBN 978-1-912622-01-6

Typeset in Baskerville and Calibri.

For Rob

'A man has got to learn everything –'
JOSEPH CONRAD, *The Shadow-Line*

PART ONE

Among the Bodies

Chapter One

Gouache

I DIDN'T NORMALLY NOTICE THE SEASONS – whether they stuck around, how they came and went. I left that to poets and doomed lovers (who often turned out to be the same people, or so I read on the back of a book), and to my Dad, who noticed everything now that he was nearing the end of the road.

It was late, late summer. *See, Billy, how the flowers in Holland Park is climbing over each other in their hurry to fall down and die.* Her name was Véronique. She was French – that's all I knew then. At the time it was enough to know just that. There was nothing more I needed to learn. I didn't try to find out about her. Mostly she was in my last thoughts as I endeavoured to fall asleep, or in my first dreams after I did. Who knows where these things begin? Who knows which day is the day that counts before all others?

One morning as I was rolling up the sleeves of my jacket (at chest height across this garment, a kind of janitor's uniform I loved, the fingerprint stains from the processing liquids we used paraded like medals) I saw Véronique appear below with three sketchbooks under her arm. Soon she began to draw. I was looking down on the sunlit scene from the hatch of the storeroom where I worked. The storeroom was a giant cupboard at the bend in the stairs above the doors to the college. You could see a lot from there. You could see the students arrive like corduroy kings and velvet queens sporting scarves and gloves and hats regardless of the season or the weather. I watched Véronique, smartly dressed, rather grave, document the statue of David in the lobby. She sat cross-legged on the flagstones with her sketchbook perched on her lap and her crayons spread out in a thoughtful arc like a fan alongside her. She didn't look like the other students. She looked as if she didn't care what people made of her. She looked like she already knew people had a high opinion of her – as if they always had. Then the weasel student (I had seen him around the place, always by himself, never with the herd) knelt down beside her and examined her drawing and admired it. You could tell he was admiring it by the way he nodded, and she smiled, in a pattern or a sequence. She wasn't convinced. I could see she wasn't persuaded by his flattering comments. She had introduced a frown into their sequence. From now on it was a nod and a smile, then a frown, as far as she was concerned. Perhaps the weasel boy just wanted to shaft her. You couldn't blame him for that. Abruptly he jumped up and began to declaim as if he was in a play. He was practically shouting now, as if he intended what he said to go down in history, as if he wanted the gods to hear it one more time before striking him dead. Look at me, he was telling us. Behold – a bullshit artist. Some people are arseholes first to last. Others are in a hurry to harm their reputation or to undermine their status long before you do it for them, particularly if they are clever or ugly or both. I could see the weasel boy wasn't pretty. I knew that already, and so did he. He was no oil painting. Véronique saw it too, of course. But (together with me and much of the civilised world) she didn't know how smart he was. Not yet.

'Hey, beautiful French art student in London – can I buy you an absinthe after school? Can I do that, love? Might I do that, pet?

Because I fully intend to paint you naked in line with an established European tradition, and we should probably think in terms of, say, gouache at this early stage, shouldn't we?'

This was in September, at the start of the college year. A low sun stole through the branches beyond the towering sash windows of the lobby and pierced my chest and ran amok in the photographic storeroom behind me, scraping cameras, scratching lenses.

'Gouache?' she said, exploring her part now, amused but wary, as if taste and judgement still mattered where she came from, or as if she wasn't prepared to sanction a new idea at any cost.

'You don't approve?' The weasel student grinned. He didn't smile, he grinned – which is to say there was something about him that was hard to like. He hooked his thumbs through the hoops on either side of his belt buckle and planted his desert boots wide apart like a gunslinger. He didn't stand a chance – he had a puny beard about two inches long curling down from his chin that you wanted to yank all the time.

'Toulouse-Lautrec,' she said, cocking her head as if weighing up a shortlist of finely balanced naming options plucked discreetly from a history of modern art. 'Taller and thinner, perhaps, but that wouldn't be difficult. No, I really don't think you should paint me naked, Toulouse-Lautrec.'

'Give me three good reasons why not.'

'Well, you're way too forward, for one.'

'You don't think it's just a brave front?'

'You're also on the wrong side of the line. I mean the line of beauty. Which brings me to the third reason why I don't think you ought to paint me naked. Don't you think you risk looking a little pretentious, or foolish, even, standing there *without any clothes on* while the paint drips from your brush?'

I saw the weasel student hang his head and tug his beard and nod. 'Ah,' he said, 'a kind of play on words – we like that. There's also the subtle sexual implication of the dripping tool you cite. At least you didn't say *little* brush, which is sweet of you.' Now she held out a hand and he took it and pulled her to her feet. He helped her gather up her crayons and, as she turned away, he called after her. 'I suppose a preliminary study in charcoal is *hors de question* –'

She was gone. I could no longer see her from my vantage point on the landing. The clock buzzed on the storeroom wall beside my head. Soon it would be time to open up the store. All this is fixed in my imagination, or buried in my memory, ready to be recalled day or night like a boyhood slight or a perfume. Every voyage begins in sunlight, with the people waving their goodbyes from the headland and a coastline glinting on the horizon. That's how I want to think of this whole episode or affair and the mess I managed to sail right into. That's how I prefer to view it – in sun. There was a queue of third-years waiting to collect the equipment they had booked out from the storeroom. Their patient line went up the wide steps from the landing to the studios above. In the lobby below me the weasel boy lingered alone, outlined in gold, with head lowered and arms lifted towards heaven. Suddenly he did a funny thing, or a couple of funny things. First he slapped the replica buttocks belonging to David. Then he looked up at the landing and winked at me. I put it to you now – can a wink be trusted? With that small, sly gesture of concord and complicity the gouache king actively sealed my fate.

CHAPTER TWO
The Only One

JANUARY ARRIVED AND I KNEW I WASN'T ready for her. She was sixth in the queue, with a tartan scarf in one hand and a rolled-up newspaper (it was a French newspaper – although I couldn't see it clearly I knew it was French) in the other. I didn't look at her, not directly. Instead I busied myself with the students in front of her, gripping, for example, an earmarked tripod and sliding it carefully across the storeroom counter alongside a scuffed MPP field camera and a couple of double dark slides before registering the items and initialling the log book in the right-hand column, as required to by Jacobson, out of respect for the apparatus. It was about respect for things, he said. If you couldn't honour a mere *thing*, what might you be like when it came to cats and dogs? Or people, he meant – that was plain enough. We had the best equipment money could buy, Jacobson insisted. If you were intent on carving out a vision of life in art then you had better have the right tools for the job – that was where he was coming from when he tried to explain it, his world view as seen from our storeroom. I don't think he was interested in art or visions. He was more interested in life and death, and what he called human progress or the lack of it. He had turned his back on God, he said, but only after God got in first and pulled the same stunt. To Jacobson every political idea or belief system you cared to espouse counted for less than our cameras or lenses or tripods with their noble names – Leica, Manfrotto and Sinar. His faith in the college's photographic toolbox had the strength of a physical truth, but it had very little to do with shutter speeds and apertures and focal lengths, it seemed to me. It was a kind of love. It wasn't about, say, the heart-rending sensitivity to light of silver halides, or certain chemical reactions in a blacked-out chamber. It was about you and me, and how we might live.

'Hello,' I said. 'What can we do for you today?' She was there, by herself, in front of me. She might have been with someone else, chatting and laughing, but she wasn't. What do I remember that was different? Nothing. There was the same fine dark hair, not too long and not too short, which she let fall across her face and then tucked away gracefully behind one or other ear (in this simple but equivocal gesture, at once involuntary and contrived, I imagined I saw reconciled all the petty contradictions of the soul) and the same dark brown eyes, sadder somehow than they had any right to be. There was the same well-bred face, open and interested, with the same nicely judged mouth, teeth, tongue and lips. It was wrong of her to look as good as she did and not be a thoroughgoing bitch.

'Véronique Lamartine – I booked some equipment out. At least I hope I did.'

I turned away and consulted the log, running my finger down the pages as if I didn't know what she had ordered. I had seen her name in there. I knew exactly what she had ordered. I held off for as long as I could because I wanted to give her enough time to clock the paperback novel I had positioned, after much deliberation and a few misgivings, at the edge of the counter.

'Here we are,' I said, sneaking a peek at the hatch. 'That's the Nikon F body with the 35mm f/2.' I bent down to collect the camera and lens, which were waiting where I had put them, on the bottom shelf beside the film fridge. 'Do you need any stock to go with that?'

She didn't come back to me about the film. I could see from the log she had used up most of her free units. Her scarf was around her neck now. She had her newspaper tucked under her arm and my Kensington & Chelsea Library copy of *Devil in the Flesh* in her hands. It was a silly idea to plant the Radiguet novel under her nose like that. It was Toulouse-Lautrec's idea – I swear it was. It was pure T-L. Again and again in the course of two or three uncomfortable seconds I cursed my clever new friend. But the strange thing was this – Véronique seemed to sense it wasn't my fault. Or maybe that was just the way I read it. She put down the novel. Then she looked right through me.

'Which one interests you more, Billy – the devil or the flesh?'

It was a perfectly reasonable thing to ask in the circumstances. There was nothing remotely smutty or cheap about Véronique's question. Coming from anyone else it might have sounded like a provocation, or a proposition, but she made it seem like a choice between apples and pears.

'I don't know,' I said lamely. 'How about neither, which is to say both?'

She put down her newspaper and picked up the Nikon, and as the newspaper fell open I saw a French headline that used the 'Tet' word about six inches high. Véronique pointed the empty camera at me and fired off a couple of notional frames and now it felt like a provocation. It didn't feel like a proposition, but that was OK. That was all right.

'Let me know when you come down from the fence,' she said, slinging the college SLR, the single-lens reflex, over her shoulder and scooping up her sexy French newspaper.

'Did you know you've nearly used up all your free film units?' I asked her like an idiot.

'Yes, I did,' she remarked coolly. 'That is probably why I won't be drawing any stock today.'

She had uttered my name. It was a useful start. As I shouldered my tripod and my backpack and set off southwards on foot towards the river I played the tape of our conversation over and over in my head. Conversation is too strong a word. Dialogue is far better – I see that. There was the unhappy matter of the Raymond Radiguet book to consider first. In dangling the novel in front of Véronique, without having read it, I had made a schoolboy error. I blame T-L. I didn't need to read the book, he said. No one else had read it, but everyone else had an opinion about it, so it was enough just to be associated with it in a generalised fashion. It ticked the boxes, T-L said, by which he meant it said Francophile and sophisticated, and said it in capital letters six inches tall. Perhaps I had got away with it. Doubtless I was beating myself up about something no one else would have bothered about. I had tried to trick Véronique, or at least to fool her. I had behaved in a way that was inauthentic (when I put this to T-L he told me it was acceptable, or necessary, or even desirable, to be inauthentic on the journey towards authenticity) but she, intelligent and perceptive creature that she was, had rebuked me only lightly. *Let me know when you come down from the fence.* She had left the door open. I was to *let her know.*

I quit the King's Road and followed Oakley Street and the rush hour cars crawling south. It was only half-past five, but all the headlights were on. On either side the white faces of terraced houses took on the early pinkness of street lamps, and behind the windows of the raised ground floors the rocking horses roamed in an electric heaven. It was frosty – I could see my breath. I pulled up my hood and adjusted the load on my back. Across the river, floating low over Battersea Park, the moon was small and hard with a corona of astral fog around it. You could see the moon's breath.

There wasn't really a plan as such. By the time I got close to Cheyne Walk I could smell the foul river at low tide. In front of me, lovely Albert Bridge was lit up like a little Las Vegas or a budding Blackpool. The bridge was just an excuse. It was the river, running slowly, bending blackly, which drew me on as it always did, as it always had done. To lean, looking east, from its bridges and spit at police launches and refuse barges and watch my spit carry like gull shit towards St Paul's and the sea – then I was content. Then my hair was in my eyes and my heart was in my hands and the river whispered – jump, don't jump, fly, don't fly. Then I was the only one. The cruel city was mine.

There is a plaque on the south side of Albert Bridge that tells marching troops to break step as they cross the river towards this or that battle in Chelsea or Fulham. It was next to this directive that I planted my tripod on the pavement, facing due north now with the brilliant bridge before me. I unfastened my backpack and took out the Gandolfi, beautiful camera so dear to me, and folded out the lens plate and mounted the box on the tripod as rapidly as I could. I don't like to make a scene. People are kind, but I don't as a rule like to draw attention to myself. My hands were getting cold because I didn't have any gloves on. Even so, I worked quickly. I took off my coat and threw it over my head to cut out the light as I examined the image – upside down, laterally reversed – on the ground glass screen at the back of the camera. I had the bridge in prospect. I had the illuminated girders in my sights. I took a meter reading and worked it out from there – a full minute's exposure at f/8, allowing for reciprocity law failure (when the light falls below a critical level all the silver particles suspended in the film's emulsion cry out for extra time). Now the curious cars were slowing and the cyclists rang their bells and it was time to take the picture. It would be a new self-portrait with my Mum.

'Excuse me, sir –' I called out.

'How exactly can I help you?'

The man was leaning towards me, framed by the car window. He was pushing fifty, maybe, with slicked back hair and glasses. He had braked hard and then stopped. He had to reach across from the driver's side of his car, the smoke from his cigarette making him squint, in order to wind the window down further on my side. Now the traffic leaving the bridge behind him was honking, and he had to pull over on the pavement just beyond me.

'Hello, sir – any chance of giving me a hand here?'

'I should think so, yes. Why not? Why not, indeed?'

'Only, I need someone to hold the shutter open while I stand on the bridge with my Mum.'

'I see. I see. The boy stood on the burning deck –'

'He did, sir – with his black and white Mum.'

I stood at the plane of focus with the lights of the bridge all around and hugged a life-size blow-up of my mother (this image I had mounted on hinged plywood for ease of transportation) as we counted out the seconds together, me in my head, the rush hour fairy with his watch. For a full minute I stood motionless, as relaxed as the situation and the creeping cold allowed, while the lights of the crawling cars traced their passage in streaks across the surface of the film. As for my mother – she seemed relaxed enough too. She had on her jacket or short coat of fake ocelot. The Berlin Wall of her hair rose up thickly lacquered from her forehead to scrape the lowest stars. In black and white her red lipstick smile hovered, sensuous but decent, in a region just beyond slate grey.

'That's a big tripod, I must say. I wouldn't want to lug that monster all the way home.'

'It is big, yes. But it's not as heavy as it looks.'

'How far have you got to go, son?'

'Not too far – North Ken or Ladbroke Grove.'

'Perhaps I can offer you a lift –'

'If you want.'

'I think you know what I want.'

'Your motor's facing the wrong way now.'

'How much is it, anyway?'

'It depends, doesn't it?'

'Come on, then. It's cold.'

From the ashtray the crushed cigarette continued to give out its smoke. Even so, you could smell the leather inside the car, the leather of the seats. In the glove compartment was a small round tin of boiled sweets dusted with powdered sugar. I took one of the red pastilles – the driver had two.

'Gift from the wife,' he told me.

'Lucky you,' I said. 'Smashing –'

I went up the steps, the few communal steps, and opened our front door. The hall was dark. The house was in darkness. I waited for a moment at the bottom of the stairs. I could hear my father's snores, disrupted now, from behind the living room door, which was ajar.

'Son?'

I closed the front door, heart heavy. I knew right away what was happening, upstairs and downstairs, in our little house. I had the feeling my father had just been pretending to be asleep. I am quiet in a house, any house, at night. I don't think I would have woken him up. Or maybe he had waited for me to come home and then drifted off, despite himself, on the settee in our living room.

'Only me, Dad.' I laid my tripod down on the carpet next to the skirting board. On the wall in front of me was a painting, once popular with my absent mother, of wild horses on a moonlit beach. I took my rucksack in my arms.

'Billy?' He was standing at the edge of the door, three quarters in and one quarter out of the room. I couldn't see his face. Only his loose vest was plainly visible. He still had most of his clothes on – I could see that much. 'The two of them is upstairs, son,' he said.

Above the pale vest his presence was deeply shaded. Was it cold? Was he cold? I could hear the dull clicking of his belt buckle against the edge of the door. He was twisting and then releasing the door handle as if he was trying to get in or out of the room.

'I know, Dad,' I said. 'Go back to sleep now.'

At the top of the creaky stairs in our house were two bedrooms and a bathroom. All three doors were shut. I waited on the landing, but I couldn't hear anything. Then I heard it – the deep murmur of his enquiry, the stifled laughter of her assent. They must be talking about me now. In my bedroom the curtain hung quite still at the open window. There was no wind or breeze out there – there was only the frost and the same old moon. I closed the window and, when I pressed my forehead against it, the glass was too cold to feel. Beyond the glass the gasometer squatted on the sombre bank of the canal like a time machine whose systems had run down. All its lights had gone out. The navigator was missing, presumed dead, in North Kensington – now the machine would never go home. I spilled the contents of my backpack on the mattress. There was the Gandolfi camera, all hardwood and brass, which gleamed in the moonlight, and the dark slide, black as midnight, which housed the exposed sheet of Plus-X film. The collapsible portrait of my mother I opened and slid behind a wardrobe piled to the ceiling with boxes that never got taken down and suitcases that never got used. Inside the wardrobe were the three big bottles – old lemonade bottles or American cream soda bottles – that held the liquids (developer to exhort the shy image, stop bath to put a lid on that process, fixer to render the image stable in light) I respected, trusted and loved. I had a thermometer and a one-bar heater. With these indispensable tools, plus a cloth to wipe off the thermometer, I set about bringing the chilly chemicals up to so-called room temperature, which for photographic purposes is sixty-eight degrees Fahrenheit, by the light of a bare bulb. I still had my duffle coat on.

In our small, windowless bathroom I laid the three little trays side by side on the floor of the bath. I turned the key in the door. I didn't have to worry about someone switching on the light from the landing – you operated the bathroom light, and a droning air vent, using a cord hanging from the ceiling inside the room. Nevertheless, I rolled up the damp towel and pressed it against the bottom of the door to stop any stray light leaking in from outside. Everything was ready. Hello, darkness. It was important to move quickly – soon the liquids in their plastic dishes would begin to cool down again. I slid the single sheet of Plus-X film from the sheath and slipped it into the developer bath and began counting, one-crocodile, two-crocodile, while I rocked the dish gently to bathe the emulsion in a uniform way. When I got to sixty seconds I stuck my thumb out to mark the first minute. After two minutes I stuck a second finger out, and so on (each of us arrives at his or her own preferred method of counting silently and accurately in the dark) while the developer coaxed and cajoled the latent image into revealing itself, as yet unseen.

I heard a knock, very soft, at the door. I heard the handle go, too. You can't come in. Not now, not yet. I called out in a whisper, but the residual droning of the ventilator was too much. As to why I was whispering inside the bathroom of my own house, I can only imagine it didn't actually feel like my home. How else to explain it? I opened the door and drew Dad inside. I had to do it in a way that was both gentle and firm. There could be no other way. No light came in – none to speak of. I sat my father on the edge of the bath. Now he was whispering too.

'Will you take a drink, son?'

I could hear the whisky in the bottle as he shook it close by in the darkness. I could smell the whisky. 'No, thank you, Dad – I'm all right.' We were together. We were bound together by pity and shame and a quiet disgust. What at? Each other? All the time I was counting, counting. I lifted the film from the first tray and shook it and plunged it into the second tray and then the third.

'Are you doing the toilet there, Billy Morton?'

'It's OK, Dad – you'll have the light back on soon.'

Soon it would be safe. The film's emulsion – soon it would be stable. Suddenly the drone of the ventilator dropped off and in the roaring silence we heard it – the sound of love, very physical, from beyond the nearby wall. I pulled the cord. The light came on and the ventilator whirred, and in the same instant the soundtrack of love was banished, drowned out.

'That's quite all right, son.' My father offered up the bottle and I shook my head. 'That's just your stepmother bringing home a little bit of bacon.'

'She's not my stepmother, Dad.'

'I know. I don't know what she is.'

'It doesn't matter – not tonight.'

'Did you see it, son? The first snowdrops is in Holland Park.'

I put the whisky on the bedside table in my room. I peeled back the blanket and watched as my father lay down on my bed. Immediately he rolled away, his eyes shut, towards the pictures on the wall. I closed the door and went back into the bathroom and fished my sheet of film from the fixer and shook it off and when I held it up to the light I exulted. I washed the negative under the cold tap at the basin until my hand was numb – all the time I was listening for the further music of love and asking myself what I was going to do about it. I waited for them to come out, but they didn't do that (turning off the tap I admitted it – I was glad they hadn't). Later I lay downstairs on the settee under a quilt of moonlight, and then pulled my coat up to my chin. As I waited for the man to go I counted the stars above the cranes on the Westway. I tried to think of something nice, but it was difficult. I thought about Véronique, of course. It was already my habit to devote a special interlude to her on this or that side of midnight. I thought, too, of my mother – watcher over my Dad from behind the wardrobe, and subject of a new double portrait with me. In my mind's eye I only ever saw her in black and white. I don't know when, at what time, the client, or the punter, left our house. The moon had scarpered by then, and an uneasy peace descended slowly from upstairs. So little was right, so much was wrong with the world – with my world. Something had to give – a blind man could see that.

CHAPTER THREE

An Alternative Guide to London Living

'MAY I REMIND YOU I AM ALREADY IN possession of a manifestly ludicrous name? I have no need of a silly sobriquet, sunshine.'

We were sitting more or less opposite each other but at different heights on a ridge of stuffed coffee sacks rising up from the floor of Toulouse-Lautrec's room in the Gloucester Road squat.

'Marshall Marshall?' I said, positioning a nail carefully on the upturned biscuit tin clamped between my ankles before striking it once with a claw hammer. 'Just as well they didn't give you a middle name too.' I looked up then, eyes widening with sudden possibility. 'They didn't, did they?'

'Don't worry.' Toulouse-Lautrec laughed and shook his head. 'It's Thomas.'

'Marshall T. Marshall – you know exactly where you stand with a name like that.'

'Pressure to succeed, my son – there can be no other rationale for my parents choosing such a moniker, so unapologetically self-serving and tautological. A fellow must make his mark with such a name, don't you see? A chap should journey to the moon with a handle like that.' T-L raised his scalpel in the air and described the lunar mission's would-be trajectory with a bitter slash. It must have been around midday, but the shutters were closed at the great bay window, and the only light leaked from an arrangement of paper cups, brought together ingeniously to create a kind of conceptual daisy since variegated with scorch marks, which clung dangerously to the bare light bulb hanging from the ceiling at the centre of the large, empty space. 'How can a mere mortal hope to live up to such a name?' the weasel student complained. 'How might he manage the burden of expectation?'

'I imagine you've given it a fair bit of thought over the years. The fact remains she insists on calling you Toulouse-Lautrec.'

'She won't let me paint her. Life is cruel. But she's French and must be forgiven.' Discarding his artist's scalpel, T-L laid the latest fragment of canvas on the floorboards beside the others and raised an empty picture frame in front of his face. 'What do you make of this, lover boy?'

'Ah.' I tilted my head this way and that in consideration of the weasel features corralled surrealistically by a wooden rectangle. 'It's a reasonable likeness, I suppose. And yet –'

'And yet?'

'I can't help thinking it flatters you, if you want to know.'

'Intriguer!' At once Toulouse-Lautrec scrambled to his feet and stamped his boots. 'I invite you here to my gaff – to the inner, so to speak, sanctum. I make you privy, without strings, to all manner of esoteric knowledge.' He nodded sternly at my pierced biscuit tin. 'How to make an inspirational yet eminently practical lampshade –' He snatched up a portion of canvas and held it like a mask over his mouth and nose. 'How to salvage a decorative masterpiece from an indifferent still life –'

'Oh? How's that?'

'Using creative cropping, *mon brave*. It will all be in our book.'

'It will? Which book is that?'

'Why, it's our alternative guide to London living, of course. Survive the slings and arrows of outrageous capitalism on a budget. Chock full of hipster's tips – the *Daily Sketch*. No self-respecting squat should be without a copy – the *Manchester Guardian*. Here – take one damaged canvas from a junk shop in Kensington Church Street. Liberate most attractive fragments of said canvas from ugly frame, and reframe to create miniature gems with resulting profit. Indispensable – the *Mirror*.' T-L flopped down on a sack and rolled off it and stretched out on the floorboards, eyes shining. 'Time for another,' he announced breathlessly, reaching behind to locate the bag of weed and lobbing it over his head towards me. 'You do the honours, squire.'

'Not for me, thanks.' I didn't want to smoke a second because I was still feeling sick from the first. What I wanted was to be alone in a city park or municipal garden with a large-format camera and certain delicate snowdrops to hand. 'Is that enough holes now, do you think?'

The weasel boy raised his head and examined the biscuit tin through narrowing eyes before flopping back down again, evidently content. 'Don't you dare grow old and wise on me, Billy Morton,' he whispered, closing his eyes and folding his arms momentarily across his chest. 'Are you hungry?' he went on, rolling towards me and fixing me with just one eye. 'Because I'm ravenous.' Suddenly he was on his feet again and plotting aloud. 'First, we flag down a Saturday omnibus. Naturally, we invoke pretty girls on our quest for victuals with potential to match our constrained budget. We feed your imagination with cake, and possibly Mallarmé, and we forget about those beastly Americans for an hour or two.'

'I thought it was the Russians –'

'Look – I want to show you something.'

He seized the biscuit tin and ran to the door and switched off the overhead light, and I heard him plug something in at the wall. It was a table lamp without a shade – when T-L switched it on with my pierced biscuit tin held over it the walls and ceiling shimmered with improvised stars.

'Have you actually slept with a member of the fair sex, Billy?'

No doubt it was right to ask these questions, at once coded and blunt. It was always going to be necessary to field them. There was the loaded reference here to the fair sex, which seemed to take for granted the idea or the fact of sleeping with a less fair sex. That was fine. That was T-L. That he was one step ahead of me at any given time was something I took pleasure in. I never resented it. I didn't begrudge him his smartness verging on cunning. I wanted more of it. And, in any case, we had struck an unlikely bargain – its nature and spirit coloured everything we said and did.

'You can take my silence as an admission of guilt. I mean the answer to your question is no.'

'Guilt? Doctor Freud will see you now. But you're OK by me, honey pie, because big boys don't brag.'

'Can we focus on the matter at hand, please, as in the future not the past? As in exactly when and how am I going to do it with Véronique Lamartine?'

'You don't need to know my plan. You just need to accept my terms, and I think you already agree to them, right?' T-L passed the biscuit tin over the table lamp again. 'See that, Billy-boy? With enough of these stars we could give heaven a run for its money.'

We caught the number seven towards Bloomsbury and sat upstairs above the driver with the windows open, and as the cigarette smoke dispersed I began to feel better. T-L amused himself by scribbling

MAN IS CONDEMNED TO BE FREE and ONLY COMMUNISTS ARE PRETTY in capital letters that read backwards through the heavy condensation on the glass. You couldn't really see out. Every time you wiped the window it steamed up again. At the gates of the British Museum a group of demonstrators waved their handwritten placards at us – they wanted us to help protect an ancient valley in a faraway country from the sons of America dropping their leaflets and their bombs. Suddenly there was the smell in the air of chestnuts roasting at a pavement burner. It made me feel happy, but when I looked at T-L I saw he was crying over some unscheduled beauty or a humiliation or injustice that had been served on him young. I didn't ask. It seemed wrong somehow to intrude on his moment of maximum authenticity. Then someone sitting behind us asked us to close the windows, and we looked at each other and bolted towards the stairs and jumped off the bus at the lights.

'So you've already done it with Véronique, then,' I said finally, holding out for T-L's denial. To go where he led, to follow in his gifted footsteps – doubtless that was my role in our relationship as he saw it. We were sitting at a Formica table against the wall in the L-shaped refectory at the School of Oriental and African Studies a short distance from Russell Square. It was still lunchtime – we had to shout above the hungry roar.

'Billy, please – that has nothing to do with our arrangement as I recall it.' It was the idea of Toulouse-Lautrec boring into her that struck me with unexpected force as I paddled my broth distractedly with my spoon. It was the notion of T-L boring into anyone at all. The weasel boy – he was altogether too *pointed*, surely, for that soft assignment. 'Unless,' he said, 'you want to make it an integral part of our understanding.'

'Meaning?'

'We could both do it to her at the same time. Oh, Billy – you poor, sweet thing.' T-L pushed his soup bowl away and shook his head and threw a pellet of bread at me across the table. 'As if she'd let us.' He was shedding his skin again. He was slipping or sliding – always ahead, ever in front. 'Oh, dear – I only came here to gossip about Cocteau and Stein. Or anyone else you care to mention. But the truth is you're not likely to mention anyone at all because that charming little head of yours is stuffed with f-stops and film speeds and, well, not much else. Ah – shall we talk about Cartier-Bresson?'

A muscular youth (he was black – I don't know if there is any way to tell you that other than by saying it, and I don't know if it matters whether I tell you, or whether he was black) who had been plating up food behind the counter approached our table now and presented us extravagantly with a large portion of carrot cake. He had on a tight T-shirt with the usual portrait of Che Guevara.

'Oh, my giddy aunt, Marshall – won't you introduce me to this pale urchin so easy on the eye?'

T-L sighed ostentatiously for my benefit. 'Lancelot by name, lance-a-lot by nature –'

After we had finished our cake the weasel boy lit the remains of a cigarette he had picked up outside the British Museum. 'Don't let Lance fool you,' he said. 'Seems his old man is banged up in the Congo or some such paradise while young Lancelot here takes up a journalism scholarship at our very own College of Printing. Plotting a coup back home, probably. Thinks he's Martin Luther King –'

'So?' I didn't want to give anything away. Any sense of anger or resentment or hurt I might have felt at T-L's casual put-downs I set aside. I don't mean for a rainy day. There was little in the weasel boy's extreme brand of cleverness – brave and funny and cruel – I wasn't ready to accept, warts and all, come what may. It seemed to me then as it seems to me now – you take it all or you take nothing at all. 'Bully for Lance,' I managed. 'More power to his elbow.'

'So Lance *prints* – and that could be a very useful thing to the aspiring editors of the alternative guide to London living. Want to hear the scam, Billy? First, you contact dear Mama to ask if she'd like her daughter's name to appear in our directory – for a small consideration, naturally. That's the debs' directory, in case you're wondering. Then you simply print the posh names up in our lovely brochure and cash all the postal orders and Bob's your uncle. Who cares if it's not quite the vehicle they had in mind?' T-L sat back in the local silence. 'You don't believe it will work?'

'Please don't imagine you really know what's going on inside my charming little head,' I said calmly, evenly. I wasn't truly riled, I don't think. I just needed to state my case for the record.

'Now we're getting down to it,' T-L came back, stubbing out his secondhand cigarette with a shudder of distaste. 'Look, Billy. I don't know what it is with you. Or, rather, I do. Shall we see if I'm getting warm? I know you want to bed our Véronique – at least you say you do – and I know I agreed to help you do it. What is it with her, anyway? She's some kind of unattainable ideal? She's going to rescue you from yourself? Is that it? We don't know. We don't care. We only know that as soon as you ball Véronique we get to bang you, Billy-boy. Now, you can walk away from that at any time, but you're reluctant to do so because, deep down, it's what you want. Are we right so far? Know what? You need to stop lying to yourself and start being who you are.' He leaned closer and cocked his head sardonically (when I think of this I commute sarcastic to sardonic in order to be kinder to history) and stroked his puny beard. 'Not that Billy would contemplate reneging on a deal – *any* deal. Hell – he'd walk a million miles to avoid going back on his word.'

A flashbulb popped. At the back of the food queue a group of Zulu warriors milled about with ceremonial spears and zebra skin shields. It was impossible to know what they were – a stag party beginning early or an anti-apartheid delegation lunching late. The celebratory flash went off again. There were whistles and cheers – one way or another we were a part of these.

'I really like you, Billy. I *know* you. Guess what? You'll be all right. You don't need my help. Trust me – you're the tops. Take a look in the mirror, why don't you?' At this the weasel boy reached inside his sports jacket and extracted a strip of card. 'Here – come to a special screening at the Film Co-op.'

The title on the ticket meant nothing to me. 'I don't know that film,' I said.

'Of course you don't,' T-L said. 'Oklahoma it ain't.' He stood up and pushed his chair away emphatically, as if to signal a turning point had been reached. 'She'll be there. Véronique will be at the screening – in case that still interests you at all.'

'How do you know she's going to be there?'

'I imagine she's going to be present because she's invited me to introduce the film.'

'What – she's asked you to make a speech?'

'Someone has to stand up and be counted.'

I watched him pick his way through the tables on the way to the counter and when he got there he gave something to Lance at the till. What – cash for cake, or a directory of debutantes? Then he looked back at me across the animated dining hall and cupped his hands around his mouth and yelled.

'Billy, love –' he said. His hands came down. He was camping it up for the Zulus. The large room fell rapidly silent. The bemused warriors had their trays in their hands. They had laid down their spears and shields. 'It's all over between us, Billy. Our arrangement is O-F-F, cancelled, withdrawn, because –' Here T-L paused in the service of melodrama. 'Lordy, lordy –' He hung his head and shook it slowly and sadly before he looked up, grinning at the fascinated world and at me. 'One day you'll thank me for this, I know.'

I walked and I walked. As I went, my thoughts were up in the air, or all at sea, or both. I followed the route of the Central line from Tottenham Court Road at Oxford Street towards Marble Arch and Speaker's Corner, dodging Baptists with bibles, ducking prophets with pamphlets, and hugged the north side of Hyde Park, skirting Bayswater on the way to Notting Hill Gate. My bargain with T-L – it was an ugly business. It was a sordid affair – I admit that. I won't try to excuse it except to say I had entered into it in good faith and for a just cause. That cause – it was me.

Portobello Road has a kink in it. There is a pronounced bend in the road at about the point running north where the handsome houses give way to the famous street market. I sat down there on an antique chair with horse's hair spilling from it like entrails until the manager of the shop came out and asked if I was all right or I was ill. People care. They don't want trouble from passing strangers.

It was T-L's fault. It was T-L who had made a good thing go bad. That was his talent. I had to be clear. I had to get it straight in my head, then and forever (some choices strike you immediately as cursed, and half a lifetime isn't enough to undo their damage). To me it was simple. If I could make it with Véronique I could make it with anyone – any girl. We would do it once and it would stand for all time. It would go down in history. I would be OK. I would get on with life, doing it with men, or doing it for money, which didn't count. But T-L *knew* me. He actually said that, did he not? After I asked him to help me (I really just wanted to be his friend) he knew I would consent to his terms because it would force me, or free me up, to confront what I was. One day I would thank him, he'd said. Not for ditching the deal, but for proposing it in the first place. Oh, T-L – you would screw anything.

I had left behind the antique furniture section of the market and reached the upper ground and now I could see Jacobson's stall, or rather I could see Becky manning Jacobson's stall, in the shadow of the Westway. I had to wait for a funeral procession to go by. The procession had a musical theme. There was a yellow wreath behind the glass of the hearse in the shape of a violin, and the women that followed, superbly veiled, were like operatic beekeepers. What did it mean? Surely it meant something. After the veiled women came the weeping men with three white whippets on a leash.

'Where's your Dad?' I asked, kissing Becky's hot cheek with my cold lips.

'Gone to fetch a tea,' she said. 'Here – you can share mine.'

She had on her big army surplus coat, which she unbuttoned now in order to wrap me up in it, and I remember shrinking, stiff with self-knowledge, from her sweetness. We stood there side by side behind the trestle table, waist deep in photographic equipment labelled Brownie, Ensign, Praktica, Perfekta and Voigtländer. There was the neon sign saying Ilford, plus stereo and 3D curiosities and pretty much anything with a folding bellows design for whole-plate or half-plate format. Alongside the daguerreotypes and the framed cartes de visite was the box of old prints wrapped in cellophane that Jacobson attributed speculatively to Fenton or Atget or Sander or Julia Margaret Cameron according to the prejudices of interested parties. What I enjoyed most was the life-size cut-out of the Kodak girl in her shorts looking cheekily over her shoulder (inspiration, of

course, for the portable blow-up of my mother), which was marked
DISPLAY ONLY because Jacobson refused to part with it.

'I'm not stopping, Becky,' I said.

'Oh – I thought you might help us pack up.'

Hanging from the end of my nose was a bead of snot, which
Becky wiped away with a glove. As I say – she was sweet. She even
smelled sweet, like a warm kitchen on Sunday morning. She had a
sunny smile and a red birthmark at her throat in the shape of the
Caspian Sea. She was a loving and dutiful daughter, and I knew I
had to end it between us right away.

'Will you tell your Dad I'll be round at yours to print a new
negative? It's a beauty, tell him.'

'I'll tell him as long as you promise to tell me.'

'Tell you what?'

'When we're going to do it –'

'I thought you said you wanted to wait.'

'Did I? I don't remember that.' They were packing up the stalls
on either side of us, and now the street lamps were coming on. I
saw a bulldozer on the flyover behind Becky hunker down under a
tarpaulin of purple sky. 'Is anything the matter, Billy?' she said.

In my pocket was the ticket T-L had given me – ticket to the
screening of a film I didn't know. It had meaning. Even then the
ticket meant something. On the one hand it was a kind of pay-off.
It was T-L's way of drawing a line under our grubby deal. It was
also a passport to another world, the world of T-L, of Véronique –
as such its significance was sensed rather than understood. Had you
told me it represented the key to a door between the past and the
future I wouldn't for a single moment have doubted what you said.
I hadn't looked at the ticket. I kept touching it. I had the crazy idea
it had cut me – a little paper cut at the tip of my finger, in the worst

place, the most awkward, debilitating place – but when I checked, finally, everything was all right.

'Nothing's the matter,' I told Becky. 'We can do it whenever you want.'

<u>BILLY</u>

It begins with Bobby Kennedy. It has to start somewhere, so let it begin with a newsprint photograph on the wall of my bedroom in North Kensington in London in the year 1968. You already know this modest room, which has a teetering wardrobe inside it and a rusting gasometer outside it. There is a youth – no, a young man – on the narrow bed pushed up against the wall below a collage of pictures. How to be sure of his voice after so much silence? How to make the past live again, to make history news, without betrayal by false memory, a burdened imagination, the recriminating heart? The young man in the room is listening to his radio, a transistor radio complete with batteries and earphone. Will you envisage me now on this narrow bed, face turned from our house towards the wall? I am scanning a suite of monochrome cuttings of the Kennedy clan, but in my mind's eye I see T-L and Véronique and Becky line up – their heads, at least – like clowns at a fun fair inviting you to toss a ping pong ball into their open mouths. What does this image mean? If we can't justify it or explain it without recourse to voiceover we must abandon it, remove it. Surface details are what we must focus on in order to recreate the texture of the times. That's why I return to the black and white pictures on the bedroom wall. That's why I cite the song on the radio, whatever that song turns out to be.

Clockwise from top left – JFK in the Oval Office at the time of the Cuban Missile Crisis and the Bay of Pigs debacle, then Jackie in a one-piece swimsuit in happier days on the deck of a yacht off

Cap d'Antibes (I don't want my father, or anyone else, to conclude my interest falls exclusively on the Kennedy *men*), then the clincher, a stolen telephoto shot of Bobby jogging barefoot and shirtless at the edge of the Atlantic with a devoted hound on one side and the incoming tide on the other. It is this image that catches our eye and holds our attention as the radio, buried under my pillow but wired to an earphone, announces the appointment of Alexander Dubček as First Secretary of the Communist Party of Czechoslovakia, before reporting that Ali, the boxer, has refused the draft. The Radio Lux signal wanders again, but when it returns more strongly with Mrs Robinson I know we have our song. Is it Mrs Robinson, or have I misremembered that? No matter – I am more than happy to accept it begins with Mrs R, the clamour of world events, and my tender feelings towards Robert Kennedy. These contextual reference points I affirm and approve. I don't expect to recall more than that here, given the distance between my old room and where I am now. We know how it begins – with a picture on the wall and a song on the radio. How will it end, if not with madness and with fire?

CHAPTER FOUR
The Pressure Project

ON TUESDAY TOWARDS THE END OF MY SHIFT I closed the shutter at the hatch and locked it temporarily, taking my brush and pan with me upstairs to the still life studio. In addition to my roles as photographic storekeeper and sometime processor of colour film on behalf of our students I was also a willing cleaner of studio spaces, darkrooms and other shared resources. I didn't mind the cleaning detail – I enjoyed going among the lucky boys and girls with their hipster talk and their smart ideas about art, love, peace or freedom. That they never got round to debating these subjects in a manner hipster, smart or otherwise, at least not in my presence, preferring to smoke alone or to consume snacks avidly in laconic huddles on the stairs or in the corridors beside the lockers, didn't matter. I gave them the benefit of the doubt. In all likelihood they had spent their night in heated discussion, and now they were merely regrouping or recharging intellectually. With my janitor's coat, targeted heavily by institutional stains, and my brush and pan, I could never be one of them. Even so, I had my place within the student body. I had my road to run, just as they did. Had we all been made to stand, naked and white, against a wall, with a dove of peace in our hands, which of us would have been picked to put an end to war? No doubt that was the type of thing they kicked around once I was out of earshot.

Tuesday at college meant pressure project day for second-year photography option students. You collected a brief first thing in the morning, delivering a finished piece of work – a 35mm black and white contact sheet, say, or a 10x8in print, or a 5x4in transparency for processing – by the end of that working day. So, good morning, reportage loving people – this week we want you to document a day in the life of one of the capital's great railway termini. Greetings, still life devotees – for today's pressure project we ask you to deliver an image of advertising quality on the theme of fish and chips. All morning and all afternoon the brave second-years had marched up the stairs in front of my storeroom armed with reeking foodstuffs wrapped in newspaper. It takes time to conceive, compose and shoot an image to marketing standards. Thus it was that fresh and cooked produce, arranged and rearranged with wonder under fierce lights all morning, had wilted before lunch, so that replacement subject matter was required and sourced throughout the long session.

'Fancy a cold chip, Billy?' asked a weary student sitting cross-legged on the floor of the still life studio at the end of the day with his congealed supper spread before him. On the table above was a map of the British Isles made up of hard little fish and thin chipped potatoes with here and there a pickled onion of the small, pale type denoting London or Glasgow or Belfast.

'At least no one goes hungry,' I said either too casually or too earnestly, accepting one boy's kind offer in my desire to please all. There was glamour in what they did – even their detritus had a type of glamour for me. As I swept up around my poor, tired second-years I wanted to be them. Naturally, I couldn't hope to cross the Mississippi between us unless I had a guide, unless someone invited me to shoot the rapids as either partner or passenger. Only T-L had come close. Be more like you are, he had instructed, by which he meant be more, I concluded, like you want to be. Doubtless it was only the first lesson in a lifelong programme of study, but in this I was a model student, a fast learner. T-L's brief, and my own private pressure project, was to be truer to myself each day. That Tuesday afternoon I felt it more keenly than ever – the need or the desire to break with the past, here represented by random glimpses of Becky, in favour of the future, which was all T-L. No, T-L and Véronique. 'The still life studio will close in ten minutes,' I called out.

Before printing my new negative I wanted to check on Dad. This much was honest and true. On the packed bus home I read my Radiguet (it was only right I assign this slim novel, already part of my story, an ongoing role in my sentimental schooling) alongside a striking woman with a beauty spot quivering on her cheek and a chihuahua shivering in her roomy handbag. The woman read her bible aloud and chain-smoked No. 6, directing the blue smoke away from the dog towards me, until she got off, still spouting psalms and puffing away righteously, at Earl's Court. This was how it would be from now on. Every encounter brimmed with portent.

'Hello? Anyone at home?'

There was a profound silence in our house. I started up the stairs to collect my negative, and then, cursed or blessed by second thoughts, I went back down to the living room and crossed the dark space towards a suspicion of light that glowed beyond the full-length curtains and the sliding doors to the balcony. He was sitting on a stool in the doorway of a hut shaped like a sentry box – a cubicle that had housed his beloved pigeons until they flew away one day – with his sheepskin jacket around his shoulders, a metal torch in his hand, and what looked like a copy of *Penthouse* on his knee.

'Come inside, Dad. You'll catch your death out here.'

'I don't believe so as such – not tonight at least.'

'Where is she, anyway? Is she out?'

'She's gone out. She's away out –'

'Please come inside now.'

'I will, Billy, I will. What are you reading there?'

'A kind of love story.'

'Ah – me too, me too.'

'Shall I bring you a blanket?'

'Thanks, son – we'll be getting the television again, so we will.'

'That's good, Dad. I'm very glad.' You could smell the pigeon smell. The pigeons had gone away, but you could still smell them. You could smell their shit – a hard, dry smell I had long ago tied to the idea of dying. 'Can I bring you back anything to eat?'

'I don't think so. Well, maybe. You could fetch me a bite of something hot from the darkie.'

The 5x4in negative with paper sleeve was in my hand as I climbed the spiral staircase at Chalk Farm station. Outside, a cold rain was falling – I held the delicate parcel inside my coat until I reached the big house in Adelaide Road with its raised porch set among creamy pillars and Jacobson's van drawn up above the pavement and wall. I could smell the meat in the pan before Becky opened the door.

'Don't tell me –' she said. 'You're not stopping.'

I shrugged off my coat and let it fall across a chair in the hall, but Becky scooped up the coat and hung it on a rack designed as a musical stave with a treble clef at one end and a notation of hooks or pegs in the form of crotchets and quavers. I didn't trust that rack to support a coat fully. To me the coat rack, whimsical, structurally suspect, set the wrong tone for the rest of the house. It was a dark house lined with deep red wallpapers or fabrics, heavily furnished in a traditional style and dressed with so many ornaments of obscure provenance that the effect was iconic, almost religious. To me the house was a refuge, or a sanctuary. When I was cold it was warm in there. When I was hungry there was always food on the table.

As Becky led me downstairs we heard her father call out to say supper was almost ready. In the cellar, which was also a darkroom equipped with running water and safe lights, the chemicals waited for me in three trays standing on a duckboard in a vast sink. First up was the exposure test strip. I placed my negative in the carrier of Jacobson's hallowed De Vere enlarger, tore off a two-inch strip of Grade 3 paper, and gave it five, ten, twenty and forty seconds, my hand exposing the paper to the light beam in cumulative tranches, with the lens stopped down to f/16. I can't really say how or why it happened. As I focused on the image of my mother growing rapidly denser in strips in the developer I felt Becky approach from behind. She wrapped her arms around me and then, virtually in the same movement, slipped her hands inside my underpants at the front.

'Five minutes,' Jacobson called out cheerfully from the top of the stairs.

When I turned round Becky sank to her knees and got to work on my trousers, loosening my belt and undoing my fly with the quiet determination that was her trademark. My first instinct was to halt her progress in order to return to the test strip, now floating fully developed in the dish, but within a second or two Becky had my cock in her mouth, and I resolved, in the name of authenticity, to let nature take its course. As expected, and in spite of Becky's best efforts, there was precious little development down there – I mean there was no firm basis for negotiation – so I helped her to her feet, pulled up my pants, and apologised using a few simple words.

'Don't you dare apologise,' she said. 'I should never have taken matters into my own hands like that.'

'It's probably because my mother is watching,' I said, picking up on Becky's tone and holding fast to the comic line.

After that we worked chastely as a team, giving the full image nineteen seconds on Grade 4 paper for additional punch, and then observing patiently side by side as the familiar magic took place in the developer dish.

'The mystery dame –' Becky said. 'At least we know who she is now.'

'She's the Kodak girl grown up. Does it matter who she is?'

'You don't think it's a bit weird – or sick, even?'

'What?'

'Taking self-portraits with your dead mother.'

We heard Jacobson call out again. 'Come and get it,' he said.

'She isn't dead,' I said. 'Not to my knowledge, at least.'

'Pity. I thought you might care to be a founder member with me of the dead mothers society.'

'She's probably on a large yacht somewhere nice – off Cap d'Antibes, for instance.'

'We'd better go back up. How's she looking, anyway?'

'She looks pretty good. Not sure about her son, though –'

After he lit the candles Jacobson reached out across the table to locate our hands before improvising a grace that made reference to absent friends, family, and the fruits of the earth. It was a typical Jacobson meal – heavy on the cutlets, with a selection of strangely matched vegetables giving off steam in an enormous bowl. 'And how is it, Billy? Your photograph?'

'It's sharp, and the negative – even with the reciprocity – isn't too far out, exposure-wise.'

'It's of Albert Bridge after dark,' Becky said. 'With a mystery woman in tow.'

'Ah, another in the series of large-format portraits,' Jacobson came back with the note of universal respect I loved. 'Shall we sell them on our stall, Billy? How many are there now? Six? Seven?' I saw the lights reflected in the black river at low tide. The soldiers marched, the bridge collapsed. I saw Becky smile at me across the table. It was all right. It was OK. Jacobson was still speaking. 'They have a convincing quality, these pictures – the irresistible force of a firm intention,' he told me. 'Don't ask me what it is, Billy. It is you. It is you.' Now he was pouring the wine into his cup. 'The mystery woman – there is nothing mysterious about her. She is the one for whom you would do anything or go anywhere.' I saw the candles, or their reflection, flicker in his interested eyes as I prepared myself for another of his meditations on life or death or human progress. Suddenly he unbuttoned his shirt at the cuff and pushed his sleeve up and there it was – a serial number tattooed very crudely on his forearm. How could I have worked with Jacobson and not seen it before? 'Do you know what this means?' he said. 'Of course, you do. Do you know what it tells me? It tells me who I am. Don't be afraid or ashamed of who or what you are, Billy. That which makes us different makes us strong.'

'Dad –' groaned Becky, gathering up the dishes and stacking them noisily in front of her.

'Did you know I used to be a taxidermist, Billy?' Jacobson went on even more purposefully. 'Exactly. It doesn't matter that I once stuffed people's pets for a living. Find the thing that marks you out most, and be that. Photograph that –'

Becky rose and left the table with an armful of crockery. I was thinking about all the stuffed animals I had seen around the house and never paid any attention to. Jacobson leaned closer and gripped my wrist confidentially. 'If you ever need help you must come here first,' he said hoarsely, with a masculine passion. 'You understand, Billy? There is no question about this.'

'Thanks, Mr Jacobson – I won't forget.'

'Now I sense you want to leave us. Rebecca – Billy is leaving.'

How could I forget? They were all out to save me. They knew what was good for me. They knew me better than I knew myself. On top of everything there was the business of Becky to sort out.

'Would you like me to dry your print?' she asked at the door.

'I'm sure I'll make a better one,' I said. 'Just look after the negative, please.'

'Is it still raining?' she said. 'Do you want to borrow a brolly?'

'I didn't realise your father had been – you know –'

'Stuffing animals in another lifetime? I know – he never talks about it.'

On the way to the station I raised the hood of my duffle coat gratefully in the teeth of an icy wind. The coat and the hood, jointly derided on occasion by this or that image-conscious student, had never felt so right. Then there was a person under a train at Camden Town, and I had to walk as far as Euston in the freezing rain before going below again, all the while being truer to myself.

It must have been getting on for midnight. It usually was. I had my eyes closed as I lay stretched out, muscles tight, below the blanket with my hands behind my head. There came four knocks, very soft, at the door. I made no sound. I heard the door open quietly and then close again. She was inside my room now. She sat down on the bed and reached her black (no, more like magenta in my mind's eye, thanks to the moonlight) hand under the rug, probing there for the erection she was looking for. She didn't find it, not this time. After I rolled over and curled up with my back to the room she left without a word, as quietly as she had come in. It meant an end to all this, an end to our little masturbation game. There was no victory in it for me – there could be no winners or losers. As I scanned the black and white cuttings on the wall beside me I played a new game, or at least I tried to play it, substituting Véronique for Jackie Kennedy on the deck of a yacht near Cap d'Antibes, but my heart wasn't in it, not least because that substitute role was the rightful preserve of my absent mother. I heard a far church clock strike twelve. Funny – I had never heard the clock before. I didn't care what Becky had done, or, rather, what I hadn't. It was nothing. I could see that. But what Jacobson had whispered in the cathedral of stuffed beasts – it was hard to view it other than as a warning. *If you ever need help you must come here first.* What did he know? He knew plenty. What had he seen? He had seen a great deal in life. Some people are put here to watch over us, are they not? All the more surprising, then, that you might choose to betray them at the drop of a hat.

CHAPTER FIVE

Acts of Transgression

AT THE HEIGHT OF THE TET OFFENSIVE Toulouse-Lautrec showed up at my house with a deluxe hardback edition of *Les Fleurs du mal*, which he presented to me on the doorstep as a gift.

'Don't worry –' he insisted as I flicked respectfully through the volume. 'I half-inched it.'

'It's the nicest thing anyone's ever stolen for me,' I admitted. 'But it's actually in French.'

'Ah – possibly because Baudelaire was a native of France.'

'You'd better come in,' I said, although T-L was already inside. We were at the bottom of the stairs alongside the kitsch painting I liked of the moonlit mustangs. I knew why Toulouse-Lautrec had come. It had to do with the film screening he had invited me to. He wanted his ticket back. Or at any rate he didn't want me to go. The Baudelaire book he had stolen – it was meant as compensation. It was compensation for what had itself been meant as compensation. As I closed the front door I told myself I didn't mind. That whole student scene – how could I have imagined it was for me?

'Nice artwork on the wall, Billy.'

'How did you know where I lived?' Now we were starting up the stairs towards my room.

'He's very protective of you, isn't he?'

40

'I assume we're talking about Mr Jacobson –'

'I had to make a sworn statement to the effect I had your best interests at heart.'

We sat down on the bed with a polite gap between us. In fact, there was nowhere else to sit. I remember thinking it was absurd that the presence of a bed – OK, my bed – in conjunction with T-L should somehow be inhibiting or awkward, but that's the way it was. As I studied my new book hard I waited for Toulouse-Lautrec to bring up the subject of tonight's screening.

'Believe me –' he said. 'That's a terrific present to receive from someone, stolen or not.'

'If it's meant to help me impress Véronique you needn't have bothered.'

'It's a gift, for goodness sake. It's an extremely cool gift from me to you as a token of the high regard in which I hold you – mind and, yes, *body*.' The weasel boy sighed, slumping forward with arms on knees. 'What can I say?' he went on with a despairing shake of the head. 'Some are born cool. Others attain coolness. Yet others have coolness thrust upon them by a caring friend like me.'

'What's your point, T-L, at this particular stage in history?'

'So I'd like to do a bit more thrusting in your direction. Oops – the double entendre. Such poor form. Slip of the tongue. No, no – nothing to do with slipping or tongues. Phew.' He slapped his cheek and blew out, then, glancing up sideways, smiled slyly. 'Someone has to take you in hand, Billy. And Baudelaire, let me tell you right now, is a colossus of cool. We're talking Nobel Prize for credibility. You cannot go wrong with this guy, Véronique or no.'

'You shouldn't have stolen the book.'

'No – I shouldn't have *told you* I stole it.' T-L was on his feet now. He reached out his hand and waited until I shook it and then he hunkered down and looked into my eyes. 'Have you been taking drugs, young man?' he asked. 'Only, your eyes look red and you do seem unusually defensive. Or have you just been beating off a lot?'

'Do you want your film ticket back?' I said. 'Is that it?'

We hit the Central line at Queensway, changed at Tottenham Court Road for Camden, and stood as far as Mornington Crescent with all the tired workers hanging from the rail beside us in a forest of newspapers, or sleeping, in the case of black and Asian cleaners, before-dawn risers at one end of the line or the other, their cheeks pressed up against the glass partitions. Seated for the last leg of our journey, Toulouse-Lautrec took out a pen and scribbled something on the back of his hand – a hurried note to himself, I imagined, in advance of his impending speech – and I had the opportunity to observe him alone, as it were, at close range but without me. I tried my best, but still I couldn't see myself doing it with him. That was the long and the short of it. I told myself it had nothing to do with physical attraction. T-L's qualities, as he doubtless recognised, lay elsewhere. No, this time the fault was all my own. It was simple (if the word can reasonably be used here) enough. For me, sex meant sex with a stranger, for cash. My inability to picture myself doing it with anyone I knew, let alone liked, was a state of affairs I expected to grow out of, like stammering or sucking a thumb, when the time was right. Poor T-L – he had a streak of red paint (gouache, for my money) in his ear below the arm of his occasional glasses, but it was impossible to know whether this was an accident or an affectation.

'OK, Valentino – before we finally get there it would help to discover the status of your fluctuating intentions vis-à-vis a certain mademoiselle.'

We were beside the canal and a row of moored narrow boats, their rooftop show of winter pansies and stencilled watering cans an assault by sheer colour on the evening chill. Across the canal, the milky arses of the Regent's Park mansions squatted above rotting landing stages and secret gardens, with here and there an old lifebelt hanging forgotten from a hook over the stream, or the ruined statue of a goddess sulking in a bower of tall bamboo. Two somnambulant swans glided closer from the direction of the zoo. For a moment the moon came out and everything shone, April-new.

'About Véronique –' I said. 'It doesn't much matter now either way.' I was first up the steps from the canal towards Primrose Hill. It was true – I had already put the whole foolish business behind me in the headlong rush to be more like myself. 'You know I never really meant anything by it,' I told T-L.

'Permit me,' he said, 'to knock myself down with this feather.'

'Véronique may be French and all that, but it's not as if she's Simone de Beauvoir.'

'Who?' Toulouse-Lautrec let out an incredulous whistle. 'You mean the well respected companion of celebrated philosopher and writer Jean-Paul Sartre?' There we were, hesitating in an agreeable way beside a lime green E-Type (that T-L knew its owner should have been obvious from the casual way he parked his rear on the bonnet) and below a flickering street lamp outside the Film Co-op warehouse in Gloucester Avenue. 'I'll give you Sartre, my son,' the weasel boy went on happily. He reached out a hand, involuntarily this time it seemed to me, before withdrawing it quickly. I could see the various comings and goings – the urge to beauty, the flight from intimacy – in his wet eyes. 'I just saw you *smile*, Billy Morton. I think I may have died and gone to heaven. Shall we get on with it now?'

Inside, the plastic seats were arranged in about a dozen rows of ten between the projector and the screen. I counted fifty or sixty people in animated groups at the walls below framed posters advertising noteworthy films from around the world, none of which looked to be Doctor Zhivago or Zulu, the last two movies I had seen (the first on an excruciating early date with Becky during which I squeezed her hand doggedly for ninety-odd minutes in the dark without once moving to kiss her, the second with Dad at a time when he could still hope to sing the national anthem without forgetting the words). In the main the assembled company was older – older, that is, than me. Véronique, for example, at the projector end of the warehouse, was nodding interestedly at a man, a demonstrative type in a pricey looking camel coat, whose gut appeared to have been laid down over years. In sartorial terms the impression was of long scarves steeped in the smoke of countless fags, and fashion resistant waterproofs in traffic stopping colours – reds, yellows, blues. If I was ready to judge these people, all of them, from now on it was using a conspicuous intolerance developed overnight in a spirit of self-defence, or in the interests of self-preservation. Would they not hurry to judge me?

'There she blows,' T-L confirmed. 'Are you coming over?'

She had detached herself from her demonstrative friend and now she moved towards us through the gesticulating ranks without actually looking our way. As she neared I began to wish my mental preparations for this fated moment had taken in a range of specific dialogue options characterised variously and in easy combinations by wit, poise, grace, maturity. I needn't have worried about what to say. Brushing Toulouse-Lautrec aside calmly and fixing her blazing eyes finally on an area just above my forehead, Véronique drew herself up and slapped me hard across the face.

I don't remember much about the next few minutes. I must have sat down close to where we had been standing, in the middle part of the hall. I saw Toulouse-Lautrec take up position in front of the screen with his hand held up against the projector beam, and heard him apologise for starting late. This was after he had called us to order by switching the house lights off and on a few times.

'The film we're about to see was made by Pontecorvo in sixty-five, and dramatises Algeria's fight for independence from France.' The weasel boy fished a folded fragment of paper from his pocket, unfolded it, and read. 'The film is shot wholly in black and white to suggest the documentary style of TV news, and critics have likened it to the neo-realist work of Rossellini while drawing parallels with Eisenstein. There you have it.' He looked up and shaded his eyes. 'I was going to say it's also been viewed as a rallying cry for Marxist revolutionaries and has reportedly been used as a how-to manual by budding terrorists, but I won't because we're already running late and I know you'll want to leave time for the usual closely reasoned discussion following the screening.' He consulted his wrist as if to check his watch, but he didn't have one – just his jottings. 'The director's achievement, it seems to me, is to present both sides in the conflict as intensely human while leaving us in no doubt as to which side he's on.' He shrugged finally and folded up his piece of paper, creasing it three or four times as his spectacles flashed in the projector's glare. 'Feel free to make up your own minds –'

The truth is I didn't know whether I should stay or leave. As the screening got underway a girl on her own sat down beside me and rustled her bag of aniseed balls under my nose in an unlicensed show of solidarity. When two strangers come together out of the blue in a context of common interest or cause – at a funeral, for example, or in the waiting room of a shrink – the potential exists, I dare say, for overstepping the procedural mark. For me the abiding image or image sequence is of French soldiers surrounding Ali's place before the French colonel invites Ali and his family to surrender or die (to this day I visualise Algiers, or any Carthage or Tunis or Fez of the imagination, under the olfactory influence of aniseed, damp wool and stale smoke). The film gave off a kind of heat. In spite of the draught from the double doors halfway down the cavernous hall I discovered I was sweating. As the movie ran whirring and clicking through the projector gate I decided it was too late to quit the scene. To slope off now would only have compounded my humiliation. For a few more anguished moments I told myself repeatedly I was out of my depth. How could I ever have imagined I belonged here, in their company, in their world? Then I fought back. To find out why Véronique had struck me should have been a straightforward enough task – I had only to ask her, surely. When, though? After the lights came on again I watched T-L take up his position front of house. I had the strong conviction this whole unsettling episode was about my future versus my past. I had to see it through. The next key step was to find out what I had done wrong.

'Where are you, V?' Toulouse-Lautrec called out, casting his eye around the hall as the audience surfaced blinking and nodding and murmuring. It was a different T-L who blew on his hands and rubbed them together in anticipation – the public T-L, even smarter, and yet more vulnerable somehow, than the one I knew. 'Ah, there you are. Véronique, as some of you are no doubt aware, was born in Algiers a few years before these events. Blue sky, warm sea – it looks like a nice place to co-exist, doesn't it? What could possibly go wrong? Any questions for V, anybody?'

In the coyly appreciative hush my galloping heart threatened to break its bonds and burst from its membranous cage. As a matter of fact I had at least one question to ask the object of our collective attention. On her feet a few rows in front of where I sat she rotated in a relaxed arc as if to make herself more generally available, her arms folded loosely, not defensively, across her tight black sweater in a place immediately below her jutting breasts and the crucifix that gleamed there coolly. She was superb. No questions, informed, inane, disturbed the silence that upheld her status and reputation. No one sought to challenge her, or her role in history.

'In your own time, boys and girls,' Toulouse-Lautrec sang out from the front of the hall. 'So, no one wants to ask what it was like to grow up French in Algeria – after watching a movie like that? It seems not, Véronique. One can scarcely credit it. What about the film, then? Would anyone care to comment on the film?'

'Yes, sorry –' I began desperately, getting up fast and gripping the back of the chair in front of me. 'I'd like to ask Véronique a question.' On the one hand it was bad. She knew it and I knew it. It was bad form for the victim of an arbitrary attack to seek redress at a moment so public. It was also very right. Few in the chilly hall could have had more reason than I had to open up a meaningful dialogue with the French art student, chic focus of our gaze. As she turned to face me, squaring up, Véronique lowered her arms and clenched her fists. I didn't ask her why she had hit me. I didn't ask how I might have offended her. I let her off because I could – I knew I had done nothing wrong. 'Can you find it in your heart to forgive?' I said in the adoptive voice of someone other, someone I was yet to be. It didn't sound like the voice of the Billy Morton I had known for all these years. As I say, I must have been acting or thinking in the future, not the present or the past. They were all rooting for me now. That was how it felt. The few friends I had known and loved, or would ever know and love, were all willing me to speak out. And Véronique went with me, alert as usual to every human possibility. I swear I saw her take my part, exploring it with her intelligence. For a fateful instant there were just the two of us left anywhere on earth.

'Can you find it in you to forgive?' I repeated, very sure of my ground suddenly. Did she see it? I was setting her up. I was learning and learning. Yes, it was a kind of turning point for me – a victory.

'What does that have to do with growing up in French colonial Africa?' she asked uncertainly, back in her role.

'Not much,' I said. 'Unless you happen to be speaking to Ali's family on a surprise visit to Algiers –'

I had worked it out, at least in its essentials, having spent the entire movie coming to a preliminary understanding of what was going on. Naturally it had something, or quite possibly everything, to do with Toulouse-Lautrec, protagonist number three in the triangular psychodrama now playing in my head with input from Véronique. Just look at the maths. It had to be T-L's fault, did it not? He was unusually quiet as we marched, the two of us, up Haverstock Hill towards Hampstead and the house party. This was right after the screening. What, I needed to know, was T-L's crime? What had he done, and, more importantly, why had he done it *in my name*? As we drew level with Belsize Park station the lime green E-type roared past us with the driver hunched over its steering wheel in his camel coat and Véronique suspended low in the bucket seat beside him.

'There were times we regretted setting forth without transport provision,' T-L called out stagily, shaking a fist at the speeding car before pulling again on his quarter bottle of whisky.

The party was established by the time we got there. Toulouse-Lautrec introduced me to our florid host, driver of the lime green Jaguar – the big, bearded Scot with the chunky identity bracelet was called Hamish – and to the host's Brazilian lover. This tiny man had a lyrical name I didn't catch. He wore his embroidered kaftan wide open on a shaved or plucked chest of terracotta hue.

'Zounds,' boomed Hamish. 'If it isn't our dashing young stand-up-and-be-counted post-screening sole enquirer.' He didn't have to boom. Although someone had upped the volume (in my head I can hear the jangly 12-string guitar sound of the Byrds doing, say, Eight Miles High, but at the time it could have been anything) of the music, it wasn't raucous as such. 'And what an important question yours was,' Hamish was telling me. 'If only I could recall it. You know – V speaks very highly of your camera skills.' The ripe vowels hung, amused, above our heads. 'I'm sure we all respect a man who knows how to use his equipment,' the big Scot continued, gripping T-L's elbow with camp complicity and aiming a long, thin plume of cigar smoke towards the ceiling. At the same time his miniature boyfriend withdrew artfully from our little group.

'Oh, we do,' T-L acknowledged, nodding gravely at thin air.

'Would you like to get into bed with us, Billy?' Hamish asked. 'I mean in a photojournalistic capacity, of course.'

'Hamish will fund our review,' T-L explained, quaffing whisky from a tumbler. 'Lavishly –'

'So I have a modest castle up in Scotland,' Hamish admitted airily, as if this excused everything.

'Politics, poetry, polemics, photography –' T-L went on. 'If it begins with a P we want to know.'

'You passed over pornography,' Hamish pointed out. 'Perhaps that's for another day.'

'We?' I said, looking doubtfully from the one to the other and gulping something that was chiefly gin.

'I shall edit,' T-L said, 'and Lancelot will print the thing with pride, passion and panache.'

'You have a wee think about it,' Hamish urged, seizing my arm protectively for a second and then releasing it.' And try to relax for uncle Hamish, chicken pie. It's a party, you know. Whatever you did to ruffle V's sleek Gallic feathers, I'm sure she's forgiven you.'

'Have you bumped into her recently?' T-L asked me, raising his eyebrows and flicking his wispy beard knowingly.

Now I was doubly perplexed. Even as I was offending her – ostensibly, at least – Véronique was talking up my camera skills, or so I had been led to believe. As far as I knew she hadn't actually set eyes on a photograph taken by me at that point in time. Nourished by gin, this new mystery grew in my head, cloaking me rapidly in an aura of wounded introspection that caught the attention of two or three older, as in twenty-something, women dancing drunkenly and alone beside the record player (Nico, I suspect, invoking All Tomorrow's Parties) while clutching, as opportunity allowed, at this or that passing partner in prospect. As I dodged a queue waiting to use the toilet half way up the stairs the aniseed girl from The Battle of Algiers stuck her black tongue out at me and demanded to know what star sign I was, pronouncing me a cusp Cancer before I had a chance to reply. Though I would have given a great deal to bail out right then, I pressed on with my campaign plan.

At the top of the house in a candlelit bedroom hedged around by irregularly sloping ceilings I found Véronique playing Cluedo on the king-sized bed beside Lancelot of the Congo and the diminutive Brazilian. Up here at altitude the noisier peaks of the party mood fell away in a monastic atmosphere of contemplation stoked to soporific extremes by the palls of incense and the sheer warmth of the room. Meanwhile the London gin coursed backwards and forwards gamely through my unpractised veins.

'Can I talk to you for a minute?' I asked Véronique after she looked up distractedly at last from the crowded playing surface that had pride of place on the bed. 'I mean can I see you alone?'

'Is it important?' she said, her tone to all intents and purposes neutral. 'You catch me at a critical time. I was just getting ready to make a declaration in respect of Colonel Mustard –'

Immediately outside the attic room I invited her to sit beside me on a carpeted stair. It was an ergonomic masterstroke designed to cast us as old lovers disdaining conflict or confrontation.

'Why did you hit me earlier tonight?' I said, nauseous suddenly and tired of looking at myself.

'You sent me two pornographic drawings detailing what you'd like to do to me. You left them in my pigeon-hole.'

'How bad, exactly?' I asked, nodding resignedly as the penny, long hanging, finally dropped. I interpreted Véronique's silence as a measure of gravity and offended taste. 'I didn't do those drawings,' I told her, before adding a more or less pointless postscript. 'I can't draw to save my life.'

'But you know a few people who can?'

If only I could have laughed. What was funny was my fiercely protective impulse in the face of T-L's wickedness. I couldn't bring myself to betray him. It was as if I had been asked to account after school for the depraved actions of my wayward kid brother. 'You don't seriously think I would send you those drawings, do you?' I managed feebly but sincerely.

'I couldn't say,' Véronique observed. 'I hardly know you.'

'So why would you promote my camera skills to Hamish?'

'Hamish asked for my opinion. I simply asked Mr Jacobson to give me his.'

There was one more scene left to play out that night. I ferried T-L in a taxi I shelled out for down to the river at Albert Bridge, my favourite place (or my favourite place that was more or less on our route). As a course of action it lacked logic – we were both drunk and sick, and the night seemed lost to me. I can only imagine it had to do with my bid for emotional honesty on the long road towards authenticity and my heart's as yet unformed desire. I had no idea what we might do when we got to the river. In my head it was all bound up somehow with the lights of the bridge and the pull of the tide. T-L didn't apologise. In the taxi he told me very lucidly he was drawn to acts of transgression because he wanted to thwart his own happiness, to kill it before it had a chance to take hold and grow. I couldn't say anything at the time. My clever friend's willingness to exalt failure over success was something I hadn't recognised. Then I saw it – success wasn't quite good enough for him.

When we got there we jumped the railings at Battersea Park and went down to the water at its darkest reach with the tide rising to meet us. After T-L peeled off his clothes (he had a towel that must have come from Hamish's bathroom wrapped tightly around his chest beneath his shirt) he handed them to me and waded into the river up to his waist before ducking out of sight below the surface. I was knee deep in the water when he finally rose up again, gasping and flailing and paddling hard for the narrow strip of shore below the wall. When I asked him why he went into the river he said he did it for me, as penance for what he had already done. When I asked him how he came to be wearing a hand towel under his shirt, as if in preparation for a midnight dip, he shrugged and said he stole the towel because he needed one, and Hamish had more than enough. I didn't know what to make of it. What struck me was the idea that all this was somehow not right, or not right for me. That's what I regretted most. How I wanted to see things differently – as a series of vivid events in the new scheme of things, or as the mark of just how far I had travelled with T-L. On the slippery rocks at the edge of the river he shook uncontrollably for twenty seconds, then pulled on his clothes without bothering to dry off. It was late, and neither of us had much dough. I didn't know where we were going – now and hereafter – which worried me in a general way. Just as I told myself there would be no turning back from this point, the Albert Bridge lights went out – I tried to view this, given the facts on the ground, as a timely show of solidarity. How dark that night was.

<u>NANA</u>

I don't remember your snapper. I remember lots of snappers. How can you expect me to elevate one photographer above the others? English? No, I really don't recall. This was in January, was it not? There was a lot to consider from the PR perspective. In preparing for today's Q&A I have drawn on historical documents, including the press briefing summaries (holds up typed page with gloved hand) I put together routinely from day to day on behalf of the so-called student leaders. Thus: (1) Swimming pool standoff at Nanterre; (2) US generals call for additional troops; (3) Robert Kennedy runs for president; (4) bomb blasts at American targets in Paris c/w burning of US flag; (5) Daniel Cohn-Bendit leads campus occupation.

Shall we start with the first prompt on my briefing list? In fact, the first item hints generously at the absurdity of the entire *affaire* as I have revisited it for this internationally acclaimed memoir (holds up signed copy, drawn from multiple stacks on bookshop table, of autobiographical version of events). Yes? In that case let us picture the French Minister for Sport as he opens a new indoor swimming facility at Paris Nanterre University. It is January of 1968. Use of a microphone would, let's face it, be hazardous in the circumstances, and the minister's unveiling speech is readily lost, drowned out by the heckling of Daniel Cohn-Bendit and others representing certain Maoist and Trotskyite *groupuscules* at the illustrious seat of learning.

The students, who are demanding an end to the segregation of male and female accommodation, approach the guest of honour to make their case, whereupon the minister, athlete and aesthete by instinct, takes refuge wittily in the chest-deep water towards the shallow end of the new pool. So, it begins with a kind of joke or jape. Who says history can't be funny when it tries? Your photographer – are you sure he was even *there* that day? I remember an English snapper, yes, since you press me on this one. How could I forget Billy? He had a serious quality that belied his appalling youth. He was a kid, really – skinny enough and with poor teeth. But that was later. The fact is I chose to omit him from my record because his wasn't, in my view, a decisive role. If it isn't in my memoir it didn't happen, or it didn't happen *memorably*. And if it did happen, I reserve the right to polish its telling, or retelling, the better to illuminate its truth. Each of us is free to challenge or acquiesce in the verdict of history as he or she sees fit. In this, Billy is no different from you or me. Young Billy is free to make his own case in his own sweet way. So, let him.

At this point I usually talk, in response to significant audience interest, about the American flag incident. Largely *je ne regrette rien*, but the flag burning I regret. I warned the student leaders about it, the populist instinct and the righteous indignation that attaches to this or that gesture hostile to a nation's idea of itself. Random acts of flag burning you certainly will find in my internationally acclaimed memoir. Today flags, tomorrow books. Next question, please.

CHAPTER SIX

Occupying Forces

THE DAY OF THE STUDENT OCCUPATION began like any other at our college. Early for work as usual, I sat on the floorboards of the photographic storeroom with my back to the film fridge and with my feet, shoes off, on the shelf bearing black and chrome 35mm SLR bodies (Nikon and Olympus, the choices of Jacobson, based, he said, on the breadth of their accessory ranges and the contrast between their handling characteristics). The storeroom shutter was down most of the way, but it wasn't locked – the padlock was on the counter above my head. Propped up against each other in front of a two-bar electric fire, my wet shoes steamed happily beside me. There was a paperback edition of *The Age of Reason* lying open on my lap, and about five minutes left on the clock. On the page Marcelle was recognising Mathieu's need to be free, calling it his vice, and he was asking her what else a man could do while she prepared coolly to give him the news she was two months late. I was strongly drawn to their world, a world of big decisions and fundamental choices, which seemed to contrast so strikingly with my own, long on moral confusion, short on heroes. It had a lot to do with being French or English – this much was perfectly clear to my increasingly partisan imagination. My fateful desire to be in Paris as soon as possible – I blame it lock, stock and barrel on Sartre and his merry band.

I heard voices, extravagantly excitable, approach on the stairs to the landing before the storeroom shutter rode up with a clatter. I got up fast, clutching my shoes protectively, and found myself face to face with Toulouse-Lautrec, wearing his most mischievous grin and carrying what looked to be an Instamatic, at the head of a small but energetic delegation of male and female students.

'Greetings, comrade Billy –'

He was gaunter. If anything, he was thinner of face. He had lost his beard and acquired a small earring on the left side since last I saw him naked and palely shivering beside a river while the lights from a nearby bridge danced on the surface of the water.

'The same to you, T-L.' He was up to something. I saw it in his body language, at once forward and relaxed, casual and calculating. In the lobby below, further students massed noisily, as if for some agreed advocacy, in a small sea of woolly hats and cigarette smoke. I saw no banners or placards bearing slogans as such. It was just an atmosphere they gave off, or an impression they created, that had to do with trouble rather than danger. T-L was no different. 'What's all this, then?' I asked him.

'One simply needs to know where you stand,' he told me, 'on the key issues.'

'Does one? I don't normally stand, I'm afraid. I tend to sit if I can – preferably on the nearest fence.'

'Yet I know of some who would vouch for your courage and conviction. We seek an alliance with the world's workers in the face of systematic oppression by the political classes and the ruling elite. On behalf of all students today we demand greater representation on governing bodies and decision-making platforms of every kind. I could go on at length and in detail about germ warfare and UDI in Rhodesia, which we condemn, but I expect you're busy.'

'I have to open up the store now, T-L.' I had an urge, which I resisted out of personal loyalty, to remind my friend he was of the political classes himself. 'It's my duty as a worker of the world –'

T-L beamed. He was enjoying himself now, although his close companions were increasingly restive. 'Smile, please,' he demanded in the manner of an impudent Scout while raising his camera. The flashbulb popped, blinding me. 'Your only duty, my dear boy,' T-L continued, 'is to yourself. So why not wander upstairs during this morning's tea break in order to find Véronique? I believe she wants to see you. In one of life's droller ironies she appears to have fallen for your charms without your having, at the end of the day, to lift a finger – or to raise anything else.'

With that he spun round and sped down the stairs with his few outriders in pursuit. After he had backed through the lobby's doors they all followed him, their leader. Two things bothered me as tea break approached. There was the idea, which I tried to dismiss as unworthy of us both, that T-L was somehow setting me up for a fall by exploiting my seasoned loyalty to him, or my ignorance of issues and ideas, or a mixture of these. There was also the fact of the flash picture he had just taken. Because of the contrived conditions under which this image was made I couldn't help imputing a base motive to it, and this irrational impulse discouraged me further, challenging as it did my notion of the camera as an agent of reason.

This whole question of T-L's motivations took on additional and unforeseen implications in the presence, upstairs in the portrait studio (an airy penthouse holed by enough windows and skylights to induce in me a kind of vertigo) during my tea break, of Véronique herself. Although her apron was crusty with paint of every hue, she managed to make of it a fashion accessory – such was the effortless versatility of her style. There was a colour snapshot, partly concealed by masking tape and intended evidently as a self-portraiture guide, on the studio wall beside her easel. I had the strange idea there and then, without having time to test it properly, that T-L might have snapped me earlier that day with a view to painting my portrait.

'You wanted to see me?' I admit it – it was as if I was seeking an audience with the student artist. That didn't worry me. She was immersed in what she was doing. I had to traverse the creaking floor from one end of the vast and empty room to the other before she finally became aware of me. She didn't turn round until I spoke for the second time. 'T-L said you wanted to see me.'

'T-L?'

'Toulouse-Lautrec –'

'Did he? I don't recall saying that. No matter. I'm glad you're here now because I want to say sorry for hitting you when I did. It was wrong, and I apologise. Slapping men across the face – it's not something I make a habit of.'

'You had your reasons.'

'They were wrong too.' As she spoke she continued to stir white paint, a little at a time, into the blob of bluish green (call it viridian) on an improvised palette (a short plank topped with white Formica) resting on a stool between us, and I found her quiet presence of mind impressive and calming. 'You know he's in love with you, don't you?' she concluded after a while, looking up. 'T-L, I mean.'

'Yes,' I said. It just came out. I hadn't given it serious thought until that moment, but it seemed to me suddenly, in the all-seeing light of the portrait studio, the most obvious thing in the world. It was Véronique, of course, who made everything clear and bright – that was her strength. 'I mean – he hasn't said anything,' I told her, backtracking naturally. 'But, yes.'

'And how do you feel about that?'

'I don't know,' I said, playing instinctively for time. At first I really didn't know how or what I felt. Instead of pausing to gather my thoughts sufficiently to confront Véronique's difficult question I decided to press on blindly. 'How do I feel? Alarmed, probably.' Now we were getting somewhere. Now we were getting closer. I let out a low-key laugh because it seemed like the right thing to do. 'I suppose I should be flattered, shouldn't I? Is that the right answer?'

She didn't get back to me on that, except to smile her general approval, and it occurred me in my innocence (OK, my ignorance) that, to a smart French girl of good breeding and mature outlook, idle talk of one man's love for another was small beer.

'As a matter of fact I've hardly seen T-L,' she revealed. 'I mean since we did the first edition of the magazine. You knew about our little review, didn't you?' She was cleaning a handful of brushes with harsh swipes of a rag she had picked up from the floor. 'By now he should be working up our banners for the Vietnam demonstration. We had you down to take pictures, of course.'

'You did? First I've heard of it.'

'You will be there, won't you?'

'Wouldn't miss it for the world.' (This conventional expression of my position was exactly half true. Although I had just this minute become aware of the Vietnam event, I would – now that I knew of its existence and the part I might play in it – have given my left arm to be there with my clever friends. Yet the prospect unnerved me.)

'So, what do you think?' It took me a second or two to realise she had moved on from the subject of demonstrations against the war. Marches and sit-ins – these were hardly natural territory for me at the time. It was a class thing, surely. Véronique would have understood that very well. By asking what I made of the unfinished self-portrait on the easel beside her she was teasing me in a way – I don't suppose she cared what I thought. 'Should I be flattered?' she went on, conspicuously reprising what I had said a moment ago.

I didn't get back to her on that one, except to smile my general approval. I could see she was happy with that – it amused her. The truth is I thought the self-portrait looked nothing like her. I mean it didn't do her *fineness* any kind of justice. In my head I was making a case for photography over painting, but in fact the snapshot on the wall didn't capture her either. There she stood, smiling in a sunlit garden, with someone's strong arm reaching out from behind the masking tape to embrace her. 'Who's the boy?' I asked.

She shrugged, stepping back to peel the snapshot from the wall before stripping away the tape. Standing shirtless beside Véronique on the grass and dangling his croquet mallet at arm's length was a lanky young man with chest hair. 'Raymond,' she said, pronouncing it the French way. 'We're engaged.'

I don't know why I found this happy news unsettling. Perhaps the emotion rode piggyback on the unease I already felt in relation to Toulouse-Lautrec, his rogue love, and his penchant for mayhem. My tea break was over. I hadn't managed to pick up my pay packet after all. As I came down the stairs towards the landing I saw the storeroom shutter was open. That was impossible, unless Jacobson had pitched up early to begin his shift. There were three of them – all nice women I recognised. They must have forced the padlock, or someone had done the job for them, and now they were making themselves as comfortable as they could beside the fire with their egg sandwiches and picnic flasks, having handcuffed (just one hand apiece) each other to the shelving. I couldn't help it – I couldn't get away from the idea that T-L had set me up by inviting me to seek out Véronique the way he had. At the same time I clung to an ideal of loyalty. Mired in doubt, I submitted to the occupying forces.

'Could I have my book back, please?' I asked one of the ladies.

'Top novel, that,' she told me. 'Had to do it for French A-level.'

That night I took Dad to the dogs at Walthamstow Stadium. We sat upstairs on the bus as usual, moving to the front seat at Chingford Road, which was when the famous neon sign above the arena came into view. The sign, with its ice cream colours, always thrilled Dad.

'Will you look at that lovely thing, Billy —' he said, wiping the moisture carefully from the window with the side of his hand.

It was worth the journey just to hear him say it. I think he knew that. I think he knew that whenever he hailed the famous neon sign I felt happy for him, and that's why he did it. In other words it was a kind of code or shorthand between us. For Dad it became a way of telling me he loved me without having to say it, or anything like it. At least that's what I wanted to believe. As our bus drew nearer to the racetrack that night the illuminated sign slugged it out in my head with the image of Jacobson, grave but stoical, at the doors to the college with, surging all around him on the steps, a restless tide of students (the leaders or prime movers wore balaclavas to protect their identities) waving placards or fists. In so far as their demands ranged across a number of issues, local, national and international, it wasn't really clear what they wanted. For example, I saw a cryptic message regarding black power in the United Kingdom alongside a sign that carried the image we all knew of the Buddhist monk who had set himself on fire in a Saigon street. From below the steps and just inside the college gates, where a second group gathered around a wheelbarrow pressed into service as a brazier (there is always the brazier), a series of satisfied cries went up as, one by one, the lesser canvases by this or that gifted student were consigned to the flames of history, and although the odd black balaclava struck a note here and there of menace, it was on the whole a festive scene. I gauged the political temperature via the policemen who watched discreetly from the pavement beyond the railings. There were two constables on bicycles, and both of them laughed at the world.

Inside Walthamstow Stadium it felt less cold but damp still. We sat sheltered by the roof opposite the finish line and consulted our programmes while the bookmakers set their trackside odds, and the music, a sad song about losers in America, blasted out from the PA. Naturally I got to thinking about T-L, about the idea that he was in love with me, as some said, and about what it meant. I told myself a little guiltily it meant nothing. It didn't matter. It would only matter if I loved T-L back, which I surely didn't, otherwise I would know it for a fact. It was amazing how quickly I made this my official view.

'Do you feel it, son?' Dad said when the song ended. 'Tonight's the night, Billy.'

'Got to be,' I said, counting out the money for our stakes and pressing it into his hand.

As six trainers paraded six dogs in single file behind a steward in a bowler hat I watched my father go trackside to place our bets. He was right – tonight was the night. I had already decided what I had to do later without quite picturing how it might play out. Then it began below, the part I liked best – the white-gloved semaphore denoting prices rising and falling in line with sentiment. A bell rang. The roof lights went down. As the hare made its run, the trap doors crashed up and the dogs appeared, drooling and leering. I shut my eyes. I imagined myself as my mother, sitting beside Dad before she ran off with a playboy and left the old pigeon fancier to die slowly of a broken heart. I was about to tell him that I, for one, loved him (this had always been a key part of my plan to make tonight more special or memorable for Dad, whether he approved or not, given that we could never be physically close and I could see the light in him was dying) when he tugged at my sleeve like an excited kid and told me how much we had won on the first race.

After we got home we stood together in the hallway for a short time with the moonlit mustangs galloping next to us on the wall. A faint light spilled down from a bedroom upstairs, and, beside us in the gloom, the living room door was ajar.

'Wait for me in there,' I said.

As I climbed the stairs I heard their voices rise up and then hang in the silence. All was as it should have been. Everything was exactly as it always was. There was no reason to think anything was other than normal unless you knew tonight was the night. On the landing I tried the door – it was locked. I knocked three times, not too hard and not too soft, and waited.

'Who is it?' she called out sweetly.

There were just two people it could have been – Dad or me.

'Could you open the door, please?'

'Not now, darling – I'm busy.'

'Open the door, please.'

I counted to ten, listening to her soft laughter. Six inches from my face the door panel confronted me with maximum indifference as if to say – I might help you, or I might not. I kicked the door as hard as I could in the region of the handle, and it yielded first time. She was sitting on top of her client, but immediately she rolled off and he jumped up and they stood side by side like Adam and Eve seen in a new double portrait in a council house in west London.

'Now, look here –' the man said, clamping his hands over his groin in the manner of a footballer awaiting a free kick.

'On your bike, mister,' I said. I was unwilling to negotiate with him. I didn't look at him. I was watching her, preparing to forget her while marvelling at the enormous scar on her abdomen – to me, in my state of heightened emotional awareness, it stood for everything I couldn't know about her and all we can't see in each other.

'Now, look here –' the man said again.

'Out. Hop it. Come on, sailor – let's have you.'

'You'd better leave,' she told him calmly, breasts swinging low as she uncrossed her arms.

'You can sling your hook and all, baby doll.'

This was from Dad standing in the doorway.

'Jesus fucking Christ,' the man said, snatching at his trousers before gathering underpants, shirt, jacket, socks and boots in at his chest. 'Fucking tart. Fucking coon –'

We heard him lurch down the stairs, cursing. Then the front door slammed. In the bedroom no one spoke and no one looked. At last Dad shuffled forward from the door and scattered his race winnings on the bed.

'What's that supposed to be?' she said.

'Right away, please,' Dad said. 'Just go –'

The rain had stopped. Now the clouds moved in ragged squadrons towards the victory hour. The monk was on fire. He was sitting in a wheelbarrow with his knees tucked up, his head on his arms. The flames were the same orange colour as his robe. I approached the monk with a pail, but when I raised it up and turned it over I found the pail was empty again. The flames climbed higher at the centre of this sacrificial scene while, a short hop away on the spark-strewn perimeter, six whippets paraded, grinning.

'Dad?'

I threw off the blanket and pulled back the curtain. There was no monk outside. There was only the gasometer and the sky. Yes, a small bonfire was burning on wasteland beyond the canal, but that wasn't unusual. It was too wet for fires, other than in dreams.

'Son?'

As I pulled the blanket around me and stepped barefoot onto the landing I could hear music, very faint, from below. Downstairs in the darkened living room my father swayed with his back to the doorway while the furniture camped sadly and incongruously in the middle of the space. Only the television and the record player stood apart. On the other side of the room, where the sliding doors were wide open to the balcony and the London night, the curtain came and went on a current of damp air.

'Dad?'

He had on his sheepskin jacket. When he turned round at last he had a pigeon in his arms – he was stroking its crop with a finger. 'Ain't seen this chap for months,' he said. Then the record stopped, and in the quiet you could hear the pigeon's coos. As he looked up, Dad's tears caught the light from the hall. 'We make a good team, you and me, don't we, son?' he said.

'That's true, Dad,' I said. 'We do. Only, why have you got all the furniture in the middle of the room?'

'Could be it's time for a new look, Billy. Could be it's time for a lick of paint and a fresh start, wouldn't you say?'

I should have done it right then. I should have told Dad I loved him, just as I had planned to. I didn't do it. I missed my big chance.

<u>REBECCA</u>

Certain story elements come together as I write, creating landmark moments, turning points, signature events. These I lob like boulders into the narrative pond before pursuing the ripples to the water's edge. Is it snowing? It snows. Look – I am getting down from my father's van on the college forecourt, the reluctant snowfall showing up nicely against the khaki backdrop of my army surplus coat. Dad switches off the van's engine. As we approach the college steps we are turned away at the brazier. It is all very civil. We are civil. The occupying students are civil. When Billy comes down from behind the line I open my copy of *Lady Chatterley's Lover* and take out several banknotes and congratulate him warmly. An anonymous collector has bought all six of his pictures – yes, the large-format portraits Dad had so much faith in he offered them for sale at the Saturday market in Portobello Road. Billy asks me to describe the collector. I won't. I have my reasons – these are less to do with confidentiality than the best interests of story. Don't ask, I say. He bought all your prints, didn't he? Then Dad embraces Billy solemnly (although they are on opposite sides of the sit-in divide they remain colleagues and friends), and asks if he is all right for money now. When I tell Billy I have been accepted by Exeter to read English he lets out a yelp of suppressed emotion and kisses me hard on the lips. Is he changed by the events of the day? Yes, his kissing is different. His hair, which has always been cut too short, is longer now. Now it looks too long for ordinary taste. At the same time it becomes a character signifier I may work on, or with, as I write this up. In so far as their eyebrows are flecked with wet snow, Billy and Dad have a comic air, but this is not right in terms of tone. On the steps above the brazier someone whistles the catchy introduction to Georgy Girl, and this, at least, is contextually fit for purpose. It's a small point, but an important one – Billy liked, and knew, his popular or contemporary music. I don't altogether understand how that can have happened. First there was his music. Then came his books. At a certain point, even the way he spoke began to sound changed by what was taking place.

CHAPTER SEVEN
Fancy Dress

ON THE MORNING OF THE VIETNAM DEMO I woke up late, driven finally to the surface by excitement and a generous helping of funk. The first thing I acknowledged as I hesitated under the blanket was the root cause of my unease, which was of an unfamiliar order (it made sense in those days to differentiate between my regular levels of anxiety and fresher incursions that might sink me from one hour to the next). The problem was easy enough to describe – I had no camera suited to the important task that fell to me. I had no 35mm SLR or rangefinder, for example, with which to do roving justice to the forces of history on the march. Under normal circumstances I could have had my pick of Nikons, say, from the college storeroom, my second home, but that was impossible in this age of occupation. The second thing I registered that charged morning was the smell of paint from downstairs, where the harsher gloss of the woodwork had superseded the emulsion (or distemper, as Dad called it) of the walls. The paint smelled good. It smelled fine in so far as it stood for progress, and the feeling it evoked in me helped me rally. The third thing that came to me was of a different order again. Today was, I decided with welcome conviction, a shaving day.

I jumped up and fitted a fresh blade to the razor I still shared with Dad. As I lathered my face it struck me – it was quiet in the house in a way that, with hindsight, is often meaningful. Acting on impulse I rushed downstairs to admire Dad's paintwork advances. It was done. The living room, bright and cold, was almost empty. There was the new TV on wooden legs, and the old settee, and the record player sitting on the carpet as before. The walls were starkly white. I had to put my face up close before I could see the paisley pattern below the paint. There was no sign of Dad – he wasn't in the house and he wasn't on the balcony. Why this should have the effect, today of all days, of deepening my disquiet wasn't evident to me then. Here were yet more feelings to be thrown off alongside the sense of failure and, yes, guilt that continued to unsettle me. I was a photographer without a camera. It was wrong. What made it worse was the idea that I should have seen it, this last minute absence of camera scenario, coming. Indeed I *had* seen it coming, but I hadn't done anything about it. Why not? Either I was responding to the fear I might not be talented enough, photographically speaking, to meet the expectations of my companions, or I had decided I didn't need to prove myself one way or the other. Then the absurdity of these absurdly defensive instincts rose up to meet me and, thanks to a sudden excess of self-regard (that there was actually a strong whiff of destiny in my decision to attend the demonstration with neither camera nor film I couldn't have seen at the time), I connected fairly and squarely with the emergent, the more *engaged*, Billy Morton of tomorrow. That was probably Mister Sartre's fault. The truth is my defensive posturing had less to do with pictures than politics. On Vietnam, and much besides, I was out of my comfort zone. Hadn't I already admitted to myself that my real motive for attending the demonstration was to impress my friends? Two songbirds fussed on the balcony rail – harbingers of spring, I wanted to believe – before they flew away one after the other towards the equator. Oh, I had done some homework on Vietnam and the savage war that barely ruffled the surface of my narcissistic self-absorption – of course I had – but still I didn't feel much in my heart.

They were waiting for me in an overflowing Trafalgar Square, pressed up against the plinth of the southeastern lion below Nelson's Column. As I worked my way around the base of the monument a couple of questions suggested themselves to me for the umpteenth time. What would they make of it, my presence without a camera? What personal validity had I in their eyes sufficient to survive this unfortunate error of judgement or lapse in taste? I had expected to join a small group. In fact there was only Lancelot and Véronique, plus a good thousand of their scholastic brethren including, nearest our inspirational lion, the vocal representatives of Essex University and the London School of Economics with placards (in my head I see only the face of Ho Chi Minh, little known to me then, although there must have been many other varieties) bristling, impatient for the off. I shook Lancelot's hand, resisting the impulse to ask where T-L was. If he wasn't here, what other business did he have that was more urgent or compelling? Véronique was a tad cool towards me, but she was often on the cool side, wasn't she? When she raised her camera, as if to suggest that some people were more in tune with the progress of events than others, I saw it was the Nikon F with the fast (meaning it had a larger maximum aperture that made it better at scooping up the shy English light, thereby helping to freeze rapid action in dull conditions) wide-angle lens she had booked out from the college storeroom on a rolling basis over the past few months. It made me feel foolish in a first-class way because it was so obviously the right tool for the job. You couldn't argue with that.

'Where's yours?' she said, shrugging fine shoulders eloquently.

'Under occupation,' I said, shrugging in turn. 'Where's T-L?'

'Not here,' she said, shrugging again, a little more impatiently this time, as if it was plainly my business to know more than I did about everything under the sun, including Toulouse-Lautrec and what made him tick. If I wanted to be part of that particular scene, their scene, I would have to try harder, do better – that was what she seemed to be saying. That was OK. I had no problem with that. In all this she stopped short of hostile – she was too perfect for that. Then I got it. She was competing with me now in respect of T-L, for his feelings, his favour. A splinter of something like resentment had pierced her lovely armour, leaving her prey to basic instincts. Even as I glimpsed the truth of the thing it was gone. 'Don't you know he disdains crowds?' she added for good measure.

Now the hubbub around the square was impressive. It flowed from speeches greater and smaller, cascading down the steps of the National Gallery and scouring the grand frontages of embassies and high commissions on its journey towards Whitehall and Admiralty Arch and Northumberland Avenue and the river. It went over the heads of the youngest with their balloons. It blew through the hair, or what remained of the hair, of academics and intellectuals, priests and pacifists, trade unionists and teachers bearing thermos flasks of tea. I heard grandmothers sing. I saw harlots in furs. We were all in the square that day, flying a flag, or swelling the numbers, or selling a point of view. An expectant hush imposed itself gradually from the north. We saw the woman with the headband (everyone concluded, correctly, it was Vanessa Redgrave) approach a microphone on the stage, but it was the man behind her (everyone decided, wrongly, it was Omar Sharif) who proceeded to speak strongly on behalf of the Vietnam Solidarity Campaign. I missed Toulouse-Lautrec. It was a revelation to me, a shock. Quite simply I had expected him to be there. Suddenly it saddened me that the seething crowd, so present all around, should count for so little. I actually missed T-L, sinner or saint. That's what I remember most about Trafalgar Square.

We marched, our chants orchestrated by cheery cheerleaders, west along Oxford Street on a carpet of discarded publicity material bearing slogans and blandishments on behalf of this or that interest group. It was a massive day for organisational acronyms and lapel buttons. Whereas, thanks to my modest research, I recognised NLF as National Liberation Front for South Vietnam, I was temporarily undone by NSA, which turned out to stand for the National Student Alliance. Armed with her loaded Nikon, Véronique scouted ahead, and I had an alarming vision, for which I couldn't account, of her fleeing a baying mob in her wedding dress at dusk. Every now and then she turned and focused on us – Lancelot and me – proceeding side by side under the censorious eye of disapproving shoppers with, between us, a handwritten banner saying no to something dreamed up by T-L. I remember feeling faintly silly (though this sense didn't last long) and let down somewhat by the marching experience. I had expected much more meaning. Lancelot, cool, calm and unfailingly courteous, viewed the whole business with just the right amounts, it seemed to me, of scepticism and belief.

'The NLF –' I said out of the blue. 'What's all that when it's at home?' That I already knew the answer wasn't the point. I wanted Lancelot to tell me what he knew, to persuade me, to convince me. What did he know? What did any of them know about the war, or about any war? 'Are they the good guys?'

'It all depends which side you're on.'

'They're the Viet Cong – am I right?'

'Pretty much – they side with the north, but in the south.'

'Remind me – why are we pro-NLF?

'Why? Because they're anti-America, of course.'

'But we don't blame the US soldiers –'

'We don't blame the war machine, no.'

'What do we blame if not the war machine?'

'We blame the society that licenses it.'

We were at Selfridges now, heading westward still on Oxford Street in the direction of the American embassy. From the pressmen fielding twin-lens reflex cameras on the canopy above the doors of the department store came the sporadic fire of flashbulbs and the banter of put-downs. Ahead of us the double-deckers were stacked up as far as Marble Arch and Hyde Park. As we approached North Audley Street we heard two roars go up close together in the vicinity of Grosvenor Square. That was the start of it.

We picked up Véronique in the portico of the Commonwealth Church at the margins of the square. From there we could see the grey bunker of the embassy building with its Stars and Stripes and its eagle above. It began as a localised protest in the forecourt area between the embassy steps and a protective hedge. It was here the first contact was made amid angry shouts on one side and whistle blasts on the other. When an agent provocateur in the crowd set off a smoke bomb the whistles of the mounted police merged to form an aggravated shriek, and the people surged blindly forward, hands outstretched, towards the square, or the idea of it.

'Over here! Over here!'

I fell through the hedge. I was pushed through it. The hedge was torn. I saw Lance's face come and go in the gaps in the smoke.

'Get down! Get down!'

We had lost Véronique. There was far too much to hear, and not enough to see. Although I wanted to abandon the hedge I found it increasingly difficult to gauge distance and, bizarrely, time. That was down to the smoke, which robbed the immediate environment of meaningful outline and contour from one second to the next. I started forward on my hands and knees. Where to? I didn't know. I only knew I felt safer down there. Beside me, above me, three men made a run, having come to the city by train to submit to a shared feeling. They went forward arm in arm, jettisoning their Ian Smith cartoon on a stick, so that it dealt me a glancing blow to the head. I saw two policemen drag a girl. She had mislaid her shoes. She had an urge to self-destructiveness. Two nuns stumbled, yoked together like a pantomime horse in the mist. They had lost their way, having come to say a quick prayer between masses. Then I saw Véronique. She was kneeling on a concrete slab below the statue of Roosevelt with her camera swinging from her neck and her fingers plucking at her eyes. I tried to warn her that the police horses were coming, but, whatever it was I yelled, she didn't hear it. The horses were in her part of the square now, very skittish. They formed a battle line of sorts, and then charged, although it was hard for them to get up speed. The cries and whistles were all around as I crashed forward, keeping low – crawling or rolling, really – and pulled Véronique up. She shrugged me off without looking at me. My impression was she had forgotten about her camera, so I dragged it over her head. As I peeled it away from her, I pushed her back down. A policeman was above us with baton raised. He was gliding past on his magnificent chestnut mare (there was, or is, no record of the sex or type of the horse other than the one presented in my photographic account of this episode) when I fixed him with the fast wide-angle lens. As the shutter tripped, the baton came down hard on my arm. I wound the Nikon on. As I pressed the release and wound the camera on again I saw a young man rise up and seize the horse's reins and hang on until the snorting beast fell down, filling the viewfinder and casting off her freelance outrider indignantly as she pitched forward. These snatched glimpses of Lancelot would become my last recollections of the protest activity in Grosvenor Square.

It was dark when I woke up in the porch of the church not far from the embassy. I listened, but I heard no whistles, except maybe the ones inside my head. What I heard was the engine of a taxi at the lights. My head must have been resting in her lap because now her hair hung down towards my face. She had a halo around her of golden light from a bulb high up on the wall of the church. Of the recent past I recalled key details – these included the Nikon, which I found, using one hand then the other, in my pockets. The body was in one pocket, the lens in another, which struck me, stretched out on the flagstones and strafed by shadows cast by the lights of imagined cars, as a kind of miracle. I had an idea I should make a stand on behalf of poor Lancelot, but I didn't stir until Véronique did.

'Is he all right?' I asked her as she licked her cracked lips.

'Lance?' she said. 'I don't know. They arrested him and took him away with the others.'

'Are you OK?'

'Of course – I just feel sorry for the horses.'

'What do you think we should do?'

'Nothing. It's too late. It's over.'

Doing nothing – it struck me as an irresistibly attractive course of action. My whole body felt numb, as if it had been paralysed or anaesthetised by a dart fired from a second floor window at the US embassy. The sheer physical comfort I experienced with my head in Véronique's lap was at odds with the anxious tide still lapping at my brain. In fact, my stubborn discontent had little to do with chaotic events in a smoke-filled square. Its defining psychology was personal not political. It was about who I was and what I might be. Having crossed the river to reach the other side I felt the tug of old forces. I was thinking about Dad. He was looking down on me. For a happy moment I felt closer to him than I had ever felt, and that worried me. Dad was telling me to go on. Go on, son, he said. No, I wasn't thinking about poor, brave Lancelot. I wasn't even thinking about lovely Véronique, who must somehow have saved me from myself.

'Look,' I said, pulling an orange from my coat. 'Want some?'

'As a kid I thought a tree would grow inside me if I ate a pip.'

'Me too,' I said, reaching up with a segment of peeled fruit.

'Will you come with me tonight?' Véronique said, pressing my gift to her lips.

'Sure,' I said, sitting up and wincing. 'Where do you live?'

'Oh,' she said. 'I meant will you come with me to T-L's party —'

Reclining at almost full length in the huge bath I turned the tap off with my toes and slid down until my chin reached the water. Above the basin a mirror continued to mist up nicely, and on the sill of the frosted window, beside a black and white poster depicting a youth on a yacht (Knife In The Water, Roman Polanski, 1962), a display of bottles and phials in blue or green glass struck a therapeutic note. I was weighing the merits and demerits of a windowless bathroom like the one I shared with Dad — how it had certain photographic advantages, for instance — when she came in carrying a scallop shell with a lighted candle on it. She set the shell down carefully between the taps, switched off the overhead light, and sat beside and behind me on the edge of the bathtub.

'Sit up a bit, please,' she said, probing my shoulder above the surface of the water. 'Tell me where it hurts.'

For a few minutes she gently bathed my back and bruised arm with a face cloth soaked in witch hazel, after which I thanked her, stood up in the bath, turned dripping to face her, and asked her to pass me the towel from behind the door. It had come to me about fifteen seconds earlier that she should see me naked, here, now, so that she could get to know me as I was, as I was always going to be, and as she looked me up and down like a trainee nurse on exam day I saw she understood perfectly the message I gave out.

'Now it's your turn,' I told her, ending this awkward episode by wrapping the towel around me.

'How's that?' she asked laughingly, as if this was the prelude to a game she didn't know.

'I don't think you want to go to a party with congealed blood on the back of your head, do you?'

'Why not?' she said, patting her hair. 'Did I forget to mention it's supposed to be a fancy dress party?'

After she had bathed (she used the same bath water I had used, which I found touching), and I had sponged the crusty blood from her hair, she made cheese on toast, and we sat opposite each other at a square table covered in red checks with the oven and grill on beside us. This was in the basement, or the lower ground floor flat, of a mansion block in Maida Vale with the high heels clicking back and forth, just out of sight, on the pavement above the window.

'Did you get some shots today?' she asked, not looking at me.

'In the square?' I said. 'I don't know.' This was true and untrue at the same time. It was untrue that I didn't know. I did. I knew I had some shots. What I didn't know was whether they were good or bad. Correction – I had the strong feeling they were good, but I didn't want to take anything for granted. 'I only snatched a couple of frames,' I said, suitably offhand, 'before I passed out.'

'But you must have some idea –'

'Nope. What you get is never what you saw. It's always either better or worse than you expected, it seems to me.'

In the silence she appeared to weigh up this pretentious claim before dismissing it for what it was.

'Would you like,' she said, opening up a fresh line of enquiry, 'to borrow some clean trousers for T-L's party?'

'You mean as a kind of fancy dress?'

'God – I loathe fancy dress.'

'So do I.'

'What do you like, Billy? I mean apart from photography? Do you like T-L, for instance?

'You mean *love* T-L, don't you? Isn't that what you mean?'

'Just because a man loves you it doesn't follow you love men.'

'Are you speaking from personal experience?'

'Maybe,' she said. 'Anyway, I'm pregnant. I'm going to have a baby.'

Certain features of our journey stand out. I remember feeling very close to Véronique, and it seemed possible she felt close to me too. We rode the bus along Edgware Road as far as the top of Park Lane, changing for Earls Court, and after we got off at Gloucester Road Véronique took my arm and we walked on in silence towards T-L's squat. I had the loaded Nikon around my neck, and she held her Françoise Hardy LP inside her jacket to protect it from a light rain. We picked up two bottles of pale ale and a single Woodbine, which Véronique paid for, at an off licence we had to ask for, and all the while the whole question of the baby hung in the air. To me, the unborn child counted for less at that point than the question of who had helped Véronique make it. Why, given that an outstanding frontrunner was available in the shape of her fiancé, last seen on a croquet lawn, did my unconscious mining for candidates go beyond Raymond, and what did that say about us as people, or about the times we lived in? The music reached us first. There was no melody or tune to speak of at this remove – just the beat. It wasn't difficult to find the party house. Through a batik drape at the raised ground floor window we saw supple silhouettes merge and part, merge and part again, in the context of what looked to be a stroboscopic light show, or a road traffic accident at the edge of the highway. Here at last I thought about T-L, not yet as the father of Véronique's child, but as subject of the idea, twice championed by her, that he was in love with me. I wasn't sure how such an emotion might make itself known, if not via a furthering of T-L's lyrical instability, and as we crossed the road towards the squat that night, Véronique releasing my arm at the steps, I told myself to be on my guard.

'What's your hunch?' I said. 'Looks like he's got a small fleet of ambulances in there with him.'

'Don't joke about it,' she said. 'We may need some of them.'

The door opened on a Gina Lollobrigida type wearing lipstick, headscarf, sunglasses and long gloves while protesting (*no photograph, please*) in a film star accent. We didn't know the fellow, so we pressed on towards a struggling actor at the foot of the stairs – he set out to be an orientalist parlour feature, a performing statue complete with bikini of parrot feathers and blacked-up skin. Common sense told you he was an unblinking mime artist, a skinny kid from the Central School getting steadily colder in the draught from the open door, his raised arm drained long ago of blood. On the salver he held out for us, a symbolic Durex packet kept company with Liquorice Allsorts, sugar almonds and jelly babies in an eye-catching lucky dip.

The kitchen, full of smoke and party people, was at the back of the house beyond the stairs. We squeezed hand in hand past the harlequin leaning prominently in the doorway and found ourselves in the presence of a gangster, his moll, a large Tarzan, a diminutive Jane, assorted pirates and cartoon characters, plus a strongman in a leopard print leotard. Véronique drank some beer and decided she wanted to dance. She meant alone, without me, with someone else. Smacking her LP like a tambourine against her thigh she drew near to the lonesome harlequin and lifted her face towards his mask and said something, just two or three well chosen words, as if to a secret lover. Then she was gone, and I started drinking from both bottles. Someone asked me for the cigarette behind my ear before helping herself and lighting it anyway (confident people in fancy dress think they can get away with anything, especially if they come as Alice of Wonderland fame with no hookah-smoking caterpillar in tow) while explaining, as if this excused any amount of sloppy behaviour, that Robert Kennedy had announced his candidacy for president of the United States of America. This was news about which I had mixed feelings, doubtless because, though no longer under the full-blown spell of my teenage preoccupation with JFK's brother, I remained in some subliminal way reluctant to share him with Alice and the rest of the world. Meanwhile, peeling his mask off as if in an opera, the harlequin revealed himself to be T-L (who else?). Framing his face with hands and forearms he let out a mock scream, highly stylised, for my benefit. Then he too was gone.

In a front room devoted to dancing, the flashing lights (these turned out to be roadside hazard lamps in line with the party's car crash theme) continued to lash the energetic pack grouped flexibly like shoaling herring in the middle of the space. There was no sign of Véronique, no sign of T-L, on the dance floor. Instead I saw the tiny Brazilian, boyfriend of Hamish who had the castle in Scotland, give it his everything with lithe limbs writhing skywards in imitation of a belly dancer or, just possibly, Salome at the feast. Now Salome beckoned, inviting me to join the fun, using little hands and wrists. Although it was sweet of the chap to think of me like that, I moved quickly to disappoint, holding up my near-empty bottles defensively and shrugging like a prig. Upstairs in a cushion-strewn hashish den I found the blacked-up mime artist with his tray of bonbons beside a Ku Klux Klansman and Gina Lollobrigida, the film star swigging warm Babycham from the bottle. Also there and swelling the circular set-up with his considerable presence was Hamish himself.

'Come away, son,' he boomed. 'Come away and lay yon weary camera down and rest.' He had one hand on the mime artist's bare knee and in the other he held a smouldering apple. 'Sit in, man,' he urged. 'Sit in and speak to us of heroic deeds in hostile parts.'

When the apple came round with grains glowing on the foil I passed it on politely.

'So, Billy —' the big Scot went on. 'Did you capture any choice images for uncle Hamish today?'

'I don't know yet, do I?' I said pleasantly.

'But I'll wager you do,' Hamish said, transferring his interest momentarily from the mime artist's knee to mine. 'Who knows what secrets lie tucked away inside that bonny wee heid?'

'I keep my eyes open.'

'Aye — stops you bumping into things, doesn't it? Like horses, I dare say.' The Scot was enjoying himself. 'Police brutality, Billy —' he went on, recalling the smoking apple with a gesture. 'It's an ugly thing, is it not? It makes a mockery of citizenship. Could be worth a few bob to us, though, if we had any pictures of it taking place. Ah, you young people of today —' He shook his head contentedly and tipped the ashes from the apple into a crumbling fireplace. 'Egging on our brave police officers with their truncheons —' Here he fished a finger of hashish from a shirt pocket and began toasting it with a cigarette lighter. 'What the devil were you thinking about — gadding around Mayfair trying to fashion a sense of change when what you probably need to change is your sense of fashion. Ha, ha, ha.' Now he patted the ill-advised trousers – slacks, actually – I had borrowed from Véronique. 'As for Lancelot –'

'What about Lancelot?' I said, listening harder.

'Lance really ought to know his place by now, the cheeky wee monkey. Don't take me the wrong way here –'

'Don't take him *any* way if you can help it, Billy.'

Here was a new voice – new to our little confab. As he spoke, the Ku Klux Klansman lifted his white hood as if raising his hat to a passing hearse. That's when I noticed his hand – I mean I noted the colour of his skin at that moment. I admit I was taken aback to discover Lancelot of the Congo below the headdress. His party look went too far. It didn't suit him, or my ideal conception of him.

'Spooky, *n'est-ce pas?*' Hamish attested, summarising on behalf of decent society.

As I got up it occurred to me I still had a long way to travel to be like my clever friends.

'Come and see me, Billy,' the Scot called out.

'Just try and stop me, Hamish,' I called back.

It was unaccountably dark on the landing. When I found the light switch I discovered the light wasn't working – either that, or someone had removed the bulb. One floor below, the music died suddenly, and in the hush I caught a whiff close by of love, of love suspended or interrupted. As the music took up again strongly (for the record I hear White Rabbit replaced by the more dance-friendly Somebody To Love), I shuffled towards a cordon, faintly luminous, of police incident tape barring the door to T-L's room. The room, like the landing, was in darkness, but by this time I could see what I needed to see. They were sitting opposite each other, but far apart, at a large table pushed up against the shutters and the bay window, and in the half-light I imagined I saw it all plainly enough. In fact, I hadn't seen quite everything yet.

'Good night, Véronique,' I said. 'I think I'll go home now. I'll hang on to the camera, I guess.' There was something else I wanted to say. Then it came to me. 'I'll get your trousers back to you –'

An uncertain silence, vulnerable at all times to outside attack, greeted these prosaic statements. There was the added implication, which Véronique didn't pick up on, that she would have to get my trousers back to me.

'Did you work it out?' she asked finally. 'About the father –'

'I think so,' I told her. 'You don't have to be Einstein.'

'Aren't you going to congratulate us?' T-L asked.

'Thanks for inviting me to your party, T-L,' I said.

'I'm sorry –' he said. 'I didn't think you'd like it.'

'You weren't wrong there,' I said. 'Congratulations –'

'Turn on the light, Billy,' T-L said.

'Why?' I said.

It might easily have been beautiful. It covered the whole wall with its grinning likenesses, its unlikely colourations, and as it made its appeal it kicked me in the stomach. At the centre of the mural a foaming stallion dragged its broken leg across a lush landscape, and where its head should have been was a portrait of me. Everything was finely drawn in this cruel paradise. I saw an elephant bloodied by dive-bombing birds in a gorgeous clearing. I saw the leopard and the gazelle come together in forbidden congress. I saw twenty faces on twenty beasts and each face looked like mine. Abruptly it came back to me – this image of T-L with an Instamatic camera trained on my person, and, in the same instant, the popping of a flashcube.

On the landing it was darker than ever. Three hands rose up and pulled me down, and for a moment I was on a mattress among the bodies. As I lashed out blindly I heard and felt my camera strike bone covered thinly by protective tissue. There was a shriek. When I reached the front door I heard a song kick in randomly, as for a game of musical chairs, but I couldn't think what it was.

I didn't find out what time it was until I reached the river. The city was wide-awake. For half an hour I stood on Waterloo Bridge with the dome of the cathedral behind me and watched the traffic crawl towards Big Ben, then turned my back on Westminster and peered the other way, all the while wondering which view was the nobler. What I wanted to do most was scrape T-L's disturbing mural from my eyes. What did it mean? What was he saying, the crazy father-to-be, and did it matter? Of course it didn't. The whole thing was a staging post on the weasel boy's self-directed flight into transgression on a trajectory of indiscretion that had at its new zenith Véronique's unwanted pregnancy. Was the pregnancy unwanted? Surely it was, I told myself. The truth is I didn't know. I couldn't tell from what I had just seen of the key players. Again I tried to put myself in their shoes in order to review their options. Forget the macabre mural – this was what counted. The ease with which I managed to implicate myself in the matter of Véronique's child by T-L struck me as proof suddenly of an obsessive identification with them both. The baby – it might as well have been mine. A man was approaching, hat low, collar up, from the direction of the National Film Theatre. He was lonely, or he was worried I was going to jump, or both.

'Everything all right here, son?'

'Everything's fine, thanks.' I held up my camera. 'Just waiting for the light.'

'Looks like you missed it.'

'Story of my life.'

'Are you looking for company?'

'I don't think so.'

'Right you are. Well – I think I'll get on now.'

'Yep – me too.'

I retraced my steps as far as Trafalgar Square. It had the sky above it – this much you could rely on. All evidence of today's rally had been removed. The platforms had been dismantled, the leaflets sucked from the fountains and hosed from the paving stones. There wasn't enough money for the bus, but that didn't matter – it was a lucky bus on its way to Paddington. The first thing that hit me was the smell of paint inside our house. I had forgotten about the paint. The second thing was the idea – no, the fact – of the photographs on the walls of our freshly painted living room. I didn't have to look at them to know they were my shots, my large-format self-portraits with Mum, on sale until now at Jacobson's stall in Portobello Road. The thought of Dad going out and acquiring *somehow* my pictures of her and fixing them to *our walls* – there was a tragic improbability about this that made the tears well up in my eyes. Maybe it wasn't so odd. He had always counted himself blessed until she left him for a man with a Ford Zodiac. Now I got a clear sense of it. This wasn't about her. It was about my pictures. He did this for me. From the back of my mind an unsettling notion, which had to do with images and walls, or with their thematic recurrence in a single day, started forward, picking up pace and momentum. There were two pigeons in the living room – that was the third thing that got me thinking. I left the birds and the pictures and went out to the balcony through the open doors. Dad sat, cold and dead, in his beloved cubicle. He had on an out-of-the-box shirt with button-down collar I had never seen before. For the historical record, and in line with the narrative truth, I had to scrape a medallion of pigeon shit – at the end of the day it seemed neither right nor fair that this should be there – from his chest in a region just above the heart.

VÉRONIQUE

You ask me about the baby. The fact is I didn't know if I wanted it or not. That knowledge came after. The baby was different from the pregnancy. At the time they were separate things. In choosing to be pregnant I chose to be free. That's what I believe. One more thing – if you asked me whether T-L forced himself on me in the college's portrait studio I would have to say no.

Billy's garden of remembrance in Holland Park was scarcely a garden, but then Holland Park is barely a park. Not so far from his Dad's favourite bench was the budding chestnut tree below which we scattered the ashes. This would have been towards the close of March 1968. When I say scattered I mean Billy shook his father's remains out like bath salts before kicking them over carefully with a toe to disperse the dunes. There was no breeze as I recall it. There had been a late frost, though – against the ridges of mud at the base of the tree the ashes piled up sparsely like London snow. I had on my hunter's cap, the kind with furry earflaps, and Billy's trousers, which I had formally adopted as a mark of my growing feeling for him. In between strong silences we discussed guilt and redemption in a way that followed closely the scripts of our young lives. When Billy said he felt rotten about not experiencing grief over his Dad's pathetic passing I suggested calmly that what he really felt was guilt – a misconceived guilt that stemmed largely from the sad context for his father's death, which had been an affront somehow to his finer sensibility. What I didn't say was that all this was simply the honest product of his sexuality, of his disposition towards men, women and life. (There was no need to lecture Billy – I mean *on anything*. He was

85

naturally disinclined to believe he was as smart as he was – no doubt that was partly why we were all in love with him a little.) Instead I urged him as lightly as I could not to feel guilty about feeling guilty. When I said it was better to sin again and again and repent than to sin once and not repent, he laughed. I guess we had been avoiding, with our fierce loyalty to higher feeling, the subject of an abortion. Dearest Billy – he asked me how pregnant I was with the anxious expression he reserved for moments of real or imagined crisis. How likely was it, he meant, that Raymond could be deceived by a false conception date if I had sex with him in Paris tomorrow? See what I mean about Billy? You had to love him a little.

CHAPTER EIGHT
Maximum Jeopardy

INSIDE THE BUSY OFFICES OF THE *Kensington News*, sole commercial tenant of a drearily modern three-storey block sandwiched between antique shops towards the Notting Hill Gate end of Church Street, I waited to see the picture editor as the couriers came and went. In fact I had been waiting a long time, my monochrome print (a 10x8in enlargement at once proudly solitary and sheepishly alone) nestling increasingly damp, thanks to hands ready to sweat at the mere idea of introducing myself upstairs, in a manila envelope bearing, in case of loss or accident, Jacobson's name, which I had prefixed 'care of', along with his home address in Chalk Farm. It was with Jacobson and Becky that I had been staying since Dad's funeral took us west via Kilburn to the crematorium at Kensal Green where the chapel of rest turned out to be a cheerful bungalow, contemporary in look and temperamentally uplifting (above head height around its white walls the chunky lozenges of stained glass marched in gladdening ranks of red, blue and yellow), the whole service passing off with a light touch in accordance with the instructions issued by Jacobson, who had paid for it, having consulted me properly *in loco*, as he put it, *parentis*. No tears were shed on the day. No eulogy was delivered. Aside from our row of three the mourners comprised Véronique, sitting discreetly perfumed and similarly pregnant behind us, and a young chaplain, standing immediately in front in order to bring us closer together while wringing his pink hands as if to rid them of a painful affliction – eczema, perhaps – that was subtly commensurate with our loss. Someone else was in attendance – we couldn't know this until we got up to leave. She sat alone at the back of the chapel below a wide-brimmed hat with black veil descending, and I knew who she was right away. Hadn't she lived with us once upon a time – with Dad, the pigeons and me – until we banished her just before midnight? How did she find out Dad was dead? It was impossible to know without asking her. I didn't ask her, nor did I thank her for coming, and as I stepped into a hard light of reckoning beyond the chapel's doors I saw this second omission was a mistake, something I would come to bury among the regrets.

'Miss Laurie will see you now on the first floor.'

As I climbed the stairs I had my envelope in my hand and my Nikon (more and more I had come to regard the college's SLR as my own) slung like a bandolier across my chest. Half way down a corridor towards the rear of the building was a partially open door with her name on it. For a few moments Miss Laurie failed to look up from a desk strewn with photographic prints, so that I was able to observe her freely, without prejudice. Her one arm, cocked at the elbow, held at a prudent distance the cigarette whose teetering ash threatened to plunge at any time. Her other arm was missing – the empty sleeve of her cardigan she attached to her chest by means of an ivory brooch in the form of an elephant. Half-moon glasses, set extravagantly low on the nose, were insufficient for her purposes – there was a magnifying glass, of the sort used by amateur sleuths, on the desk with all the prints. Deploying these details she made an impression on me for several long seconds. Although I was looking at her, I had the feeling it was she who watched me.

'Well?' she drawled finally, glancing up and losing the battle to retain her ash. 'What were you expecting – a one-armed *man*?'

'I'm sorry,' I said, stung. 'I didn't mean to stare.'

'Wondering whether to shake hands?' she said, not unkindly.

'Not quite,' I told her. 'I was trying to imagine what it would be like to do certain things – to be a photographer, say – with just one arm.' It was impossible to lie to her. In this small, bare room the truth was king. 'Is that so wrong?'

'Sit down, please, Mr Morton,' she said, indicating the orange plastic chair on my side of the desk, 'before your youthful candour, charming though it is, trips you up and breaks your neck.'

Conversational niceties, beating about the bush – these were clearly alien to Miss Laurie. Her freedom of speech was hard won, having something to do with her lost limb, surely. As I slipped my solitary enlargement from its damp envelope and placed it the right way up for her on the desk she reached down towards an enormous ashtray on the floor and crushed her cigarette savagely.

'Just the one image?'

It was the question for which I had prepared, if only loosely. Ignoring the blood that rushed hotly to my neck I fixed Miss Laurie with what I hoped was an honest smile, a smile that pitted quality against quantity before coming to important conclusions about the value of one relative to the other, and said nothing.

'Just one image,' she confirmed, raising her magnifying glass and carving the air between us with a slash. 'Describe it to me in as much detail as you can.'

'You're looking at a horse,' I began, voice faltering briefly then rallying defiantly. 'A horse and a policeman – they fill the frame, or almost.' I saw what Miss Laurie was doing. She didn't know me, not as such. She couldn't even be sure it was my photograph in front of her. This was her way of finding out who I was and what I stood for in life. 'There's a young man hanging from the horse's neck –'

'Tell me about the horse.'

'It's a chestnut mare, very strong, very beautiful –'

'This young man – describe him to me, please.'

'He's a coloured student, passionate, courteous, well educated – better educated than me.'

'There's a young woman in the picture –'

'The young woman is French. She's going to have a baby.'

We stopped there. Miss Laurie put down her magnifying glass and gave me back my print.

'Ever been to Paris on assignment, Mr Morton?' she asked.

'No,' I told her.

'Passport? Visa? Cholera jab?'

'Not exactly.'

She was searching her desk for something, rummaging among the images. She scooped up two 5x7in prints and turned them over briefly to take in their captions typed on adhesive labels. 'Protesting students invade all-female residence, Nanterre University,' she read as if at random, shaking a cigarette from her pack before looking up with narrowed eyes. 'Does it mean anything to you?'

I glanced at the pictures on the desk. This was it – the moment of maximum jeopardy. Inside my chest my heart was duffing up my ribs. I saw a US flag on fire. 'Yes, it does,' I told Miss Laurie.

'Good luck in Paris, Billy,' she said, amused by the quality of my lie. 'Naturally, I can't promise you anything in advance.' She reached out her hand and I shook it, and as I slipped my print back into its envelope she returned to the others on the desk. 'Oh,' she took up again distractedly. 'Your picture is good. I think you know that, don't you? As a matter of fact Grosvenor Square is already old hat, which is a pity. I dare say you could place the photograph with any number of bleeding-heart journals destined to languish, by and large, in a toilet under the stairs. Or try the Sunday supplements.'

On the train I stood, exhilarated, exultant, from High Street Ken to Fulham Broadway, one hand on the rail, the other gripping my picture in its envelope. The image was legendary, iconic. As for me – I was already the associate of hardheaded picture editors. My creative destiny lay, as it had for so many others, in Paris, a city I didn't know in a country I had never visited. Oh, I had read a few things. I was also an accessory to stolen French goods in the form of Baudelaire's poems, gift of T-L in what now seemed like another lifetime. Again I saw his scribbled epigraph (it was typical of T-L to bury this, like a guilty secret or an unpleasant surprise, deep inside the volume, instead of presenting it on the title page for all to see) – ART IS LONG AND LIFE IS SHORT, AND SUCCESS IS VERY FAR OFF. Again I dismissed this message as unhelpful. No, I set it aside. I wasn't then in the business of dismissing anything.

As I crossed the King's Road I saw the occupation was over. The placards had been removed from the college's gates, now flung conspicuously open, and the pickets withdrawn from the steps above a forecourt scorched here and there by braziers. Inside it was like a new term, or a new year. Only the potted plants, dying in the lobby, spoke for time lost or wasted as first-years mingled unusually with second-years, and second-years with third-years, all of them milling excitedly about like freshers, canvases clashing, or flashing smiles of recognition, relieved smiles, in my direction as I hesitated beside the statue of David. Looking up I saw the shutter was raised at the store – I pictured Jacobson at work between the shelves on an inventory of stock. It was then I acted on an unworthy impulse. It would be a temporary betrayal only. Holding my famous photograph between my knees I eased the Nikon from my shoulder and separated lens from body, sliding each into a pocket of my coat (in fact I had been concealing or denying the SLR in certain quarters for days already, as if in subconscious preparation for this dread moment, but it was only now I resolved to follow through fully on my duplicity). Then I bounded up the steps towards the store.

'And where did you disappear to this morning of all mornings without so much as a by your leave?'

Jacobson moved between the racks of shelving with a sheaf of typed pages in his hand.

'Sorry about that,' I said, propping up my envelope and then shrugging off my coat heavy with contraband. 'Man about a dog –'

'Meaning mind your own business, I suppose.'

'Is it me, or do people look different today?'

'Your friends don't. That's twice they've asked for you –'

'Oh?' Standing at the counter, my back towards Jacobson, I opened the ledger, located the relevant page, and picked up a pen. I inserted two ticks alongside Véronique's name to indicate she had returned the camera and lens she had booked out long ago, adding my initials in the right-hand column, and with this the betrayal was complete. Although I felt bad I smiled hard at the universe. I was letting myself down, I insisted in the face of a new self-loathing, not Jacobson. 'Which of my many friends is that?' I asked him.

I found them at Jimmy's, a local diner whose house specialities included sticky banquettes arranged in booths and a permanently rank atmosphere built on fags and bacon fat. I didn't have a lot of time. I was conscious of Jacobson, my betrayal, and an urgent need to do the right thing. Something stirred, imperfectly constituted, in my imagination. It was barely an idea, far less a plan. It had to do with Paris, Véronique, her baby and me. Oh, and destiny, too.

'Billy-boy!' Toulouse-Lautrec was on his feet, hugging me as if I was his kid brother recently released from jail, from the Scrubs. 'Sorry to hear about your old man –'

'I appreciate that, T-L.' I didn't mention the monstrous mural, and neither did he. If the artwork stood for anything it stood for the end of something. There was no future in it. I had expected T-L to look different – more like the prospective father, say, or a husband-in-waiting. He was the same, and so was Véronique. It might have been me that was pregnant. No one else cared. 'What's happening about the baby?' I said, waving my hand in a bid to order tea.

'We've decided – Véronique's going to have an abortion.'

'What?' I slumped down opposite her, seeking her fingers out among half-empty cups. She looked straight at me – there was no attempt to dissemble. 'I thought you wanted to keep it.'

'What gave you that idea?' she asked, shrugging.

'I don't know,' I said, body temperature rising.

'What gave you that idea, Billy-boy?' T-L repeated, wresting Véronique's fingers smoothly from mine. 'It's the best thing for all of us, going forward –'

'Except for the baby, you mean.'

They were wrong, totally wrong. I was right – that Véronique wanted to keep the baby was a matter of record, wasn't it? Hadn't she told me from the start? *I'm going to have a baby.* Why would she have said that unless she intended to keep it? Hadn't I told Miss Laurie? *The young woman is French. She's going to have a baby.* After Véronique withdrew her hand from T-L's she squeezed mine briefly, as if to signal it was time to get on with the challenging business of living life. Then she picked up a set of keys lying carelessly on the table in front of Toulouse-Lautrec and held them up for inspection.

'These are for you,' she advised me.

'Keys to my former palace,' T-L chipped in.

'We're staying at my place now,' Véronique explained.

'But I've already got somewhere to stay,' I reminded her.

'In case you want to make a new start,' she said, tapping the keys on the table. 'Later –'

They stood up together, as if in line with an agreed schedule. I had imagined I would leave first, but in the event I had to switch to their side of the booth in order to watch them wave goodbye to me from the glass door. In fact, they had dictated the terms of our little meeting from start to finish. I sat there, sad and lonely, even though the surroundings here at Jimmy's were familiar. Then I saw it – I saw T-L put his arm around Véronique and Véronique throw it off. In this way it came to me that things were not necessarily as they seemed. How could they be? Nothing made sense. Everything was waiting to be written. It was something she said. What had she said? *In case you want to make a new start.* It was code, surely – it had to be. A move to T-L's squat could hardly be described as a new start. *Later*, she had said. Later when? Today? Yes, today. The stakes – it fell to me to up them after all. What had stirred, imperfectly made, in my imagination began to gather speed now. Soon it took on an unstoppable momentum. On the table in front of me were the keys Véronique had tapped so negligently. The tea was cold in the cup. The two sugar cubes were as dice in my hand. Famished suddenly, I ordered a bacon roll, and when it came I ordered another.

That evening, as he drove us home (his home was mine now) after work, Jacobson returned to the subject of the missing apparatus, of the photographic equipment that remained unaccounted for, and I cited again the high levels of confusion created by a series of sit-ins at our college. I still had the large-format Gandolfi out on loan – he knew that, because it said so in the ledger. All the while I was sure he was giving me a last chance to admit my crimes in respect of the Nikon. As he changed gear beside me, the college SLR and its lens lurked hidden in my coat just inches from his hand.

'Could you let me out here?'

We were at the traffic lights below Chalk Farm station, waiting to turn left. It wasn't quite dark in north London. The daffodils had come and gone, and now the days were getting longer.

'But we're almost home.'

'I said I'd look in on a friend in Hampstead.'

'Another man, another dog?'

We stopped in Adelaide Road, half on, half off the pavement. After Jacobson killed the engine I had the urge to jump down from the van and run. The door was open. This instinct for flight – it was about rejecting what had been, in favour of what would be. And yet everything I had done or said or thought or dreamed had brought me precisely here, to the threshold of decisive action, to the prospect of fundamental choice. The past – didn't it merit some credit at least for a job well done? Then let me renounce all that tomorrow.

'Is something wrong?' Jacobson said. 'Are you in some kind of trouble?' He didn't give me time to answer. Doubtless he couldn't bear the thought of my guilt, the idea of my confession. 'We worry about you, Rebecca and I. We love you, so we worry.'

There were many things I liked about Jacobson, not least the fact that in my feelings towards him the impulses to love and respect came together indivisibly as one emotion. Among the things I loved and respected most was that he did no special pleading on behalf of his daughter. He never expected me to *like* Becky, and I believe this made a big impression on me at the time.

'Thanks, Mr Jacobson,' I said. 'I won't be late.'

So it began – the countdown to tomorrow. I rode a Northern line train for two stops, and when I reached the red front door and rang the bell I felt strong. Although I had made no appointment to see Hamish, something told me he would be at home. It wasn't just that he was so obviously of the leisured classes. It was more a case of rightness under the circumstances. He had to be there. He opened the door in what looked like a Japanese robe, a kimono, black and shiny with a dragon motif in gold. After he made us tea (chamomile, the first and last time I had it) I showed him my Grosvenor Square photograph, which he seized on with a natural feeling for what was involved, and then I asked him for fifty pounds. Call it an editorial down payment, I reasoned.

'There's so much happening in Paris at the moment,' I said, as if this was justification enough for a cash investment.

'Fifty quid?' Hamish said, letting out an ostentatious whistle. 'That's a lot of bread, man.'

'Is it?' I asked ingenuously. 'As a matter of fact I just plucked that figure out of the air.'

'I tell you what we'll do, Billy,' he came back. 'We'll strike us a wee bargain, shall we?'

After he had cleared the cups from the kitchen table he bent me over it, worked my trousers and underpants down to my shoes, spat on me a few times, and then entered me from behind without further preparation or preamble – without small talk. He asked me to call out various names that meant something to him, and for the next three or four minutes we carried on like that while the table migrated in harsh lurches towards a window, and the radio fed us Louis Armstrong's What A Wonderful World. In between events I was thinking about T-L, about how I would have to distance myself from him now, and that's what hurt most. To be on the cusp of the new without my crazy mentor – it saddened me suddenly. I felt a loss. Ten minutes later I was heading towards Belsize Park and my temporary home with one hundred pounds (Hamish was a generous man) in my pocket and a clear sense in my head of how it would be.

There was no sign of Jacobson. It was as if he had removed himself so that everything might happen according to plan. Becky was in the dining room with her typewriter and a pencil case on the table in front of her and a dictionary on the chair beside her. When I asked her what she was doing she said she was writing a romance called 'Late Summer Rain' for a competition in *Woman's Own*. She found me a white envelope, and I wrote the short note there and then with Becky watching me out of the corner of her eye. DEAR MR JACOBSON, I wrote (my use of capital letters must have been a spin-off, surely, from T-L's Baudelaire book epigraph), PLEASE SET THIS MONEY AGAINST WHAT YOU PAID FOR THE FUNERAL, YOURS TRULY, BILLY MORTON. P.S. SORRY I TOOK THE NIKON CAMERA. Now Becky sat back from the table, her arms crossed defensively or accusingly in front of her. By this time she would have worked it out for herself. Why else would I be writing her father's name on the envelope and propping it up against the stuffed stoat on the mantelpiece?

'Where are you going, Billy?'

'Away – just for a few days.'

'Where to?'

'Paris.'

'Paris? With her?'

'I don't know.'

'Why?'

'I'm taking pictures for a newspaper.'

'Which newspaper? Are you serious?'

'There's a taxi waiting outside.'

'What – you're going right now?'

'I'll collect the rest of my stuff when I get back.'

'But you don't know any French –'

That was it. That was as far as we took it. Becky watched me round up some clothes and assorted effects, including Baudelaire's poems, but not my kitsch painting of mustangs on a moonlit beach. As for the paltry balance of my stuff – I was already kissing goodbye to it. There was something I had to remember. It was the Gandolfi camera – I asked Becky to give this back to Jacobson. When I went to embrace her at the end, Becky stood there passively. She didn't return my embrace, and I couldn't blame her for that. The truth is I was in a tearing hurry to get away. I felt bad, abandoning my post without notice like this and sneaking off, a thief in the night. It was pretty low, I admit. If I was letting anyone down, I argued feebly, tendentiously, and not for the first time, it was my guilt-riddled self. As for the Nikon buried in my coat – I was only borrowing it, I told myself, for as long as I had to. Yes, that was it. Having confessed to my crime and apologised for it, absolution was mine. Then the flaw in my thinking came back to haunt me. If I was only borrowing the camera, why didn't I ask Jacobson to lend it to me? What possible motive or reason could there be for not asking unless it was the will to destroy the things I loved best?

No taxi waited outside. I had invented that bit to make things quicker, or easier, for everyone, especially me. I picked up a black cab outside Camden Town station, and when I reached the squat I saw the place was in darkness. When I tried the first of my keys the front door gave. I flicked a light switch, but nothing happened. After I called out, with the noise of the Gloucester Road traffic behind, I saw the glow of a candle, high up, and heard a man's voice.

'Who's there?'

'Billy Morton – I've got keys.'

'Ditto half of London. Know your way around here, do you? Bastards have gone and cut us off –'

I couldn't recall a lock on the upstairs door, but clearly there was one. When I tried the second key the door yielded. At the same time the candle withdrew behind me. In front was the familiar bay window leaking light from the street. When I opened the shutters the orange light fell in. I was alone in T-L's room. There was the big table and two chairs, and, beside the mattress on the floor, a plank of wood with its charred end in the fireplace. The mural was gone. The mural had been painted over – now the wall was black, except for a segment in the middle, which carried in large capital letters the legend THERE IS A WAR BETWEEN THE MAN AND THE WOMAN. Stuck to the table was the stub of a candle, but I saw no matches. That didn't matter – I was in no mood for Baudelaire, or Sartre, or any of their tribe. I lay fully clothed on the mattress, the warm light comforting me, and waited for Véronique to show up. I didn't doubt she would come. This was how it was supposed to be – she felt it too. Such certainty I based on my strong sense of kinship with Véronique. Again I saw it from her point of view. Although she was escaping something, hers wasn't a blind flight. She was running away from something towards something else. So was I.

J\ACOBSON

Either you are trying to hurt us, or you are trying to hurt yourself, or both. It's impossible to know which from such a distance. Four little words I commend to you, Billy. Thou shalt not steal. There is no excuse for this. What good could come of it? Had you asked me for a camera, any camera, I would have given it to you willingly.

Had you asked to go to Paris for any practical purpose I would have given you my blessing. How are we to view your actions, Rebecca and myself, other than as a betrayal of our trust and love? A man gets very few chances in life, Billy – I mean to make mistakes and be forgiven. I don't expect you to think kindly of me – to me your actions are those of a young man bent on burning bridges. Think rather of your late father and, yes, your mother. Try to be worthy of their love, or their undying regard. Try to ration your mistakes – I mean your biggest mistakes. The fast wide-angle lens you took – it's a rare prize, isn't it? Its extra speed is its special virtue. In admitting extra light it admits more truth. Use it wisely, Billy, and use it well. Don't you know people have died for a glimpse of that truth?

CHAPTER NINE
The English Sky

WHEN I WOKE UP, THE DARKNESS HAD A CHANGED quality, a new
look or feel. The orange colour had gone from the light. Night itself
was withdrawing – now I could map the rugged continents of damp
on the ceiling of T-L's old room. I began to doubt. I went over the
ground again, and all the signs were uncertain. I thought – soon it
will be morning. Still she didn't come.

I heard a noise at the window. It might have been a small stone
lobbed up from the pavement, or a fragment of glass from a broken
windscreen. I jumped up and pressed my forehead against the pane.
No one was down there, as far as I could make out. Then I heard it –
a knocking, softly purposeful, on the front door below. When I got
to the landing someone was already on the stairs to the hallway.

'It's OK,' I said. 'It's for me –'

'No – don't answer it.'

'No, no – it's all right.'

I pushed past and rushed down the stairs. Just as I reached the
hall someone's parked bicycle fell down on the loose tiles. When I
opened the door Véronique was standing very close to, as if she had
been pressing her cheek to the wood, or kissing the paint. There was
a suitcase beside her on the step. After I picked up her valise I drew
her inside and closed the front door. Then I righted the fallen bike.

'Martin Luther King is dead,' Véronique said.

She followed me up the stairs, hesitating in the doorway while I padded across to the big bay window. Day was arriving fast now, unpremeditated, without conditions. It was a new morning. On this question of the news of the world I was clear. I didn't want to think about it – not here. It had no business with us – not today. In the street directly below me a whistling milkman carried four empties, two in each hand, from a doorstep to his waiting float.

'I wasn't sure if you'd come,' I said.

'When are we leaving?' Véronique asked.

I turned my back on the window and the English sky. She was still standing in the doorway, toying with the buckle of her trench coat, her suitcase at her feet. It was as if she chose not to enter the room. She didn't want to. Yes, that was it – she didn't want to step back. In respect of where we might go together, nothing had been declared. Nevertheless, it was understood between us. As for what we would do when we got there – we left all that to tomorrow. The rattle of milk bottles rose up from below – to me it was a poignant marker for something lost, or something I was about to forsake. At that moment Véronique picked up her valise and held it in front of her knees using pale hands.

'Well?' she said, rocking her head from one side to the other.

'Now –' I said, shouldering my backpack and stepping into my shoes. 'We're leaving now.'

PART TWO

City of Love

CHAPTER TEN

The Price of Everything

WITH THE PROPRIETOR'S NAME EMBLAZONED discreetly in seven gold letters over its illuminated window, Zwimmer's photographic studio stood at 13 carrefour de l'Odéon at the point where the lesser streets came together in an awkward delta just short of boulevard Saint-Germain. Hesitating for a moment on a cobbled island at the confluence of thoroughfares I examined the shop and surrounding terrace from roof to roadside and wondered again what I was doing there – not simply at that precise location in the city of love, but in the city of love itself. Above Zwimmer's studio the apartments were ranged in hostile, low-ceilinged tiers, tall windows with wrought iron balustrades clustering starkly side by side like the gills of a shark. I say hostile. My most naked appeals to Paris to accept me, to take me to its vain heart, had fallen on uninterested ears. I had said nothing of my bitter disappointment to Véronique. What good would it do? Obviously I wasn't trying hard enough to adore Paris. There comes a time in every quest when the next stone turned must be the last – the last, that is, that fails to uncover the prize. I couldn't go back. Back home – for me the idea had no meaning. It was a measure of how much I wanted to belong that I was still looking for a job in the city of love. I would make Paris like me – I had to. If I hadn't quite given up on my hunt for a post (I am not speaking here of shooting pictures according to Miss Laurie's hypothetical brief), I was ready to do so. Zwimmer would be my last roll of the dice. To be rejected by my adoptive city – it felt harsher, more desolating, than anything I knew. As I crossed rue Monsieur le Prince with my faithful Nikon slung desperately across my chest I was close to angry tears, most earmarked for myself, with the balance reserved for the indifferent streets. In Zwimmer's shop window, hanging spotlighted on narrow wires and backed by a drape of red velvet, was a colour photograph, poetically charged and politically resonant, of a sensually handsome youth wearing a beret in the style or attitude of Che Guevara. Why I should take particular notice of this image wasn't exactly clear. It was there to be noticed – of course it was. From the photographic standpoint it had a lot of interest and merit, reconciling as it did the colour temperatures of flash, tungsten and further lighting at dusk. The youth was pictured in front of a warmly lit café. From above his head a fluorescent sign that said 'La Goutte d'Or' in peppermint green sang out memorably, the whole luminous outcome giving me hope while stiffening my sagging resolve. Fishing a worn fragment of paper, my jobseeker's crib sheet, from my pocket, I pushed open the door beside the shop window and stepped resolutely inside.

At first there was just the dark bulk of Zwimmer, back turned to the door, at the centre of the room beside the tripod. Pouf! His flashgun went off. The flash was only there to impart sparkle to the eyes of the woman and the dog, joint focus of Zwimmer's attention, posing together in period dress (the spaniel included) under fierce floodlights against a painted Arcadian backdrop featuring idealised trees and shrubs on a low stage towards the rear of the studio.

'*Bonjour,*' I said, directing myself, in the absence of any more reasonable target, at the model on the platform beyond Zwimmer. After the dog barked twice and the woman on the dais shouldered her parasol interestedly I pressed home my advantage (no need at this time to invoke the glossary of useful phrases jotted down for me by Véronique). '*Je m'appelle Billy —*'

Now Zwimmer turned away from the platform so that I first saw his features silhouetted against the photofloods. Above a large body, which sat on uncommonly short legs, his round head seemed to hover without recourse to the usual connecting tissue. There was no neck as such — just a head and protruding ears edged with silver light below the unruly hair, cut notionally *en brosse*, which reached up and out as if in response to electric stimulus. The effect, boosted benignly by Zwimmer's thick, round spectacles, was of an avuncular snowman. '*Bonjour à vous, monsieur,*' he came back to me fastidiously (I already knew he was German). '*Vous voulez?*'

'*Je suis anglais,*' I explained according to an established routine developed or adapted from Véronique's helpful notes. '*Je m'excuse — je ne parle pas bien français. Je cherche du travail.*'

'But my dear boy —' began the woman from her station beyond Zwimmer, addressing me in English before stepping down from the stage with spaniel in tow and gloved hand extended. (Although we were already known to one another we pretended otherwise, as if in deference to the principles of a marvellous game.) 'How perfectly charming — you know, there really is no need to apologise here, of all places, for being as you are.'

I took the gloved fingers in mine and, moving instinctively to brush them with my lips, I saw the Adam's apple of a man got up as a woman, a woman of a certain age in the garb of a bygone era. I was in a carnival, or a circus, or a play. That was fine by me — there was nothing unsettling in all this. It was unexpectedly comforting in a dreamlike way. We were actually smiling, Herr Zwimmer and the lady with the lapdog and me. I was about to kiss the proffered fingers in a nod to good manners when the spaniel, now in the big German's keep, barked three times and the shop door burst open, a delivery boy sweeping in like a waiter exiting a kitchen.

'Ah, Lafcadio,' Herr Zwimmer said. 'Take off your helmet and meet our new friend Billy.'

Again, this was in accented English. Although it struck me as highly improbable he would comprehend anything but French, the courier confounded me by peeling off his crash helmet and tucking his parcel under his arm before removing a soiled gauntlet with his brilliant teeth and holding out his hand.

'You speak English?' I asked him, his close physical presence conspiring to strand me between question and statement.

He shrugged then in a way that made it hard to know whether he understood me at all. Suddenly I saw it. He was the young man with the beret in the photograph suspended spotlit in Zwimmer's shop window. Now the handsome youth (his beauty had an Arabic quality, the quality of, say, a gazelle) exchanged a few rapid remarks with the man dressed as a woman, grateful recipient of his parcel, before putting on his helmet and backing away towards the door, where he waited. He waited, I sensed clearly, for *her* – to help her, or to protect her, or to honour her somehow according to the rules of the game we were caught up in. Here, she was king, or queen.

'Time now for Madame Georges to slip upstairs and take her medicine,' she explained then, evidently for my benefit, patting her paper package before presenting me with the furled parasol. As she cupped my chin with her gloved fingers she let her voice, pitched until now in a region between contralto and tenor, sink to a manly bass. 'We will be your new Paris family, Billy – Herr Zwimmer and Lafcadio and Madame Georges. We will care for each other, won't we? You – you were sent here among us. But why, I wonder?'

As soon as I was alone with Herr Zwimmer I returned to the pressing business of landing a job. In fact, we weren't quite alone together – the spaniel, panting hard now, was at our feet.

'I'll do anything,' I said, raised camera lending useful context to my wild offer.

'Are you all right?' Zwimmer asked me. 'You look sick. Your face is white.'

'Is there a job going here?' I persisted. 'The only thing I can't or won't do is process colour –'

'There's no job here – except, maybe, with the tourists. Wait – first I bring water.'

'I'm OK – really I am – but thank you anyway. How do you mean except with the tourists?'

'I mean taking their picture in the park. Wait, *bitte*. The water is intended for the dog.'

Perhaps I was sick. Perhaps Zwimmer was right. As I crossed the river at Pont des Arts, the Polaroid instant camera around my neck, I pictured the mighty Thames flowing out to sea with, here and there, a low-slung barge ploughing, minnows below and gulls above, due east by Poplar. It was unhelpful as an image. Nostalgia, homesickness – these were fatal to my cause. Nanterre, the political fact of it, had brought me here with a loaded Nikon. That was just an excuse, surely, a trigger for the personal transformation destined to take place here in Paris. When I thought back to my audiences in London with Hamish and Miss Laurie I didn't recognise myself as I was then. Unformed and unfulfilled – these were just two of the epithets I found to use against myself. Half a person – that's what I had felt like mere days ago, or so I told myself. Now I was nothing at all. It was no joke. With Notre-Dame and Île de la Cité behind me I eyed the prospect of the Louvre and viewed the photographic task that awaited me in the park beyond. This would be my job. It was a noble calling. In any case, I couldn't simply plunder the city of its meaningful images, at Nanterre or anywhere else, and retire. First it was necessary to pay certain dues. First it was necessary to honour the place fittingly (in the way Lafcadio appeared to honour Madame Georges, for example). Only by earning the city's respect and trust would I access its secret life or unlock its special quality.

From the Louvre I tramped west from courtyard to courtyard until I reached the Tuileries, where, finally, I was sick at the base of an old plane tree. Above the gardens in all directions the sky was a novel blue, a French azure untested by cumulus or cirrus. Suddenly they were there beside me, beside my tree, two tourists from Japan, from Hiroshima, I imagined, or the blasted hills of Nagasaki – two lovers, no longer young, one crying in the sun. When I took their picture and gave it to them they giggled and bowed, thanking me in their outrageous French. Two lost dogs, both trailing leads, were stuck to each other back to back behind a slatted bench.

It was in place de la Concorde that I first saw her. I picked her out. She was on the Champs-Elysées side of the obelisk, smoking, alone. Who was she waiting for? She needed no one. She had on dark glasses. There was something dyed about her hair. Discarding her cigarette she stepped onto the crossing, ignoring the signal, and advanced unperturbed, the traffic all around her, until, framed by the Arc de Triomphe and followed by me, the itinerant portraitist, she made the far shore, her suede handbag gathered in closely now. I was about to give her my little speech – Zwimmer's speech about the role and value of instant photography – when a scooter rode up on the pavement beside us, inaugurating a fast-moving sequence of events. First, the Polaroid camera went off unexpectedly. Then a helmet flashed in the sun. Finally, the rider of the scooter snatched the suede handbag away and roared off unsteadily in the direction of the westerly gardens and the Seine.

I don't know what I was thinking when I elected to give chase. I suppose I judged myself to blame somehow. I was an accomplice, an accessory. For all she knew I was the one who distracts you even as an associate steals the bread from your mouth, or the gold from your teeth. I ran and ran. Soon I began to feel sick again. The thief was getting away. I wasn't myself – I had to stop and retch, hands on knees. Now something was wrong – that is, something new was wrong. The whine of the engine – it was getting louder. That was because the scooter was coming directly towards me on the central path of the park. There was nothing to do but wait. It took about five seconds for the scooter to close the gap between us, scattering boulevardiers and separating dogs. After the rider came to a messy halt just a few feet away he threw down his scooter, by which time I had all but recognised him, using my strong feeling for destiny, as Lafcadio of the medicine parcels.

'You –' I said, relief and surprise trumping my trepidation at the last moment.

'*Quoi?*' he said, hurling away the suede handbag and snatching off his helmet before seizing me by the throat and kissing me hard on the mouth. '*Mais que veux-tu que je fasse?*'

There was something else that might easily, in circumstances less freighted with existential responsibility, have made me laugh. I must have nudged the magic button unwittingly, or hit the plastic knob, so that now Zwimmer's Polaroid gave out its latest offering, an abstract composition not yet fully developed but moving rapidly towards that state of affairs in the blue afternoon.

'That bag you stole –' I said, pointing in front and behind to indicate the scope and range of my concern, while Lafcadio cocked his head at me pityingly. 'I'm asking you to return it to its rightful owner immediately.'

When I opened my eyes it was growing dark. Véronique surveyed me from the edge of the bed. In the soft light from the window, and from my coordinates of physical frailty and emotional suggestibility, she appeared to me as a kind of apprentice Our Lady.

'Feeling better?' she asked, switching on the bedside lamp.

Closing my eyes again in order to explore the question in detail I tried to picture my surroundings as far as I recalled them, running in my head a potted topographical slide show that featured avenue de l'Observatoire and the nearby Jardin du Luxembourg, landmark locations during the several days and nights I had been staying here as a reluctant house guest. Don't get me wrong. I was very grateful to Véronique's parents for putting me up – I just couldn't be sure how genuinely welcome I was under these circumstances. To me, I was a clear signal to the parents that something was wrong with the daughter. That was another thing. The question had plagued me using half a dozen or so conceptual disguises as I tossed and turned these past few hours in the big, high guest bed – how pregnant did you have to be before it became obvious to the rest of the world? It was a question to which I felt I ought to know the answer. Shouldn't everyone know the answer? Did Véronique? When I looked again she was still watching me, her face bathed in the reassuring glow of the lamp, smiling patiently. 'Yes, loads better –' I told her.

'Hungry?'

'Starving.'

'You've been out cold for the best part of twenty-four hours.'

'How rude of me.' I was thinking about the parents and what they must have made of me so far. She was Canadian. I liked her, and I felt she was prepared to like me. He was much cooler towards me in a style and manner that befitted his lifelong station as a civil servant. No doubt he had made a career success of circumspection. What I mean is he was probably cool towards any and every male friend to his daughter if he didn't recognise you as Raymond, the betrothed. It was at this very moment, pulling on my trousers while Véronique continued to watch me, the hint of a frown on her face now, that I readmitted to the uncertain realm of my senses the idea of Toulouse-Lautrec. This brief glimpse – it was just a flash in the sky. Even so, I saw it as an unfortunate lapse, an error from which I was keen to move on as quickly as possible. 'How long did you say your parents had lived here?' I asked, making immediate reparation while casting a polite eye over the tasteful collection of masks, rugs, drawings and other decorative objects, including a giant ceremonial hookah, which made of the guest room a miniature museum.

'Since we got back from Algeria,' Véronique said, shrugging and then swatting this notion aside in favour of something closer to the surface of her mind. 'You look thinner,' she told me, the source of her frown made evident.

'Almost certainly the result,' I said, 'of not eating enough chips in recent days.'

'Supper's ready,' she said, getting up and kissing my cheek.

At the table Mrs Lamartine spoke on behalf of her husband, but without looking at him – it was as if he had been temporarily detained in another part of the house. In answer to my promptings she listed couscous and canaries in gilded cages among the things she missed most about the Algeria they had left behind more than a decade ago. She missed the little things, she said. It was probably a code, I felt. She missed the days when she had loved her husband. The wasted nights were her biggest regret. She had exhausted her stock of loving – all but a reserve she held back for emergencies. He too had used up his store. Now he inched respectably towards his pension at the ministry on the bank of the river and, had you asked him what he missed, he would have listed the sea, the sun, and the savage stars above diplomatic receptions at a time when his wife was the best hostess to be found anywhere decent, meaning anywhere *French*, between Marseilles and Alexandria.

'But you must stay on with us here, Billy,' she was saying. 'At least until you find your feet.' I didn't speak. I only looked at her, wide-eyed, open to everything. 'Of course, there's the wedding to come,' she went on immediately, thus conflating the event with me, me with the event, in a way I found dangerous and alarming. Had someone set a date? Had she brought it forward behind my back? How much did she know? Did she suspect? 'We can see how fond of you Véronique has become in London –'

Still I said nothing. I took no chances. Instead I focused on my physical surroundings in a renewed attempt at fitting in. There was the crisp white tablecloth with, at its centre, an elaborate ornament (in the absence of detail recollected what remains is the impression of quality) picked up for a song half a lifetime ago in a backstreet bazaar. There was the heavy cutlery and the charged candelabrum and, on the distant sideboard, a fragrant terrine with, above it on the wall, two oils, dark and lustrous, in ornate frames with the little strip lights over them. Only the maid was missing.

'Billy's been commissioned to make a photographic record of the latest developments at Nanterre.'

We had agreed not to mention this at all, so that Véronique's intervention here marked in my eyes a new phase of our household arrangements. I shot her a glance, but she gave nothing away. I still couldn't quite believe what was happening. She had said it herself.

The idea that an unmarried French girl of good family could have sex, get pregnant, and not be punished for it was absurd. Why then had she come back to Paris, to the family seat, in her condition – up the duff, and with a bun, courtesy of T-L, in the oven?

'Would that be the frankly unpleasant housing developments, I wonder, or the even uglier political developments?'

'Oh, Papa, *honestly* –'

'Forgive my little joke, Billy. What we really want to know is whether you'll be taking the pictures at our daughter's wedding.'

There was no love there – not for me, at least. Suddenly I saw the thing differently. By getting pregnant Véronique was punishing them for something, something I couldn't expect to understand. It could never be described or discussed. It was carried in the blood.

'I'd be extremely honoured –' I said, gulping some of the thick red wine. 'If that's what Véronique wants.'

Later I stood at the bedroom window, looking down on the shared garden – there was the fountain at this end and the tall railings of the Luxembourg Gardens at the other. To the south, at the corner of boulevard du Montparnasse, the famous Closerie des Lilas was emptying out in a splurge of neon light. Véronique had mentioned it in passing, and now it was part of the world of possibilities here in the city of love. She said you could go to the famous brasserie and flash your wallet or the proofs of your latest masterpiece and ask for Hemingway's table, or the alcove favoured at one time by Verlaine, and feel better about yourself at a price. Everything had a price.

As I lay in bed, hands behind head, and stared at the painting, a desert scene (the sand dunes, the mushroom cloud, the blinkered dromedaries, the canaries with the banner saying First French Test, Sahara, 1960) in a naïve style by the younger Véronique Lamartine,

I slowly became aware of it – the sound of an engine ticking over, regular and low, in auditory competition with the working fountain (eight cavorting horses with fish tails, plus the spitting turtles) in the Jardin Marco-Polo beneath my window. When I looked down I got a shock. He was sitting astride his scooter, crash helmet under his arm, a cigarette hanging from his lips, gazing up at me like a punk. My first instinct was to step back, to turn away in recognition of the heat taking sudden hold in an area near my heart and lungs. The bedroom seemed much too light now. Wildly I registered the camel stools, the camphorwood chest, and the empty birdcages. Then I heard a revving of the scooter's engine from below. When I looked out again Lafcadio had disappeared from view. There was only the fountain, impossibly loud now in the relative quiet. Force-fed by the blazing street lamps, all the trees were coming into fulgent leaf.

Madame Georges

At all times his appeal was well judged. It had both a physical and a psychological dimension. He was agreeably put together in what I would call a working-class way. He was also self-aware in a painful or punishing degree – I would say there was a struggle happening inside him between the fact, or truth, of who he was and a model conception of himself. In other words he was a young Englishman, naturally fair-minded, the best of his type. It was his first night in Paris. He had taken it upon himself to find an inexpensive hotel in the Port-Royal district because he didn't want to stay at his friend's house. She did offer, but he told her he would manage. He had his useful French phrases ready, the few she had given him – these he directed at the hotel's receptionist, a man dressed as a woman. I am, or was, that hotel receptionist. I invited Billy to wait beside the fish tank while the night porter was summoned, after which I led our guest to the uppermost room (I levied no charge for the use of this garret) in the house, uncovering there my medicine kit and laying the works out on the bed. After I had taught Billy various phrases to boost his meagre repertoire – *à moitié mort de faim, il se mit à ramer de toutes ses forces,* for example – suggesting these would stand him in good stead because the idioms they used were readily transferable from one circumstance to another, he slept like a baby beside me. I myself rarely sleep when the medicine is on me. Shortly before first light I wrote down for him the address of Zwimmer's photographic premises, located directly below my own household apartments in Saint-Germain-des-Prés, indicating he might try his luck there. The boy's hunger for knowledge and experience was plain to see. At the same time he had a remarkable feeling for *what was exactly sufficient* to every situation or need. In this way he quickly came to represent for me an ideal of English youth at that time.

IN THE MORNING I ACCOMPANIED VÉRONIQUE to the University of Paris-Sorbonne where she was due to hook up with Raymond (I never did discover his subject there, but it was bound, I feel sure, to have been in the physical sciences). Things were getting serious for Véronique now in the sense that time was slipping by, and she had yet to confront the consequences locally of her pregnancy. As far as I knew she hadn't actually met up with Raymond since returning to the city, which made this an important moment in her story, and in mine. The truth is I regarded Paris as a hopeless case. The whole thing was a mess, or a mistake, and I was in the middle of it. There were three things that disturbed me. There was Lafcadio with his uncanny ubiquity – I couldn't work out whether this was a force for good or bad. There was my inability to get to grips with Nanterre, a location that, although notionally the starting point for this entire misadventure, remained a mere dot on the map to me. Crucially, there was the business of Véronique's pregnancy, and the growing conviction I had that the truth shouldn't, or wouldn't, wait. In this last case my unease was tied in with my domestic situation – even as I found shelter under Véronique's roof I was party to a lie. In fact, although I couldn't have known it as we descended deeper into the Quartier Latin, this was the day everything would change.

'What's Raymond *like*?' I asked Véronique with a sense, which she probably picked up on or shared, that my seemingly superficial question went to the heart of the matter.

We had left busy boulevard Saint-Michel behind, and now the dome of the Richelieu chapel rose like a dark sun over the academic bookshops in the place de la Sorbonne. Around my neck I carried Zwimmer's Polaroid camera – a reminder, if any were needed, of the disappointing reality of my encounter thus far with the city of love. In my head was, among other things, the abiding image I had of a fiancé equipped with a croquet mallet in a snapshot taken down from a college wall in London.

'Raymond?' Véronique came back at me, as if she needed to remind herself of who we were dealing with here. 'He's old school, or old money, like his people. He's a cat person. He loves cats.'

As we sat, waiting for the appointed hour, on the steps of the chapel in the Cour d'Honneur we had the statues of Victor Hugo and Louis Pasteur, eavesdropping heroes, on this side and that.

'Is he capable of forgiving you?' I asked, because this seemed to suggest a way forward for Véronique.

'I'm not sure I know,' she said. 'You meet someone you think you like. You allow yourself to fall in love just a little and then you discover who or what that someone is. You only get to know after – after things go wrong. I think we can take that as a no, don't you?'

'There's something you haven't told me,' I said.

'You mean whether or not I *want* to be forgiven?'

'I mean how you got pregnant in the first place.'

'Don't they teach you the facts of life over there?'

'I'm not sure they taught me.' Fundamentally, there were two aspects to the whole business that had to be addressed either jointly or separately. This was my settled view. On the one hand there was the news (news to Paris) that Véronique was in the family way. On the other there was the small matter of who the father was. It was with this second consideration that I engaged more closely. As each hour passed I wanted to make it clear, not least to Mrs Lamartine, who had been kind to me, that I was not the father of Véronique's unheralded baby. Of course, there was a third, hugely important, element to the story, which I had struggled from day one to ignore (indeed I had just touched on it with Véronique in the shadows of Pasteur and Hugo). What we still didn't know, those of us who knew anything at all, was whether the baby was, or ever had been, in any meaningful way, a love child. Wasn't this the most significant factor in play here? We had received no briefings in that regard. We were obliged to make it up for ourselves. Funny thing – in their ongoing consideration of Raymond's feelings, Véronique's sympathies could best be described as chilly. At the same time there was no evidence of a love pact with the baby's father. The fashioning of Véronique's pregnancy struck me as a personally destructive gesture, and, to this extent at least, it bore the true stamp of Toulouse-Lautrec, drawn as he was to acts of transgression designed to thwart his own chance of happiness. Maybe I worried too much. Maybe my sensitive mining for motive was misplaced. After all, I was a man – perhaps the only thing that counted was the fact of the baby, growing larger inside Véronique from one minute to the next. 'What,' I asked urgently, in the uncertain knowledge I had just glimpsed him, or someone who might easily have been him, 'are you planning to tell Raymond in a few seconds from now?'

'The truth, of course – what else?'

'Toulouse-Lautrec included?'

Then he was upon us, taller than I had imagined, older than I had remembered, and lightly bearded. After they had kissed, and

Véronique had introduced me to Raymond as her English friend, he said something witty about the instant camera (only the Nikon defined me) I had raised to my eye before shaking my hand coolly and inviting me immediately to dinner at the family home.

'A friend of Véronique's is a friend of mine –'

'You'd better tell Billy how to get to Auteuil.'

'I know that. Or perhaps you'd like to do it.'

'Just jot an address down, please, one of you,' I said, firing off another shot to suggest a relaxed approval of unfolding events.

'Shall we throw a surprise party, Véronique?'

'Yes, let's – you know how I adore surprises.'

So it was done, arranged. As I took myself reluctantly towards Zwimmer's studio to confront another day of stalking tourists in the city's parks (or, just possibly, to resign my Polaroid commission in response to an inner voice that railed at futility) I pictured the scene – the polished dinner table, the candlelight, the wine, the laughter of family and friends, the polite enquiries of me in formal English, and Véronique's bombshell revelation that she was pregnant. Did she perhaps intend to surprise Raymond earlier so as to manage the fall-out? Yes, that was it. Why ruin a perfectly good nosh-up?

I found Herr Zwimmer at the enlarger under safe lighting in the darkroom, an extension in the form of a lean-to at the back of the shop. When I asked him how best to get to Nanterre he told me not to bother – I wouldn't find any tourists to shoot there because it wasn't remotely on the tourist trail. About Auteuil he was far more positive – there were no tourists to photograph here either, but at least it was a nice location. I was about to hang up his Polaroid and reclaim my Nikon forever when the lamp went out at the enlarger, Zwimmer moving placidly to immerse the paper in the developer along with half a dozen other sheets already exposed. These sheets were small – about the size of a tarot card, or a passport. It was the moment of discovery, the moment beloved of all photographers. As I leaned over the tray to take a closer look at the ripening images I got a couple of surprises. First, I felt Zwimmer's fleshy hand caress the nape of my neck. That was OK – he was a nice enough old boy, very affectionate, I could tell, towards young people. Second, I saw the image of Lafcadio appear rapidly in black and white on six or seven sheets of paper (these were identical exposures) as Zwimmer rocked the developer dish periodically in the dim red light. What emerged from the gloom was a full-length study of Lafcadio posing naked against a decadent backdrop, which I had observed at some time or other in Herr Zwimmer's hand-painted collection, depicting a landscape of jutting pyramids and priapic palms realised with skill below a searing sun. It was pornographic – of course it was. But it was only *slightly* pornographic as I saw it that day, and in this it was perfectly in keeping with the mild disposition of the photographer.

'Do you like it, Billy?' he asked, and it wasn't clear whether he was referring to the image of Lafcadio, now stabilising in the fixer, or the action of his fingers at my neck.

'Very artistic,' I said, investing as best I could in a prevailing ambiguity relished harmlessly, I felt sure, by the big German.

'It could be Billy in those images,' Herr Zwimmer suggested encouragingly, 'instead of Lafcadio.'

'That's a flattering thought and a generous offer,' I told him. 'I'm not sure I've got what it takes physically, though.'

'Why not think about it?' he said. 'It pays better than shooting pictures in the park, I can assure you.'

Afternoon found me tired and hungry, burdened by two cameras (that I had chosen to carry the talismanic SLR with me at all times from now on, as you might a teddy bear, struck me as a mark of my growing alienation) in the Luxembourg Gardens, sharing my bench with two strangers. Any attempt to interest either or both of these parties in the features and benefits of instant portraiture would have been futile, I knew – the average person would sooner die horribly and alone than squander his or her money in the cause of art. Just as my sinking emotions threatened to reach their nadir (it occurred to me then and there I might even return to London), it kicked off – the next in a series of events designed to set the day unforgettably apart. As she approached my bench, fingers flirting at the limits of discretion with those of a younger man beside her, Mrs Lamartine was laughing happily, joyfully, so that I had difficulty recognising her as the woman I thought I knew. Had they been arm in arm, two friends or acquaintances meeting in the park, it might have looked different. As it was, their hands came together and parted in a way that put me in mind of courting birds on the wing, and I understood immediately they were lovers.

'Ah, Billy –' Véronique's mother said, smiling approval, as if it was the most natural thing in the world we should bump into each other like this in the middle of the park. 'Still trying to separate the lost from their savings?'

'Can I talk to you?' I said. It just slipped out. She had made it come out, turning up out of the blue like that, the way she had. She didn't bother to introduce me to her friend. She simply asked him to take my place on the bench before sliding her arm inside my arm and pointing up ahead, as if to suggest a horizon with which she was familiar, one she could recommend. Soon we fell into step together. There was no awkwardness between us. In fact, she made me feel glad suddenly, or grateful for the sky above. 'Véronique's pregnant,' I told her at last. 'She's going to have a baby.'

'I know,' she said, 'but thank you for saying it. You wanted to, didn't you?'

'The baby –' I said. 'It isn't my baby. You do understand that, don't you? I mean – I'm not the father.'

'My dear boy –' she said. 'From where do I get the idea you're not the fathering kind?' By this time we had turned around – now we made our way back more purposefully towards the bench. It was as if Mrs Lamartine had calculated the likely value of our exchange intuitively, in advance, from the word go, and matched it effortlessly to our orbit of travel. 'Nanterre –' she announced with her sudden warmth of feeling. 'Shouldn't you be out there somewhere?'

'I don't know what I'll find,' I told her. 'What if there's nothing there?'

'That's a lovely idea,' she said. 'I've so enjoyed our little talk today, Billy.'

Because it was too early (we had said eight o'clock for dinner) to make my way to Auteuil, I took myself back to Zwimmer's shop, not only to dump the instant camera that was weighing me down, but also to visit Madame Georges in her apartments (if I have so far skated over the details of, or failed to mention at all, my few trips to these memorable rooms it is because my early visits there had little practical bearing, it seems to me, on what happened later and more widely in Paris) on an upper floor of the forbidding tenement. I had time to kill – that was my excuse on the one hand. On the other, I suppose I felt I deserved some kind of reward for finally telling Mrs Lamartine what she already knew. The fact that she already knew was something I chose not to dwell on.

'My dear boy –' Madame Georges drawled by way of greeting, and I admit it pleased me that two different people had seen fit to address me like that back to back. 'Don't you know I work nights?'

She was belting her robe just inside the door at the top of the stairs. Behind her in the hallway – a short corridor giving onto the fading daylight at the front of the apartment – the gallery of black and white portraits made by Zwimmer over many years offered up her likeness in a variety of fanciful settings.

'What music is that?' I asked immediately, because I knew it amused her to share with me, an ignorant Englishman, her passion for certain French composers I knew virtually nothing about.

'Can't you guess?' she said, ushering me into her salon, a long room sparingly furnished with choice items brought together over decades, as the first of the lamplight spilled inside from the street.

'Debussy?'

'No.'

'Saint-Saëns?'

'I don't think so.'

'Ravel?'

'No, no, no –'

'OK, OK – I've got it now. It's Fauré – neither Impressionist nor Romantic, but modern.'

'At least you remembered something. And just to please me. How thoughtful you are.'

'Can I have some more medicine, please? Just a little –'

'Ah, I knew there must be something you wanted.'

'A small amount – only if you can spare it.'

There was a lull here in our dealings – a hiatus during which Madame Georges closed the first pair of tall shutters, doubtless as a way of foreshadowing her intent. As the music for organ fell away it left us with the traffic's hum and a bell tolling somewhere far off.

'The truth is I can't spare it, Billy – not for you, not any more. It wouldn't be right. What would your poor father think of me – or your mother, sunning herself on the deck of a yacht? I promised I would look after you, didn't I? Didn't I? No more medicine, Billy. Don't you see? We would love you to be like us, to be one of us. It would make us feel less alone, by a factor of one special person, in a godless universe. But I promised, Billy. I promised myself –'

'All right,' I said. What struck me or gave me pause was not so much the rejection, or the refusal of the drug – everything that was spoken, in accents foreign and familiar, made perfect sense. It was more the merging, within a single emotion, of the ideas of Mum and Dad. I so rarely thought of them in the same imaginative breath, as co-existing in a shared time and space – in the same heaven, or on the same yacht – and now Madame Georges, drawing on her scant knowledge of the familial facts, had done the job for me. 'I suppose I should thank you,' I told her, 'for saying no.'

'Don't be angry or sad,' she said. 'Instead, say you'll come to our next happening.'

'What happens at your happenings?'

'Nothing happens, but it does so rather memorably.'

'OK, then. Meanwhile, how do I get to Auteuil from here?'

'Oh, the Gare Montparnasse, *évidamment* –'

Rattling noisily, the suburban train carried me across the river into the sixteenth below the Bois de Boulogne. It was true I hadn't given enough consideration to what lay ahead – even now my imaginings failed to probe beyond a stunned silence that followed hard on the heels of Véronique's shock revelation. The villa was set in shadowy (thanks to the action of the rue Poussin street lights on tall trees, and the early moon) terrain behind a high wall with a door in it. Was it a side door? Surely it couldn't be the main entrance at such a classy address. The first thing was this – the door stood open, unlocked, swinging on its hinges and creaking slightly in a current of air. That struck me right away as odd. It was a big house in a large garden. Above a terraced lawn the hot light of the interior blazed brilliantly before cascading tier by tier towards me, cooling and dulling all the while. Aside from the intermittent creaking behind me of the door I heard two distinct sounds. There was the breeze, high-pitched and eerie, in a conifer above me, and the hissing and spluttering further afield, from a direction or location unspecified, of a running tap, a garden tap. Then I saw it for a split-second out of the corner of my eye – an arm descending rapidly behind me, from the direction, in other words, of rue Poussin. The blow caught me in a glancing way somewhere behind the ear, and I went down immediately with an enjoyable sensation of blacking out or fainting. When I came to a few seconds later (my impression, right or wrong, was of the briefest possible lapse of time) I was curled up on the wet ground, and my camera was staring at me a few inches from my face, as if someone, or something, had taken it from me before having a change of heart. Either that or they were telling me they might have taken it, but had chosen not to, and in this guise the Nikon served as a warning.

Once I had picked myself, and the camera, up, I checked the street. Nothing stirred. No one was there. I felt OK. That is, I felt OK considering. It seemed to me that everything under the sun (or the moon, in this instance, full and French and obscured mostly by scudding clouds) had the reality, vivid but unreliable, of a dream at dawn. Up ahead, the bold light continued to spill from the croquet lawn perched with hoops gleaming at the highest level in front of the house – down it spilled across the lower terraces, their wet grass catching the fitful moonlight when it became available. As I ran up the luxurious slopes I had a bad feeling. When I reached the top it was plain enough – the croquet lawn was the setting for a barbaric act involving cats. I didn't hang around at that time. Closing within seconds on the blazing light I banged on the glass of the vast doors that separated me from the expansive living room with its domestic scene. There was Raymond and his parents, plus his kid sister, and Véronique, of course. Had she said it? Had she told them yet? Why hadn't they seen them? The cats – how come they didn't see them, so conspicuously dead just a stone's throw from the hearth? Inside, everyone sat up or took a step towards me, all of them talking at the same time. It was Mr D–, Raymond's tall father, who threw open the heavy doors separating house from garden.

'How many cats have you got here?' I asked immediately.

'There's mud on your face,' Véronique said. 'And blood.'

After Raymond stepped outside with me we moved in silence towards the croquet lawn with its shining hoops. Beyond the gloom at the bottom of the garden the Eiffel Tower swaggered, amazingly bright and astonishingly close, as if to impress and inspire for one night only. The first item we came across was a croquet mallet dark with blood. Each of five cats had been impaled at the throat on a wire croquet hoop, so that all five were, in effect, stapled to the lawn according to what I took to be a random configuration rather than a ritualistic design. Of course, it was quite possible the creatures had been slaughtered elsewhere and transported here after the fact. We didn't recover the dead animals. We just stared at them for a while in silence. One thing I noted was the condition of the lawn. It was, unsurprisingly, closely cropped. It was also, unlike the lower slopes and terraces, dry to the touch – except, I imagined, where it looked darker with blood. It bore, finally, a set of disfiguring gouges, as if the heel of a shoe or boot had slipped there wildly.

'You didn't hear anything?' I said like a private eye ticking the key investigative boxes on his latest assignment.

'No, nothing,' Raymond said. '*Rien du tout*. You'd better come inside and clean yourself up.'

There was one scene left to enact at the big house in the leafy suburb of the city of love. While everyone else waited at the piano for the police to arrive, Raymond took me upstairs to a childhood bedroom kitted out, it seemed to me, as it always had been, as if in hope of the prodigal son's return, or in honour of the war hero, his memory kept alive in scrapbooks, who wasn't coming back.

'How are you feeling?' he asked.

'OK,' I said. I didn't know why I was there. The huge French flag suspended from the corners of the room struck a patriotic note, sombre and sanctimonious, which set a moral tone for the whole. It was like a chamber lovingly built, with front wall missing, for a play on TV. What caught my eye, apart from the massive flag, were the Tintin books – that was a nice touch. 'Are you going to kick me or kiss me?' I added with a manic confidence fuelled by adrenalin.

'It's not your baby, am I right?'

'I'm not the father – that's true.'

'Then you have nothing to worry about.'

There was an unreal, or surreal, quality to all of this – delayed effect, arguably, of the blow I had sustained earlier – married to a chilling sense of Raymond's correctness, which was both solicitous and menacing. Abruptly he turned his back on me in order to root around in the top drawer of a chest beside the bed.

'Did you see anything?' he said.

'Where?' I said. 'Down there?'

'You didn't see who hit you?'

'Not really,' I said. Again I heard the creaking of the door, the keening of the wind in the big fir tree above. There was the hissing, or spluttering, of the garden tap. Then it came at me from another angle – the matter of the grass, wet or dry, underfoot. As Raymond spun round he caught me looking at his shoes. His shoes were wet and muddy, just like mine. 'Everything happened so fast, didn't it?' I reminded him, rubbing my bruised neck mechanically as the crazy suspicion took hold of me.

'It wasn't any of these guys, was it?' he said, handing me three grainy mug shots that looked in each case to be make-do portraits cut down from some larger photographic canvas.

Time stalled. Moments lurched and stumbled. Was it possible that Raymond himself had struck me down with only the moon to witness it? If it were technically feasible, what would it signify? And what, if anything, did it have to do with the slaughter of five cats? As I stared at the portraits in my hands I worked to separate these two notions – the dead cats and the blow to my head. It was impossible to view them discretely. Meanwhile, there was the absurd here and now to consider. Had Raymond clocked my suspicions? Why show me these pictures at all if he thought I suspected him of something, unless it was part of a fixed plan or strategy?

'I don't recognise these men,' I said at last. 'Who are they?'

Now I felt nauseous and faint. I hadn't eaten for a long time. I remember studying the mug shots as hard as I could and laughing shortly before I fell down. All three men were Arabs – I mean they conformed to my idea of that. Two of the faces looked familiar, if only in a nightmarish and controvertible way, while the third one belonged, unconditionally and unmistakably, to Lafcadio.

BILLY

From time to time, when it becomes necessary to remind myself we cannot love independently of each other, my thoughts turn towards Raymond and Lafcadio, two young men of linked destinies, one a cat killer. Raymond's clear-eyed readiness to slaughter his own pets in order to create an investigative red herring still has the power to disturb. As for Lafcadio – I didn't see him as victim material until it was too late. Nana it was who gave me the history lessons I needed in Paris. Lafcadio, she said as if it was obvious, probably belonged to a clandestine network that had supported the National Liberation Front in the struggle for Algerian independence. This was the same anti-fascist crowd that opposed the colonels in Greece, and Franco and Salazar in Iberia. In Paris, Nana said, these people still woke Nazi collaborators in the night. Raymond and Lafcadio, it seemed reasonable to suppose, were on opposite sides of history. This much I got completely. What I failed to see *quite*, despite Nana's gift for contextualisation, was what any of this had to do with my life.

CHAPTER TWELVE

Soundings of a Dream

IT HAD STRUCK ME ALREADY AS A FLAWED PROJECT – now, with my stocks of wonder failing, Paris embarked on a new relationship with me. The city, until recently a damaged concept, had become a troubling *thing*. This mutation had physical shape. At the same time its dread quality was elusive. What was happening to me? On the dark seabed of my imagination the question echoed from wreck to wreck like the soundings of a dream. At any moment I might smash the mirror or switch on the light.

'Are you awake?'

Véronique was with me in the room. She was at the end of the bed, faintly luminous in her white pyjamas, with an empty birdcage suspended above her head. In the Jardin Marco-Polo below us the fountain fell silent suddenly. In my mind was a clear sense that the affair was entering a difficult new phase. Already I was preparing the ground, bidding farewell to the familiar landscape around me in order to confront another – one I didn't yet know.

'Yes,' I replied. 'I can't sleep.'

She didn't climb into bed with me. I thought she was going to get into bed beside me, but she lay on the cover and pulled it over her so that we were wrapped in a kind of S-shape, a figure of eight, me on one side of the counterpane and Véronique on the other.

132

'I can't sleep either,' she said.

'What happens now?' I asked her. I meant with Raymond, of course – Raymond and her. My strong instinct was to trust no one (when I scouted for exceptions I identified only Madame Georges and Véronique herself). Whatever boyfriend Raymond was up to, or mixed up in – it had nothing to do with me. That's what I told myself. I was a guest of the city of love. Soon I would shoot some black and white photographs in a reportage style and consider the job done and go back to London where I belonged. It was time to take a step away from Véronique and her famous baby. As for her mad boyfriend – I didn't know how I could protect her from him. Again I went over it for the record. There were the five slaughtered cats and the three Arab men, including Lafcadio. If you put them all together you got nowhere – they added up to nothing. Throw in the attack on me and it made even less sense. Either I had stumbled on events I wasn't meant to witness, or my assault was a distraction, a false trail. There was something else. It had taken a while to rise from my subconscious. It had to do with certain telltale gouges on a croquet lawn. The marks, the furrows – they weren't random ruts on the surface of the world. They took the form of a swastika. That was how I saw it. When you threw a swastika into the mix with the French flag and a trio of Arabs you began to suspect a pattern was trying to emerge. It wasn't a nice pattern – that much was clear. I felt Véronique's warmth seep through the bedspread that separated us and tied us together. I didn't know how I could help her. At the same time there was something I needed to ask her. It was about her so-called boyfriend. Had he left the big house just before eight and unlocked the side door to the garden and waited for me in the shadow of the towering conifer? 'I mean – what happens now with you and Raymond?' I managed to finish off.

'I don't know,' she said, sighing. 'He told me he needed some time to think about it.'

'About what?' I said.

'Exactly,' she said. 'I made up my mind ages ago.'

'About Raymond?'

'There's something heartless and unfeeling about him.'

'You know,' I said, 'he issued a kind of threat against me. He said if I wasn't the baby's father I had nothing to worry about.' No cats, no swastikas – I didn't want to discuss these with Véronique. Not now. In the silence between us one thing cried out. It was the idea of Toulouse-Lautrec. It bound us together. It always had. Here it seemed to signal the end of one chapter and the start of another. The world had turned. We saw that. 'You still haven't told me how it began,' I whispered.

'He had booked the room,' she said. She didn't hesitate to tell me. She had been through it in her head a hundred times and now it came out willingly. 'He had booked the second portrait studio on the top floor,' she went on. 'The door was locked. He was painting me using gouache. Gouache was a medium T-L loved. He had on a blue boiler suit crusty with paint. A soft light came down from the skylight above us. I tried to make him angry by telling him he hated women, but he just laughed. He knew what I wanted, but he refused to hurt me. Without his boiler suit he was thin and pale. For once he looked almost beautiful. Can you believe that, Billy? He was like a little boy. There was no funny stuff. He didn't pull out because I told him not to.'

Lying beside Véronique above the silent fountain I could see why she had done things the way she had. What she had done was an act of volition, of free will. It was all about her and a world she wanted to throw off, or journey beyond. Her decision not to have an abortion made sense to me too. It was the only credible course of action, given the act itself. I wasn't sure what to say. Right then I didn't know whether I regarded Véronique as a hero or a fool. I rolled over and hugged her clumsily. We both knew it was the end of something. The world was turning. Still I had my enquiries.

'Raymond —' I said. 'Did he excuse himself and go out of the house in Auteuil at around eight o'clock?'

'He did,' Véronique said. 'He said he had to go down to the bottom of the garden to turn off a tap.'

'Final question —' I said, and as I spoke I glimpsed Zwimmer's portrait of Lafcadio with the peppermint green sign above his head. 'The Goutte d'Or — is it the name of a district here in Paris?'

'We call it Little Africa,' Véronique said. 'It's where lots of the city's immigrants live — the Algerians, for instance.'

Later there were farewells and thanks, after which I trudged north with my rucksack on my back and Lafcadio on my mind. He was in danger — this I took for granted. That it mattered so much to me was more of a surprise. I knew little about Lafcadio beyond what I could see. No doubt I should have asked Madame Georges, ever discreet, to tell me more. What was it she had said? *We will be your new family, Billy. We will care for each other, won't we?* Now, with the Gare du Nord looming, it came to me — I could jump on the Calais train and be in London by midnight. At the Hotel Terminus, right opposite the station, I asked for a room with a view of the tracks that ran northwest towards the Channel and Dover. They took my passport, and I dumped my pack in a cell under the roof. Looking down on the station forecourt from my tiny window I tried to get it straight in my head. Raymond had killed his own pets and assaulted me in an attempt to frame Lafcadio and his associates. That was it in sum. It was about racism, or fascism — how else was I meant to view it? There was the swastika, of course, which didn't fit in. Why, in Raymond's plan, would the intruders gouge a swastika into the grass as a kind of calling card? It didn't make sense. It wasn't right. In my crummy hotel room I washed my face and neck repeatedly. I wanted to shave, but I had no razor. The basin had no plug.

That afternoon I took myself the eleven or twelve miles to Nanterre where I planned to initiate, and also to conclude, my photographic business in the city of love. It was what I had come here to do, after all. It mattered to me to get the job done, to deliver on a brief I had set myself, not only because I hated the idea of going home empty handed, but also because I needed to wrest a modicum of control from the situation I found myself in, which meant focusing on what I did best. To that end I borrowed a roll of black tape, of the kind electricians use, from the hotel porter (he was an old Pole who spoke harshly accented English and who immediately saw a way to help) and carefully covered up the Nikon's chrome pentaprism so that it wouldn't glint and thus catch the eye. My materials, thanks to Herr Zwimmer's store, were Tri-X and HP4, both rated at 400ASA.

The university campus turned out to be a concrete wasteland – no wonder students protested there on a daily basis. The speeches and sit-ins were designed to highlight local hostility towards certain unpopular rules and regulations – not least the segregation of male and female residences. I already knew about that one, of course. It was blatant paternalism, said Nana (her given name was Anna, but she looked, she told me, just like Nana Mouskouri) as we skirted the mobile confessional and a pinball machine outside the refectory. It was a brand of institutional violence, she said, which Daniel Cohn-Bendit was at pains to condemn, taking time out from his studies to champion the rights of *les jeunes*. Nana herself was kept pretty busy

discharging a public relations role on behalf of the leading activist
(call him Danny the Red she suggested with an eye on posterity) –
it was in this capacity that she took the time to escort me personally
to the principal campaigning event of the day, marching fractionally
ahead of me across the flagstones towards the senate building while
briefing me over her shoulder. Her fluent English seemed to fit her
for a spokesperson's duties. In fact, she would have made her mark
in any language. She had an impressive ability to make you believe,
or believe in, what she said by virtue of the quality of her speaking
voice alone. Her long straight hair was jet black, as were the frames
of her outsized glasses.

'Today's event we see as a type of rag day stunt with a political
message of hope,' she explained, editorialising freely. 'What lens are
you using there? How close do you need to be to the action?'

I saw three beds parked at the top of the senate building steps.
These were classic beds with iron bedsteads and iconic status – they
might have been World War I surplus, or cast-offs from a film set.
In each bed were to be found cohabiting, with a brazen disregard
for diktats and directives, a male and a female student. From their
supporters on the steps came a chorus of whoops and cheers. After
a tip-off from Nana I worked my way upwards through the crowd,
my hostess following directly behind, towards the central feature of
the protest, towards the middle bed, from which the spokesman (a
late stand-in for Danny the Red, Nana explained, the chief activist
being detained elsewhere by pressing duties) declaimed in pyjamas
for the benefit of the assembled journalists below a placard asking,
so I was assured, what Madame de Gaulle would think. It was all
very graphic, thanks to the uprights of the bedsteads and the stripes
of the pyjamas. The white bed sheets reflected the meagre daylight
helpfully towards the chins. Before long I had devoted a roll of film

to today's speaker and his mate, a student of sociology according to the handwritten sign that obscured her breasts above sheet level.

'What's our megaphone man saying?' I asked Nana in a bid to bring context and meaning to my work.

'He says we – no, the student leaders – expect the authorities to close down the university at any time.'

'Wouldn't that represent a victory for the powers that be?'

'Wait –' Nana cautioned as the loud hailer took up again. 'He says experience matters more than knowledge. No, not experience as such – *imagination*. Imagination is the engine of life –'

'He makes a valid point,' I said, emptying the Nikon and then moving to reload it just in case.

'We won't object if they shut down Nanterre. On the contrary – pull it down, he says. Bring the whole edifice down and raise it up from scratch, because our universities must be the models – fertile, responsible, instructive, responsive – for our society as a whole.'

'Sounds like the student leaders have given it a lot of thought,' I said. 'I just hope all these distractions won't affect their studies.'

'Do you want to interview any of them?' Nana said. 'I mean it. I have their ear, you know.'

'Not me,' I said, raising the camera defensively. 'I'm more of a snapper than a scribe.'

'So why don't you shoot a photo essay for the *Times*? Are you for us or against us?'

'I don't know,' I said. 'I haven't really thought about it.'

'What do you believe in, Billy – apart from Father Christmas?'

'Not much, I'm afraid – the jury's still out, pacing hard.'

'You don't believe in Goddard or Godot or Bardot or tarot?'

'Can't say I do,' I said before moving to strike a conciliatory note. 'Look – how will I find you if I suddenly start to believe?'

'Here,' Nana said, seizing my wrist and digging out a ballpoint pen and writing a number on my hand. 'Let me know if you want a ringside seat at the circus. That's the circus of *history*, Billy –'

She was saying she liked me, in spite of who or what I was and my facetiousness. I couldn't at first see why this mattered to me as much as it did. In fact, it meant everything. Nana's affirmation gave me the courage or the strength or the will to press on, to do what I had to do in Paris. It was still there – what I needed to do was still there, waiting for me in a region just behind what I was saying and thinking. How or when it had come to me wasn't exactly clear. The significance of Raymond's swastika – suddenly I grasped it. It was without logic. That was the whole idea. It was impossible, within the terms of Raymond's sick plan, to see why Lafcadio and his buddies might etch a swastika into the grass of the croquet lawn. Raymond did it anyway. It was as if he was enjoying his own private joke. He had to leave his signature. He couldn't resist it, imagining he could get away with anything. That was why I needed to warn Lafcadio. That was why I enlisted Nana's help on the steps of the senate as the curtain fell on the picturesque bed-in of Nanterre. All the while something else – something closer to what I might once have called home – was stalking my outlook. Lafcadio's jeopardy – in my head it was bound up with a sense I had that, beyond Paris, beyond the ramifications of slaughtered pets and swastikas, T-L was in danger too. T-L was the father of Véronique's baby. Therefore T-L was at risk from Raymond's vengeful hand. This sense came without useful detail – I had no proper awareness of what Raymond knew about T-L. At the same time I couldn't shake the thing off. It formed part of the troubled landscape through which I now passed.

'Do you happen to know,' I asked Nana, deploying my most nakedly sincere tone, 'a district of the city called the Goutte d'Or?'

'Are you kidding?' she said, laughing without evident mirth. 'I spent the best part of a year and a half slumming it in Little Africa.'

Two hours later we were sitting in the café that had the peppermint green sign above its door. Ironically, the green sign wasn't actually working at the time, but this was definitely the right place, situated more or less in the middle of rue Polonceau between a Vietnamese laundry and what I took, on the basis of the shoes stacked neatly in pairs below three steps, to be a mosque. Inside the busy café the old men sipped milky tea from small glass beakers and sucked on pipes, regarding Nana (she was the only female in the joint) frankly as they slapped their playing tiles down. We sat at the back, without a clear view of the door, because all the favoured tables were taken. It was getting on for seven, or a little later perhaps, when Nana ordered us a second round of mint tea with almond biscuits.

'What does your friend *do*?' she asked, using a precise measure of interest that reminded me she was a student of social sciences.

'Lafcadio? I'm not quite sure. I know he steals handbags from time to time and ferries heroin from A to B in polite society.'

'It's what we call a portfolio career,' Nana said. 'In an unstable world young people are increasingly keeping their options open for as long as possible.'

'It's not as terrible as it sounds,' I said, acknowledging Nana's disapproval. 'At least he doesn't take his own medicine, or so we're told. It's a kind of gospel with him, apparently.'

'Oh? And that makes it all right?'

'There's something important I have to tell him,' I said, siding loyally with Lafcadio because I had to. I was waiting for Nana to ask what that something was. If she picked up on my worried tone she didn't show it. 'Aren't you going to ask what?' I prompted finally.

'*Ça ne me regarde pas*,' she said, shrugging. 'I don't think it's any of my business,' she told me, impressing and disappointing me at a stroke. 'I don't suppose he'll show up anyway – out of the blue.'

'He'll show,' I said. I had no way of knowing whether Lafcadio would turn up, today or tomorrow. There was desperation in what I was doing – I saw that. At the same time it seemed to me the most natural thing in the world he would come. 'He has to,' I concluded. Suddenly I understood what was happening to me. It was simple. If Lafcadio *loved* me he would come. That was the deal I made with my anxious heart. 'Do you mind if we give it a bit longer?' I added.

Things moved up a gear soon after that. First, Nana set about describing the scene behind me in a spirit of cloak and dagger.

'You see those two men?' she said. 'No – don't look now. One is thirty years old, the other is younger – twenty-five, say. Are they brothers? Possibly. Both are handsome in a brutal way. Both wear ill-fitting brown suits – their Friday best, as it were. They sit at right angles to each other at a wall table below an embroidered excerpt from the Quran. Now the older brother folds his newspaper again – a police informer, naturally.'

'What makes you so sure?' I said in the spirit of the game.

'I believe his moustache to be false. His tie may turn out to be a spy camera. Don't you know this whole area has been a hotbed of dissent since the war?'

'Which war is that?

'The Algerian one, of course.'

'Can I take a peek now?'

'Wait – it looks like someone might be joining them.'

As I half turned towards the window and the street I glimpsed Lafcadio, framed by the door, approaching, peeling off his helmet. Now he was standing at the table already occupied by Nana's duo (two men in brown suits sitting, as stated, below an inscription). He hadn't seen me, but it was only a matter of time before he spotted Nana, the sole woman at hand. I started forward, pulse quickening, from the rear of the shop. Had Lafcadio seen me? It wasn't clear. I didn't hail or greet him. Instead, I pressed on towards the door and the gathering night, sent forth by a rapid change of heart. It was the two men, Nana's pair, who did it for me. I saw it right away – they were the two men in the grainy images Raymond had offered up in a childhood bedroom below a giant French flag. What did it mean? I didn't know. I couldn't think. This unexpected development had rattled me. It undermined what presence of mind I had left. Hadn't I set out to warn Lafcadio he was in danger? Now my concern for him seemed oddly misplaced. It wasn't part of these events or this context. Still Nana didn't come out. Then I got it – she was settling our bill. A full minute passed before she joined me on the pavement beside Lafcadio's parked scooter.

'What's the matter with you?' she asked immediately.

'I guess I didn't want to see my friend after all.'

'That's not what I told him.'

'What did you tell him?'

'I told him to call round tomorrow. I told him it was a matter of life and death.'

'What? You gave him the name of my hotel?'

'I gave him my home address. The fact is he already knew the name of your hotel. Looks like you're staying at my place tonight –'

Nothing was straightforward. You enlisted the help of a quick thinker like Nana, and the next thing you knew she was calling the shots. At first I resented her intervention – it seemed to put control of the situation further beyond reach. Soon I relented. Nana made me strong. I had already admitted it to myself. There was little she couldn't fix. She had the ear of the student chiefs, didn't she? There was a quiet scramble for shoes outside the mosque in rue Polonceau. Someone barked various utterances into a public address system – it wasn't so much a call to prayer as a testing of the equipment. The truth was I was content to have control of the situation taken from me, even for a night, or for a night and a morning. The more I set out to confront what was happening the more it contrived to move away from me. Nana's passing reference to the war in Algeria had taken me straight back to a film screening at which Véronique had slapped me across the face. That act was the starting gun. In many ways it was the beginning of everything. Still, I hadn't actually done anything wrong, had I? Not then, not now. This was my defence in the face of complications past and present. It was a lousy defence, I knew – a coward's defence. After I slung the Nikon across my chest I began to feel stronger. When I pulled out some money to give to Nana she refused it, as I knew she would.

'My mystery friend –' I said, buying myself precious recovery time while my thoughts hurtled from station to station like the steel ball in an arcade game of fraught possibility. 'How did you manage to single him out in there?'

'Lafcadio?' Nana said. 'I'm no expert, Billy, but are you two, perhaps, in love with one another?'

NANA

He lacked maturity – personally, politically. I don't know what he majored in at school, but I can't imagine it was modern history. He had the British talent for ignoring the way the world – the rest of it – works. At the same time he was sexually repressed – is it unfair to lay this one, too, at the door of national predisposition? On the plus side he was open-minded, brave, loyal, and emotionally honest, with just enough personal vanity to want to make everything right, even though he had no real reason to worry – the world was already his oyster by virtue of where and when he was born.

Unfolding events I rationalised for him using certain thematic groupings: (a) protesting students; (b) striking workers; (c) conniving communists; (d) Gaullists of the new backlash. My role was to help him make sense of history as it happened. In the fake revolution to come, Nana would be something real. I suppose I must have fallen hard for Billy, if only briefly. When I introduced him to Camus, trying my best not to patronise him, he trumped me earnestly with the Baudelaire in his bag. I like to think the lesser part of him was French. At any rate he yearned to be better, or other, than he was, and to this extent he could hardly be accused of excessive self-love. I forgot to mention one important thing – Billy was a photographer. I mean he was a photographer *durch und durch*. I didn't need to see the creative fruits of his labour. I didn't need to view any images as such. I would say the camera defined who Billy was. In his hands it became a living thing. He was the camera. The camera – it was him.

WE ABANDONED THE SCOOTER AT TROCADÉRO, carrying a small picnic in a knapsack donated by Nana to the cause of opportunistic love. It was a ravishing day of the order stranded superbly, without debt to logic or duty to reason, between spring and summer, and as I followed Lafcadio to the jetty beside the river it occurred to me – we (in the absence of meaningful dialogue it was necessary for me to *project* a good deal of what I experienced onto my friend) felt glad to be alive. The air was bright and warm. The gentle breeze seemed capable of bearing the lightest pollen of contentment, and I drank it all down in case it turned out to be rationed. The sky was filled with high-stacked clouds, mutating possibilities, portents. Happiness was the disposition of sunlight on the grass beside a brook. It might fade at any time. The first thing of note was this – I had come without a camera. I had left the Nikon, increasingly indispensable to my idea of myself, at Nana's flat because Lafcadio had asked me to. I didn't understand why he did that. Was it because he thought the camera might possess his soul? Was that what he was thinking when he let Herr Zwimmer shoot him, naked, for the arousal of others, against a decadent backdrop? I didn't know. I concluded my friend wanted us to be truly alone together, and in this, it is fair to say, there was nothing at all between our respective outlooks that radiant day.

We didn't speak, being ill equipped to say anything intelligible in each other's language. After a couple of bends in the river we left the Eiffel Tower and the monumental city behind, the boat taking us powerfully west towards the sea. Although Lafcadio was as grave as ever, here, away from his scooter and the streets of the capital, he appeared to me in a brilliant new light. His teeth were startlingly white. His checked shirt billowed and flapped like a tablecloth on the line. After he rolled up his sleeves he took Nana's map from the knapsack and spread it over our knees on a hot bench on deck and pointed to certain locations – Argenteuil, Maisons-Laffitte, Poissy – as we passed them to left or right. From rail to rail the passengers smiled at us until I began to think there must be something odd or funny about me, about how I looked, but in observing Lafcadio I detected nothing untoward. All around us the women tucked their skirts in while the men held their hats down tightly. I had an urge, which I resisted, to kiss my friend in plain sight of the world.

On the way back we got off at Saint-Cloud where, free finally of the throbbing deck plates, I gave in immediately to a temptation to charge uphill through the sun-splashed woods. Lafcadio followed more slowly, clutching our pack like a baby to his chest. Emerging out in front on a slope above the trees I turned, out of breath, and looked back at the river shining from the plain. All the poplars were in tremulous leaf. Far away across the river the corn swayed silently in a current of air. Above me the clouds hurried north. I wanted to shout at the sky – slow down, please! I saw the swallows swoop and rise and swoop again like the bows in the tail of a kite. All around me the earliest meadow flowers nodded their approval. Then I saw Lafcadio at the lower edge of our clearing and I ran down to meet him, chasing him briefly through knee-high grasses before jumping on his strong back. How good it felt to be with him that day.

We made our picnic on the grass beside the stream. Lafcadio, it turned out, wanted nothing of what we had brought – he ate no food and refused the wine. As he presented me with a succession of items wrapped in greaseproof paper, drawing these doubtfully one by one from Nana's knapsack, I opened the packets in turn and set each down carefully between us. There was the parcel of chicken in aspic. As well as a handful of glossy black olives there were gherkins and a wedge of Pont-l'Evêque cheese and some hard pears and half a loaf of old bread. I ate a piece of fruit and some bread and cheese and washed it down with three mouthfuls of claret, drunk straight from the bottle cooling in the shallows at our feet. Then I stretched out and tracked the clouds for a moment and closed my eyes and waited for what I thought must surely happen. It was impossible to withhold it, the Jack of Love, any longer. That was how it felt to me. At the same time I was reluctant to initiate any physical intimacy with my friend. Rather I left it to him to decide what to do beside the river. Nothing took place. When I woke up the sky was grey. I sat up, feeling cold suddenly, and looked around me. Lafcadio was in the company of two young fishermen a short distance along our bank under a willow, their red floats circling widely in the eddying stream. One by one they turned sadly towards me and waved like orphaned brothers. Lafcadio knelt down at the edge of the water. When he raised both fists I saw a small fish gleam dully in each.

Back in town, my arms reached around him as we sped down boulevard Raspail. It was unclear to me where we were going, and why. At Montparnasse cemetery we entered next to the gatehouse in Edgar Quinet, dismounting on the gravel path in order to confer with the watchman. Armed with a sketch map of the site, Lafcadio marched me in the direction of various gloomy tombs more or less overgrown, or else sheltered by bowers. Charles Baudelaire's grave lay, marked by an inscribed tablet, in a thicket of monuments and crypts. Instructed by Nana (she saw it as her duty to extend the hold already exerted on me by French literature), Lafcadio stood at the poet's graveside and declaimed for my benefit, uttering *et jamais je ne pleure et jamais je ne ris* while offering up a sense of these words, which meant nothing to me at the time, in a laborious enactment of never weeping or laughing. Eschewing amusement I found myself moved by this show, which Lafcadio repeated, pointing all the while to the grave beside him in order to ensure I made the connection between the words and where they came from. By the time I had recovered from the sentimental gratification occasioned by his sweet displays my friend had vanished. Immediately behind where I stood was the back wall of a mausoleum. I heard a gate squeak. When I reached the front of the structure the heavy grille swung open, and Lafcadio drew me inside. Above his pants, which were hitched down around the knee, his cock jutted out crookedly, curving up like the spout of a coffee pot. It was as Lafcadio pushed me down that we heard the first sirens. They were close enough to where we were, a plethora of them by the sound of it. Pretty soon it was impossible to ignore the racket they made, so I got up off my knees and we ran towards the gatehouse and the scooter, the remains of our picnic wine sloshing drunkenly in the knapsack on my back.

Because my instinct was to reach for a loaded camera I felt a pang of resentment, irrational but strong, towards Lafcadio. In insisting we left the Nikon behind that morning he was part of a reactionary tendency undermining social justice. Not for the first time I saw my trusty 35mm SLR as a vehicle for truth. No, it was the opposite – a shield protecting me from the truth, or its worst effects. Either way, I had to have it with me as soon as possible. Nana wasn't at home.

Lafcadio, desolate in the face of my resentment, climbed through a window to claim the Nikon while I did my best to inform interested parties we were rescuing our own property, in the shape of a truth-telling imaging device, from the scene. Now there was something in the air. You could smell something. On the streets, the residents of Chinatown faced grimly north towards a pall of smoke. There was heated speculation. The distant sirens wouldn't stop. Assessing the colour of the sky finally I decided to push my film to 1600ASA and have done with it. Then we roared off.

The Sorbonne was the main focus. Here, the rioting was at its height. As we approached via rue Saint-Jacques the students either ran about the place with scarves covering their faces or conferred in disapproving huddles pressed up against the hallowed walls. The cars of Paris had been abandoned in rue Soufflot where the mature citizens, closing ranks against the forces of chaos, blocked the street. Now we could smell gas. I pointed ahead, and Lafcadio nodded – although we had no plan of campaign it was understood we had to get closer to whatever it was we were looking for. What that might be remained obscure. It had much to do with Nanterre, I decided, inferring massively from the scraps of dialogue rising harshly on the suffocating air. At the Panthéon we had to stop again. A phalanx of policemen carrying shields guarded the entrance to rue Valette. In the cobbled square the shocked residents of the capital crossed from one side to the other pointlessly, shaking their heads, or wept where they stood, or coughed with hands on knees.

Already it was a case of every man for himself. Still we had no agenda. Lafcadio laid the scooter flat on the ground behind the big dome. He motioned decisively, and we ran west on Clovis. I had a powerful urge to jettison Nana's knapsack, which encumbered me just enough to get in the way of taking pictures. Then I thought –

no, the knapsack must survive. Through a gap in the smoke I saw a small church – the prelate who gripped the black rail outside it was vomiting. (In fact I remember, or remembered, few details of what I saw in Paris that afternoon, these dislocated impressions arising, in most cases, retrospectively and much later as a result of what was on the film). There was the French flag in the window in rue Descartes with two lovers embracing there, as if waiting for their ship to sink, behind half-closed shutters. At some point the sirens fell mercifully away. When Lafcadio veered abruptly left I followed him. We had to circle wider, no doubt, to get nearer – but to what? Looking up I saw a sign saying rue des Écoles. That was when we heard the pop, oddly muffled, of a proper explosion. After the second such pop we stopped running. Alone in the middle of our street was a girl, book in hand, with red hair half up and half down, one sleeve missing, a breast exposed. Bricks and rocks littered the street. Where had they come from? The girl looked down – she had lost both shoes. In the viewfinder I saw Lafcadio approach her, but she pushed him away savagely before sinking to the ground and curling up there. I had to know which book she had chosen to save. It was suddenly the most important thing in the world. She wouldn't let me see it. As I knelt beside her and tried to wrest the volume from her, someone bowled me over violently and began pulling on the camera strap. I gave up Nana's knapsack in order to keep the Nikon. I had to. Immediately I was overwhelmed, blinded, by an acute sense of shame. The girl seized her chance to flee. From somewhere very close a recording of the national anthem blared out with delirious intent.

In place Paul Panlevé we hid behind a statue of Montaigne. It was like a field hospital in the rose garden below the trees. Beyond the railing the ambulances lined one side of the square while all the police vans hugged the other. From the apartments above the trees the people looked down on the scene. I raised my camera towards them. They were all in it. There was a sculpture on a plinth beside me of Romulus and Remus at the tits of the wolf. I shot it all. Then Lafcadio pointed to an armoured car, and we ran. We jumped the railing and ran to the river via the narrower streets, now strangely deserted. Short of Notre-Dame Lafcadio pulled me up and said he was going back for his scooter. I told him he was crazy. It was as if, having steered me to safety, he felt licensed to go back. It took him exactly an hour, and I was waiting for him in exactly the same spot when he returned with the scooter and a scorched petrol can he had picked up somewhere along the way. He had Nana's knapsack on his back – that was the craziest thing of all. When he grinned at me his teeth were whiter than ever. The shattered mirrors of his scooter hung down, swinging grotesquely. Nana's knapsack was empty.

I lay on the floor in a corridor between rooms with the SLR beside me, my fingers tight around the lens. Beyond the partition Lafcadio slept soundlessly with his brothers on divans pushed together. That was who they were – the two men in the Goutte d'Or café, and in Raymond's ugly pictures, were Lafcadio's older siblings. You might ask why I hadn't worked that one out already. No doubt Raymond would have filled me in had I managed to stay upright for a little longer in his childhood bedroom beneath the flag of France. We all went to bed early, having eaten rice cakes with *tabbouleh* and patties of spiced meat, and I had felt tired but happy in the neon light. On a contentment scale of one to ten I had been nudging ten. We had the confirmation that night by radio. Disgruntled Nanterre students had marched on the Sorbonne and occupied it, and now the Odéon too was home to disaffected scholars. My reluctance to sleep right away, tired though I was, had a lot to do with certain images on the wall beyond the partition. I might have expected to see evidence of family or friends – a sweetheart, perhaps, or a pen pal from Algiers. In fact, something else caught my eye. As I lay awake on the floor I considered the unwelcome symmetry of it all. The photographs on Lafcadio's wall bothered me not because they were poorly exposed and badly printed, although they were. No, it was the fact that one of the pictures was clearly, pointedly, of Raymond. That was what got me. For a whole morning under restless clouds I had convinced myself I had been wrong about the swastika carved into the surface of a croquet lawn. All afternoon I had been too caught up in events to consider anything but the moment at hand. Without a swastika my neo-Nazi conspiracy theory connecting Raymond with Lafcadio fell apart. Now the swastika was back. It was back inside my head, along with the sirens, the explosions, a girl, her book, a wine bottle, a petrol can, the scooter's mirrors, two small fish, and Baudelaire.

Mrs Lamartine

At the time, and immediately after, he represented the possibility of love, or at least of happiness, in my imagination. It wasn't anything he said or did. His presence alone denoted such possibility. To me he was an agent, without having to act, of change. I mean change for the better. He was a kind of totem, if you will, or a symbol. His influence was emblematic. While he was with us, love grew inside me. I think Billy understood this very well. As soon as he went, love started to die. How silly of me to think such happiness might last. Thank you anyway, Billy. What's left is the long evening, and night.

CHAPTER FOURTEEN
The New Culture of Anxiety

WHEN I ASKED NANA WHAT IT ALL SIGNIFIED I HADN'T expected
a history lesson. How clever of her to take the long view, to see the
news of today as the movies of tomorrow. My role was to flounder
around in a dream world looking for answers to questions I barely
knew how to ask. It was all about *me*, a shipwreck. As I scoured the
horizon for a glimpse of shining shore I saw just sea. I had watched
the riot police blunder about, gas masks on, in the name of liberty,
equality and the rest. I had watched the young people at the Arc de
Triomphe wave their red flags in time with the song – their fathers
had paid in taxes for the finest gas masks the state could use against
them. All around me the people of Paris were singing, or marching,
or praying, or crying. I didn't know what to do with myself. I didn't
know how to act, unless it was to position a camera between events
and me (when Nana suggested again I do a photo essay exploiting
her special access I urged myself to take up my ringside seat at the
circus). If there was a moral paralysis at the heart of my doubt it was
linked to the snatched portraits I had glimpsed in the bedrooms of
the city. There was Raymond's picture of Lafcadio, and Lafcadio's
shot of Raymond. I didn't know what I should, or could, do about
them. As each day passed I sensed more and more I would end up
doing nothing, and this notion, freighted with guilt and relief, was a

boulder that threatened to drag the raft, me on it, to the bottom of the sea. Doing nothing could only end badly, couldn't it? Such was the verdict of history – Nana was clear on that. Even as I set these unhelpful deliberations aside I understood I was storing up trouble for myself – I could scarcely have guessed what kind *exactly*, or how much. When I asked what it all meant, Nana eyed me with scorn.

'It might mean any number of things,' she told me. We were crossing the place de l'Italie on our way to avenue des Gobelins. An armoured personnel carrier in front of the Mairie was strewn with hyacinths. 'Their hatred of each other – is it, perhaps, a type of self-loathing? Might Raymond and Lafcadio actually *cherish* one another because they hate *themselves*, or what they've come to represent?'

There was nothing silly about this. Nana made it seem like a pathological possibility. It was as if she placed no limitation on the follies of which men were capable. At the junction with Port-Royal she stopped me, then pointed west towards the Eiffel Tower before delivering today's history lesson using the lightest of tones.

'Over there in the fifteenth they were given an indoor stadium all to themselves. It was quite a famous place in its day – the winter stadium on rue Nélaton. They've pulled it down since. They should have kept it. The buses arrived, filled with Jews, every ten minutes, as if they were crossing a runway to board a plane. Soon the arena, its floor space, was full of old Jews. Then the upper tiers filled up with young Jews. Some jumped. Others gave birth. At last the piss ran down from the most expensive seats. At night they closed it up to shut in the stench. You ask what it all means. I think you know, don't you? Or don't they teach you anything at all over there?'

We approached the Odéon by way of rue Racine. The area in front of the pillars was the preserve of policemen, motorbikes, and assorted vans with mesh covering their windows. No traffic moved in place de l'Odéon. Observed by grim-faced witnesses at the exits to the nearest side streets, an apologist for the occupying students gave forth through a megaphone below a banner, stretched between classical columns, that read *free our jailed comrades.*

As I say, it had been Nana's idea I should shoot a photo essay describing Daniel Cohn-Bendit from the point of view of what she called a fly on the wall. Now she dragged me through the ranks of bystanders, approaching the police cordon and choosing her target as I followed doubtfully across the cobbles. After her man protested, barring the way with his shield, Nana fired off a few words, which had to do with photojournalism and we English, before raising the policeman's visor, throwing her arms around his neck, and kissing his lips. The crowd roared. Nana stepped through the cordon and beckoned to me. She had picked out the loneliest man in their line, and he had obliged her. She herself wasn't pretty – she had assured me of that already in contexts incidental. Within seconds we were inside the police cordon on the steps below forbidding pillars.

'It's going to be too dark,' I complained as we passed through a dim room hung with shiny old paintings in massive gilt frames.

'I don't think so,' Nana replied, entering a dazzling chamber where a press conference was already in progress. 'Move freely,' she advised me over her shoulder, 'but watch out for the cameras.'

She meant the TV cameras. There were two of them, cables trailing up towards a window from which the fragments of stained glass had been removed. As I hesitated at the big doors, my Nikon in my hands, I watched Nana take her place on the stage beside the student spokesman. The heat from the TV lights was sensational.

'Now – any questions from our English friends?' Nana tossed that one down at fifty-odd journalists before consulting the student activist on her left. As I raised the camera to my eye I carried in my head the famous image of Trotsky ranting at the podium. Nana too was speaking on behalf of ideas. 'Our demands are too modest for words,' she went on in her terrific English. 'First, release our jailed comrades. Second, reopen our classes. Third, remove all the police from our campuses.' Here she cleared her throat and then drew the microphone closer as if to connect with the seasoned international press corps (white men in grey suits) at a personal level. 'You know – this is only the first time since the French revolution our university precincts have been broached.' She consulted anew, her hand over the microphone. 'We are making news here,' she disclosed finally, upturned palms proclaiming this as self-evident, 'not history.'

'How surprised have you been by the vigour of police action in recent days?'

Again she conferred. Again I moved closer. I had to get closer to the stage if I intended to fill the frame with the fast wide-angle. I saw Nana lean towards the microphone again.

'A great many Parisians have been surprised by the vigour of police action in recent days.'

She was good. The student spokesman was good too. You had to hand it to them. As I took to the stage and dropped to my knees and fired off nine or ten frames, bracketing furiously by up to a stop on either side of 1/60th at f/4, I swear I thought of Miss Laurie, amputee picture editor at a news desk in London. Someone called out with another question from the floor of the chamber.

'Is it true the Corsican riot police have been drafted in in case their Parisian counterparts prove too sympathetic to your cause?'

It was the student activist who answered now from the stage. I observed him at close range through a 35mm lens. The speaker had nothing but admiration, he insisted, for the people of Corsica whose independence of spirit was as rugged as their native landscape.

'But we didn't invite you here today to talk about our summer holidays,' argued the corduroy Trotsky, enemy of the state, from the platform. 'For my part I enjoy a brisk walk in the Black Forest –'

Later I met Lafcadio north of the river as arranged. It was quieter up there. There was more money around. All the art was in vaults. It was the evening of the tenth, the evening of the latest happening hosted by Madame Georges at her flat in Saint-Germain-des-Prés.

'Kiss me, Billy.'

'No.'

'Kiss me, Billy – yes.'

Had he improved his communication skills? No, his appeal was yet more physical. He sat astride his scooter, its mirrors restored to health in a backstreet workshop in Little Africa, with a smouldering cigarette clamped between his teeth. He wore no socks and carried no helmet. His suit jacket was fastened by a single button, and he had his white shirt done up at the collar. His hair, shorter now but swept as before behind the ear on both sides, gave off a clean smell, which came to me clearly as he nudged us into the crawling traffic. Everything crawled during those riotous days and nights.

We got as far as rue du Louvre before we were pulled in. I felt my friend's stomach tense, but his voice was calm and courteous as he conversed with the checkpoint personnel, explaining, it seemed to me, we were on our way to a funeral (this rationale, which struck me at the time as a kind of schoolboy ruse, turned out, once we had reached our destination, to have some basis in truth) on the other side of the river. The fact that it was already late, as in too late for the average funeral, failed to trouble our tired policemen, and they waved us through. Ahead of us lay the river with, beyond its slick surface, the domain, shrouded in reddish smoke, of the professional rioter. Madame Georges, tonight's hostess, was in there somewhere, laying down the sweetmeats and an old 78 of Ravel. To be in that lurid here and now with Lafcadio was heaven. I no longer worried about the photographs I had seen in the bedrooms of Paris. I had made an accommodation with moral torpor. It wasn't my place to confront the historical sins of the city – someone else would have to take care of that for me. I couldn't actually *do* anything for Lafcadio, could I? Worse – I couldn't even share my concerns with him. If by absolving myself of responsibility for his jeopardy I made of him a sex object pure and simple, what of it? From our riverside viewpoint immediately below the Louvre we watched an angry mob converge, a stone's throw away across the glassy water, on the Pont des Arts. Just yesterday I had imagined I was one hundred per cent in love.

We sped westwards along the broad towpath, a police launch tracking us by searchlight, with beside us in the river the reflections of explosions blooming and fading gorgeously and in the air above us the braying of hooters and hailers coming together outrageously with the sirens and the disillusioned cries. When we surfaced again at place de la Concorde the bridge was open to traffic – we crossed the river there, the National Assembly building confronting us like a symbol, the cops running out to close us down at the last. Lafcadio swerved then skidded, and we nearly came off the scooter, hitting the western end of boulevard Saint-Germain at a screaming forty. Across the street directly ahead of us was an improvised barricade of gouged out paving stones and overturned vehicles, of looted road signs and uprooted trees and iron collars from around the bases of the trees. We were on the wrong side of the line.

As I jumped from the scooter I was aware of the armed forces massing close behind us at the parliamentary gates. I could see the protesters, faces black, arms reaching out, on the other side of the wall. I seized a panelled door, a fine old door taken from a house or a shop, and dragged it up the slope, and then Lafcadio climbed the ramp and surrendered the scooter at the top and we both fell into the arms of the people. Looking up from the ground I saw the fiery arcs described by petrol bombs. I heard the bottles smash one after the other – pop, pop, pop. As the fuel ignited beyond our rampart it gave off a deliciously sweet smell. Lafcadio yanked me up, and for a moment we watched the yellowish smoke drift towards the river in a fascinating cloud. Then we were running and pushing the scooter against a tide of hard core rioters – they wore trademark scarves at their faces and carried half-bricks in their hands. When his scooter refused resolutely to start, Lafcadio wheeled it as far as the massive church at Saint-Sulpice, which was where I fucked him as hard as I could in an open sacristy lit by candles, scotching my guilt in respect of the location by telling myself this was an act of devotion.

It was nearly dawn when we reached the raised apartments of Madame Georges. The police had moved at two o'clock against the barricades – now the mob dispersed under radio instruction from the student command. I had assumed we were too late for a soirée or a cultural happening, but there was evidently no fixed timetable on such a night. Lafcadio sounded the bell next to the boarded-up window of Herr Zwimmer's shop, and when the street door swung open we heard the sad music descend from the rooms above.

'Pavanne For A Dead Infanta,' Madame Georges explained, without prompting from me, at the top of the stairs. 'Perfect, you'll agree, for the funeral of an old friend.' She leaned forward from the waist, eyes shining under the influence of her medicine, and kissed us lightly three times in turn. 'My dear boys –' she said, addressing us both but expressing herself in English. 'I've been frantic about you these past few days and nights.'

'Has someone passed away?' I asked our hostess as she led us solemnly by the wrist along the short corridor towards the front of her accommodation. Here, surrounded by mourners bearing posies and little goblets, an imposing coffin stood on a trestle bier in the middle of the principal room. This should have been my chance to ask for advice about Lafcadio, about Lafcadio and Raymond and everything that was going to happen (I am not speaking here of the riots then consuming Paris). I ignored all that in line with the more sanguine outlook I hoped to cultivate from now on. 'Someone you knew well?' I added, drawing on dwindling reserves of manners.

'Just Marcel Proust,' Madame Georges came back smoothly. 'Passed away here in Paris in twenty-two. Ever in our thoughts, our prayers, and our hearts –'

I took back my hand. Lafcadio lit a cigarette. As I peered over the rim of the coffin I glimpsed an inert body stretched out among the folds of red satin.

'You must have been fond of Mr Proust,' I suggested seconds later. We had withdrawn towards the tall shutters, the hostess and I. 'Shall I let in some light?' I asked doubtfully, sipping the contents of a tiny glass offered up by Madame Georges on a silver tray.

'Goodness me, no,' she said. 'Plenty of time for that later.'

'I wanted to talk to you about Lafcadio,' I said, despite myself, or because I decided this intervention should, after all, be a matter of record.

'Of course you did, my dear. You're getting ready to betray the young man, aren't you?'

She didn't judge as such. Rather, she gave me an opportunity to review my options.

'Do you have to pay him?' I said, thinking and thinking. 'The pretend Proust in the coffin, I mean –'

'I don't really know yet,' Madame Georges said. 'I found him wandering alone in Montparnasse cemetery yesterday. The curious thing is he talked mostly of you —'

I took three paces towards the sleek coffin and gripped its rim with two hands. Lying doggo inside, the gaunt young man clutched a spray of violets to his chest. His eyelids were painted purple, as if to acknowledge a last bruising struggle with the departing forces of life. Between his legs, among the folds of luxurious satin, he stored his phials of holy water and a sprig of salubrious box.

'My God, T-L.'

'Billy-boy —'

It was only a stage whisper. I felt a brand of horror. The pale young man opened his eyes.

'Jesus, T-L,' I persisted.

'I know, old boy — this is just a dress rehearsal for the big one.'

If the voice was cracked, the gaze was as penetrating as ever. All the while the thin body failed to stir within its opulent confines. Abruptly the occupant of the coffin seized both its sides, a collective gasp running round the salon as he hauled his frame upright.

'Hello again, Billy,' he said. 'What on earth made you imagine you could hide from your old pal T-L?'

'Will you try to see her? You ought to see her. You're the father —'

I was just going through the motions. I didn't really want T-L to track Véronique down in the interests of the unborn child. What good would it do? Wasn't it T-L who had wanted to get rid of the baby from the start? Then there was the business, still active in my head despite my attempts to banish it, of Raymond's threats against the instigator of the famous pregnancy. In the face of this historical danger I had an ongoing duty to shield T-L from the consequences of his actions, a responsibility I was suddenly unable, or unwilling, to accept. The truth was I felt something like revulsion towards my old friend. This new emotion was bound up with a creeping sense I had that he was out to own me, to possess in so far as he could my love, or my affection, or my loyalty, or whatever else he might get his hands on. My apprehension in all this of something sinister, an obsessive factor at odds with the person or personality I had looked up to, disturbed and disappointed me in equal measure.

'*Father*, did you say? You overlook the son, Billy, and the Holy Ghost –'

We were alone together in place de la République with about a quarter of a million strikers and students and paid-up communists attesting *diz ans c'est assez* or consigning de Gaulle to the museum. It was the place to be in Paris if you weren't working that day.

'What's he saying now?' I said. I fielded the Nikon as ever. T-L carried a transistor radio like a monkey or a parrot on his shoulder, the loud speaker up against his ear. 'Is it Danny the Red?'

'Hold on a minute –' T-L said. 'These inconsiderate Frenchies insist on speaking French.'

Things felt different on the city's streets. Was it the beginning of the end, or a pause for breath? I had watched the students throw their books and their bombs. Now the factory workers would bring the country to its knees, or its political senses, while the playground philosophers went back to their classrooms. That was the prevailing mood. No doubt a revolution too was an assembly line activity – it required proper investment, management, overtime, all that.

'What's he saying?'

'He says the trade unions have been living off past glories while failing to win concessions on pay, and immigrant workers are being manipulated to weaken job security. Oh, and the communists don't really want to topple de Gaulle because it appears Moscow regards him as a thorn in the West's side.'

That was all very interesting. I held my camera over the faces behind us, but I don't think my heart was in it. Something uncanny happened. It was mysterious and chilling, but also rather beautiful. I saw Mrs Lamartine in the crowd. She was standing very close to us. How she came to be there, so close, was impossible to divine. She had a woollen hat pulled down low on her forehead as if she set out to make herself unrecognisable to the world. When I touched her elbow and opened my mouth to speak she looked straight through me, smiled like a stranger and backed off slowly as if discouraging a dog. I started after her, but soon stopped. She hesitated finally as the crowd took her, and in her blazing eyes, glimpsed memorably the instant before she vanished, I saw the end of this whole story.

'Please don't keep running off like that, Billy. You tried to run off before, remember?'

'That was Véronique's mother,' I said. T-L's hand gripped my shoulder hard – I told myself that meant nothing. 'How could she possibly be standing right next to us in this enormous crowd?'

'You must introduce me to your French friends,' T-L said.

'That was Véronique's mother,' I repeated.

'Meanwhile the gazelle boy has to go.'

I didn't comment, no doubt because I had come to the same conclusion myself, but for reasons that had nothing to do with T-L. Madame Georges had been right about Lafcadio – I was preparing to betray him, to let him down. At the heart of the regret I felt was a recognition that I had loved Lafcadio for a day, for one desperate day. Now I wanted to protect him all over again. That was part of the new culture of anxiety. There was something else that stemmed directly from the shocking reappearance in my life of T-L. For the first time it struck me that the future I was so keen to insure against might just be my own.

'The supple Arab –' T-L said, to clarify. 'Ditch him now.'

'What's it saying?' I asked mechanically, meaning the radio, or the voice on the radio.

'Not very much,' T-L said. 'The student leaders welcome the reopening of the Sorbonne.'

'You still haven't told me,' I said, 'whether or not you plan to see her. Véronique, I mean –'

'I didn't come here to *parlez-vous* with Véronique,' T-L said. 'I came to find you, Billy-boy. Now – can we quit this awful crowd?'

<u>NATHALIE</u>

If you ask me about Billy my contribution is necessarily small. At the time, my mother was writing a diary or a journal in an attempt to make sense of her feelings. Because Billy appears on page one of this journal, and then fails to reappear, he occupies a special place in my heart. For my mother this phase marks the beginning or the end of something – that much is clear from the words on the page. There is no description of Billy as such. What we have is the sense of a photograph of him taken, using his own camera, by my mother at the fountain in the Jardin Marco-Polo below my grandparents' residence. There is no photograph to look at – just the story of it as told by my mother with an understanding, extremely affecting, that she will never see her English friend again. Véronique died, as you may know, during childbirth. The Saint Barthélemy religious order raised me until my majority, at which time I changed my name and swapped Paris for Montréal. My grandmother had people there.

CHAPTER FIFTEEN

The Best Interests of the Truth

NANA STOPPED A PASSING WAITER AND ASKED HIM what time it was, and then looked at me and told me in English, which wasn't strictly necessary. My spoken French, linguistic casualty of a feeble schooling over years, had in the course of a few fortnights graduated from non-existent to rudimentary, such had been my hunger to fit in here. (Every word of French I learned was paid for, I later came to see, in blood.) After toying fretfully with the camera on the table between us my companion, her famous black hair cut rioter-short now, spread her arms rhetorically as if to acknowledge that certain factors – another's timekeeping, say – were, in spite of everything, beyond even her formidable capacity to influence or control.

'He's late,' I observed needlessly.

We were waiting for the student spokesman, by far the busiest man in Paris that day, to join us at Hemingway's table at Closerie des Lilas on boulevard du Montparnasse. But that wasn't all – there was also the idea, resisted by me to the point of absurdity, that T-L would gatecrash our little party in order to rub shoulders with, as he put it, the man of destiny. If it was a trial of wills, I lost out. My overwhelming desire to keep T-L in a box separate from everyone and everything else in Paris was indicative of my newly embattled, by which I mean *re*-embattled, state of mind, and the growing sense

I had of an increasingly extreme quality in T-L. Just recently I had imagined myself descending gratefully into the valley of respite.

'Actually, I'm not surprised,' my companion said, fanning her throat with a proprietary coaster.

'Me neither,' I replied casually, watching Nana's lips flirt with the rim of a miniscule wine glass charged alluringly with a coppery blush. Late May sunshine bounced off the leaves of an ornamental hedge on the pavement beyond the open sash window behind me, splashing her face and flashing from her spectacles. 'I'm sure a folk hero's got much better things to do than shake my humble hand.'

'That's not what I meant,' Nana said. 'At this precise moment your photo essay is probably uppermost in his mind.'

'So where is he? Converting his student spokesman credentials into mainstream political capital? Isn't that what they say?'

'Do they? Detained elsewhere by events, more like. You know – it occurs to me there's something in the air.'

'You mean it's going to be another hard day's night?'

'Maybe. Let's just say I don't think this is over, Billy.'

'Oh, look,' I said. 'If it isn't our old chum de Gaulle again –'

Nana turned to look. From the gloomy depths of the venerable restaurant a vast television glided forth, its picture coming and going alarmingly, like an experimental dessert trolley amidst the diners. A bearded man drinking brandy on his own, his soiled napkin tucked into his shirt, demanded the volume be turned up. We were used to these presidential incursions by now. For me, their chief value was as a language tool – you could learn a lot from de Gaulle on TV.

'He's appealing for civic calm, is he not?' I suggested.

'*Again*,' Nana confirmed. 'There's something going on.'

'Shall we cut our losses here? I think we've been stood up –'

'What time did you tell your mad English friend to show?'

'Six,' I said. 'We don't have to be here, though.'

'Too late –' Nana said. 'I do believe he's early.'

The whine of the scooter – we had all heard it. How could I have failed to recognise it for what it was? Before I had a chance to turn, T-L penetrated the interior like an inquisitor in a long black coat, holding forth immediately in conversation with the bearded brandy drinker on the televised issues of the hour, while Lafcadio slipped in beside me, rebuking me with his careful silence. What was happening? What was happening to me *today*? How could they be together? Such a manipulative liaison was forbidden by all natural laws. I hadn't yet moved to put my relations with Lafcadio on a new footing. I had taken no steps in that direction – on the other hand I knew now who had done the job for me, the ground shifting under my feet once again. In my beleaguered imagination I saw T-L and Lafcadio ride the familiar scooter on familiar streets – my streets, the indifferent streets whose grudging respect I had earned the hard way. Here was the twist – T-L rode up front.

'Is this one taken?' he drawled from above us now, extending fingers with nails painted black towards Nana by way of greeting or introduction. 'Billy's told me so much about you, my dear.'

'That's hardly fair,' Nana said brightly. 'He's barely mentioned you at all.'

'Isn't this too perfect?' T-L suggested without breaking stride. 'And to think I journeyed all the way here on a *moped* just to meet the student spokesman. Where is the prophet of the poly when you need him, Billy-boy?'

'Detained elsewhere by momentous events,' I said as T-L sat down beside Nana. In my mind a novel sadness was taking hold. It had to do with the impossibility of knowing one another, or some such. You might have added another soul to our party, and another and another, until the restaurant was as full as the winter stadium on rue Nélaton. Still you would have dreamed alone. 'Nana reckons it's going to be another long night in the city of love,' I added from somewhere outside myself. We were all here in this restaurant. We were together, or mostly together, at last. At the centre of our little huddle sat Véronique. Hadn't she first revealed this joint to me? I believe she did that. Back then it was a place of promise. Almost all my French brothers and sisters were present in my head. Madame Georges was arriving, equipped for her night shift with a paperback Proust. Only Raymond, tasked in another place with the burying of slaughtered cats, was missing from our virtual crew.

'But we should speak French now,' T-L was proposing, 'so that Lafcadio can join in.'

'Should we?' Nana said. 'Then Billy won't be able to follow a word we're saying.'

'Does that matter?' T-L said, without looking my way. 'I'm not sure Billy really *gets* politics.'

'Don't be a prick, T-L,' I said. 'What you can't see is a waiter eyeballing us in a hostile fashion.'

For myself I didn't care. It was Lafcadio I felt for. His ongoing silence was heroic and terrible at the same time. I couldn't read it, what it meant. Was it baleful, a rebuke aimed at me for what might have been? Or was it the studied insouciance of someone who had already moved on, having taken up with another? Sweet hoodlum – as we watched the stern waiter approach our table Lafcadio seized my hand out of sight and squeezed it tenderly. I nearly cried out.

'He says we'll have to change tables if we want Lafcadio to be able to stay,' Nana said, blushing, or flushing.

'I think we should put our foot down,' T-L said. 'What planet do you suppose these lovely people are living on?'

It didn't matter because just then history intervened, making a bloody mess of things as usual. First, Lafcadio stood up and swept the little glass and the vase with its single flower from the table (that he was obliged to present the Nikon to me for safekeeping ahead of this pained outburst appalled and shamed me, going on to break my heart in a hundred small ways). Then a brick struck the half-open window directly behind us with great force, shattering the pane and showering us with angry shards, one of which cut the waiter's face just below the left eye.

'Shall we, perhaps, move on?' T-L asked calmly after a short interval. 'This place is so *bourgeois* –'

Later the same evening I found myself running alongside Nana on rue Réaumur in the direction of the stock exchange, but I couldn't say why, unless it was to capture the one signature image, uniquely compelling and convincing, that would set me free and describe the way home. We had left T-L and Lafcadio and the scooter in rue de Rennes below a shuttered apartment T-L shared with an actor and junkie who had worked with Chabrol. It came to me in the street. The business between T-L and Lafcadio – it was about Lafcadio's medicine, or his access to it. Such was my rationale. It gave me no comfort. In fact, it made me feel worse. That was why I ran beside Nana and the others, most of these masked, shooting this, shooting that. Nana took my hand (her powerful instinct for protecting me was something I never resented) as we drew level with the Brasserie la Bourse, from which diner an ancient woman, a cook or a kitchen hand, fled with a raw steak held aloft. Without understanding why, I felt close to this woman. She threw her meat at me, and I snapped her twice, and the restaurant's lights went out. This marked the start of a local blackout. They were hurling missiles at the lights in place de la Bourse. It was really quite dark now. It struck me my camera was redundant. Up ahead, the stock exchange building, symbol of the old order, loomed in the by now familiar way. There were the columns, far too many of them, and the rooftop flag, and the iconic pronouncement, claimed by every great institution for itself, on the national themes of liberty, equality and fraternity. The flag was the thing. The flag, eminently portable but supremely difficult to reach, was the natural target or prize. Nana said so herself.

She pushed ahead and immediately I lost her inside. The fire alarm competed with the outside sirens in a way that filled the vast, dim interior with sheer noise, obviating via some odd sensory effect any requirement to act. It was only necessary to run about blindly in the limited time available, and we did this with conviction and distinction. Because I was a neutral (this is much the kindest label of the many researched in respect of my conduct in the Paris stock exchange) I turned down multiple invitations to destroy this or that telex machine or filing cabinet, preferring to shoot pictures which, notwithstanding the speculative flames rising all around me from waste paper bins, had no chance, from the point of view of the light available, of succeeding. This question of the ambient light level was significant in a number of ways. Not only did it impact negatively on my ability to shoot the one special picture that would save me, it also made it difficult to appreciate fully a highly decorative interior (more and more I had come to see the revolution as an opportunity to enjoy, from within, a succession of classical buildings one might otherwise admire only from without). There was another thing that had to do with the light. I discovered this by accident after I caught myself cowering below an array of switches set into the wall beside me. When I flicked the first switch a bank of lights suspended from the vaulted ceiling came on. It might have been funny at another time or in another place. It meant the power was on. It had always been on. There we were, stumbling around in the dark while the alarm continued to inflict on us its disorientating din thanks only, one had supposed, to the exclusive intervention of a backup power supply. In fact the reactionary lights, and presumably anything else that was plumbed in, had been fully functional all along. For a few seconds I toyed with the idea of activating all the other switches on the wall of the stock exchange, but instead of making history, or at least altering its course in my modest way, I followed Nana at half tilt towards the front of the building and the cool night air.

'Are you OK?' she asked me, lips white, face black. 'You look like you've seen a ghost.

'Thanks,' I said. 'All clichés gratefully received. You don't look so hot yourself, sister.'

Immediately behind us the boys urinated doggedly against the huge doors in the intermittent glow of the flashing red lights. Below us in the square the cops drew themselves up wearily behind their shields in lines of ten or twelve under the direction of a loud hailer. I followed Nana down the steps and towards the perimeter roadside where I lost her briefly behind a row of ambulances. Then she was there again, beckoning me from the broken window of a shop – no, a bar – and hauling me inside.

'What are we doing here?' I asked her in English. We squatted with three or four others on the glass-strewn tiles behind the bar. No one spoke. Some covered their ears. One or two rubbed their eyes. Nana accepted a bottle of water and emptied it over my head – I couldn't tell if this was her scathing verdict on my disloyal enquiry or a bid to refresh me. Either way she had to apologise for getting the camera wet. I told her it didn't matter. Actually, I was thinking at that precise moment about Véronique – how she once cradled my head outside a church near Grosvenor Square, London. Soon I began to laugh, or at least that's how it must have sounded.

'What's so bloody funny?' someone asked in decent English.

'Did you know the electricity was on in there?' I said, directing myself at Nana as if she was responsible for this particular absurdity together with a notional back catalogue of other cases. 'I mean the lights were working. We could have switched on the lights –'

'So?' she said. 'What does that have to do with anything?'

'Nothing,' I said, suitably chastened but oddly liberated. The end was in sight now. Although I would have given anything not to fall out with Nana just a moment ago, I suddenly didn't care – if it was a price that had to be paid for reason and proportion, so be it. 'Nothing,' I repeated. 'Nothing at all.'

There was one more lesson for me to learn that night on the margins of the stock exchange. It was a further tutorial in absurdity with advanced options in futility and cynicism, the whole shooting match sparked by the unlikely provenance of Nana's extraordinary revolutionary souvenir.

'What's that?' I asked, upholding my current instinct for silly questions as she fished a neatly folded French flag from inside her leather jacket. 'I mean – how did you get it down from the roof?'

'I didn't,' she said, deploying a new kind of impatience with my trademark credulity. 'Someone else got there first.'

'Really? So where did you find yours?'

'In a cupboard beside the ladies' toilet under the main stairs.'

'Don't tell me you're going to pass it off as the real thing –'

'Why not? No one will know the difference.'

'Except whoever took the other one down, I guess –'

'And me and you and a few other souls besides.'

'But we don't really count, do we? Is that it?'

'What matters, Billy, is the underlying narrative. That's why a fake or replacement flag is as good as the real one.'

'Of course – yes. And what about the truth?'

'If the story serves the best interests of the truth, why worry?'

I didn't get back to Nana on that. No doubt she was tired and emotionally drained – we all were. We were coming down from a high induced by recent events and our part in them. When I looked for the old gleam in my friend's eye I found only a strong disregard for irony. Against the dispiriting backdrop of this insight I opened the rear of the Nikon and began dragging the exposed film slowly and deliberately from the sprockets. Nothing could be more wanton or destructive. Immediately I felt foolish and sick.

'What are you doing?' Nana asked urgently.

'As you can see – I'm deliberately fogging my exposed film.'

'No, no – why? Why?'

'I don't really know right now, but I'm certain everything will become clear to me in due course.'

'Oh, Billy –' Nana said, stifling a sob and throwing her arms around my neck.

'Do you think it might be time for Billy to go home?' I asked my friend and anyone else in our company who was interested. 'By which I mean *home*, of course.' There – I had said it. Even now it was a meaningless idea. I didn't know what home was any more, unless it was that part of the world which wasn't *here*, which wasn't Paris. 'Answers on a postcard, please, to this address –'

Chapter Sixteen

Near Darkness

So it began – the final, fatal phase of my sojourn in the city of love. My big mistake was to choose to say goodbye to the people who mattered to me. I should simply have disappeared in the night. Few would have missed me – Nana, perhaps, because she cared for me a little, and Lafcadio, just possibly, if only he had been given the chance. Yes, I should have slunk off like a beast. If I hadn't tried to do the right thing by assorted others I wouldn't have got caught up in Lafcadio's squalid, pointless death. By choosing to quit Paris in, as it were, broad daylight I aimed to draw a clear line under local affairs in order to put the remainder of my life on a firmer footing. It didn't work out like that. Had I already left town I might just have persuaded myself there was nothing I could do, or could have done, to save Lafcadio. (The point here is I believed, naively but honestly, I was getting ready to bow out conclusively and for good – I didn't expect to hear from, or about, these people again.) As it turned out I was still in Paris when Lafcadio died. Somehow I managed to let him down again, this time forever. When the tawdry finish came it had nothing to do with Raymond or swastikas or dead cats. In fact, these ghosts left me alone for a spell, so that I began to feel free. On the other hand, I don't believe I could have done more to protect Lafcadio from T-L. At least, that's what I told myself at the time.

The final sequence of events began at Au Vieux Colombier, a restaurant of the old school close to T-L's temporary home on rue de Rennes, where we had arranged to meet. Because Lafcadio was unwelcome there we decamped almost immediately to La Palette, a different sort of eating place located in rue de Seine just below the river and a brick's hurl from the École des Beaux-Arts, operational HQ of the student rabble-rousers at that time. His gunslinger's coat swinging low, T-L led our little march via Saint-Germain-des-Prés. As I trailed marginally behind on the narrow pavements I rehearsed anxiously in my head the farewell encounters with this or that Paris I had planned for today. Lafcadio advanced, slouching and sullen, in the middle of our convoy, an exotic charge under double escort, while, decommissioned and empty of film, the Nikon ran diagonally on its strap across my back, facing away, in other words, from life.

'You wanted to see us?' T-L began for a second time once the waiter had been summoned and dispatched.

'I wanted to see Lafcadio,' I countered using the same tone, as dry as champagne.

'Lafcadio is with *me* now, Billy —'

'I've come to say goodbye, T-L.'

We were in the old *salle de billiards*, surrounded above eye level by the crusty palettes of dead, distinguished artists. Although it was T-L I addressed, the focus of my attention was Lafcadio. He looked right past me, rolling a toothpick from one side of his mouth to the other. When I told him in French I had come to say goodbye I saw a flash of something — regret, perhaps, or a mild form of hurt — in his eye. I had been hoping for anger, or at least recrimination, but there was to be no such consolation for me. There was only a weird serendipity, too bizarre to please, which arrived at a table beside us in the shape of a woman with a handbag. It was the same woman, the same handbag. It was the woman whose handbag Lafcadio had tried to steal before I chased him down on the other side of the river half a lifetime ago. Why was she here? She had no right to be here, not now, not today. When I looked again at Lafcadio I saw a flicker of something new – call it acceptance (as I tried to do) – in the pupils of his widening eyes. Then it was gone again.

'Planning to return to London?' T-L asked without apparent interest, or, rather, with a type of feverish indifference brought on by the harsh medicine he had injected into one or other vein in his lightly bandaged forearm.

'Yes,' I said. 'I'm not sure Paris holds a lot more for me now.'

'Really?' T-L said slyly. 'Right now it strikes me as just about the most fascinating location on earth. The French communists are calling for a further show of strength, while the president is a virtual prisoner in the Élysée. The end can't be far off now, surely.'

'That's good,' I said, getting up to leave. 'That's very good.' I wanted to say something, anything, to Lafcadio, but all I could think of was sorry, and I was reluctant to say that because it would have conferred satisfaction and legitimacy on T-L. 'I think I'm going to climb the Eiffel Tower now,' I announced unaccountably instead. 'Ridiculous, I know, but if you'll excuse me –'

'No, we won't excuse you, Billy. We can't, can we, Lafcadio?'

The shift in tone, when it came, was unnerving. I felt the sweat break out inside my shirt.

'Let me see –' T-L went on icily, the thinnest of smiles playing over his face for the shortest possible time. 'Seems to me you belong here with us now. Doesn't Billy belong here with us, Lafcadio?'

In the silence that followed, T-L motioned at me to sit down again. I could either stay or go, but I had to decide quickly. In the end there was no question about which option to choose.

'I'm sorry, Lafcadio,' I said, and this was nothing less than the truth. As I backed away there came the final injunction from T-L.

'Please, Billy –' he said, with no trace this time of the smile on his lips. 'Don't make me do anything I wouldn't want to do.'

Where was the wonder? The lovers' contract I had signed with the city – what joy had it brought me? I gave up on poetry. I demanded meaning – something that would tie up my experience of Paris not with ribbon but with rope. At nine hundred feet above the Champ de Mars I met with vertigo, nausea and a sense of freedom too wild to be helpful. Nothing I felt up there bore any relation to events on the ground, and for that I was grateful. I forgot about T-L. I forgot about Lafcadio and the few others on my shopping list of farewells. Below me the city presented itself as a series of formal and informal conversations between lines, planes and textures, now animated by a feeble sun, now silenced by a vagabond cloud, the entire distorted vista arching so savagely beneath the vault of the sky it was possible to trace the curvature of the earth, as through a fish-eye lens or an extreme wide-angle, from Montmartre to Montparnasse. I shut one eye and viewed it as a camera would view it (during this disaffected period I turned my back on the act of photography itself), and saw the planes and surfaces stack up, one tight against another, as if to streamline existence or intensify experience, their three dimensions becoming two. An expensive house was badly on fire in the vicinity of boulevard Haussmann – I watched the smoke advance towards the river and break up somewhere over the Luxembourg Gardens. When I saw the flash down there I assumed it was the action of the sunlight on the fountain in the Jardin Marco-Polo. In that instant I thought about Véronique, next target in my valedictory sights, and within seconds all my highborn feelings had crashed to earth.

She came down from the apartment and we perched, holding hands, on the wall of the fountain. It seemed inevitable she would be there to receive me – these last few steps of the journey had the rhythm and tempo of something rehearsed. She looked different to me (crazy, I know, to state the obvious about a pregnant woman) even though it was only a matter of days since I had last seen her. It wasn't just the physical fact, impossible suddenly to ignore, of the baby inside her. She looked changed – yes, she did. Call it serenity, call it peace – there was a type of acceptance or submission in her warm smile. Hadn't I just glimpsed something similar in Lafcadio's eyes? Then I saw Véronique as I had seen her in the London dawn. She was on the top step between the scuffed pillars, fingers at the buckle of her coat, with her suitcase at her side, telling me Martin Luther King was dead. The kid was the thing. The baby had been everything then, and it was everything now. On the one hand I had a horror of the baby and what it was capable of even before it was born. On the other hand I loved it as if it had been my own child. I think Véronique understood that.

'Are you happy?' I said. 'You look happy.'

'Thank you,' she said. 'I'm writing everything up in a journal, and I think it helps.'

'I've come to say goodbye,' I said, ending a short silence and releasing her hand.

'Again?' she said, laughing so generously I wanted to hold her.

'What will happen to it?' I asked. I meant the baby. I meant after – after it was born. There and then I saw a succession of nuns raise the child high with no-nonsense hands. 'Will you keep it?'

'Did you know my mother likes to pretend it's yours?'

I wish I hadn't let go of her hand when I did. When I revisited the scene in my head later it was one of two things I regretted. Not hugging Véronique – that was fine. I should have held her hand for longer, though. The second thing I ought to have done was tell her T-L was in town. Perhaps she already knew. Perhaps it was none of my business any more. Have I made clear my position at this point in time, on the eve, more or less, of my departure? I had the strong feeling I would never see Véronique again in my life. All the same, it was wrong of me not to tell her about T-L. She would have told me, had our positions been reversed. That's what got to me when I ran the scene again in my head. Such a scene should be perfect. It should be written perfectly and played the same way.

'I don't know if I'll keep it,' Véronique said finally in answer to my question. 'In any case the baby will be looked after, Billy. What else would you expect?'

Nothing, Véronique, I told myself – I would expect absolutely nothing else. After I got down from the wall of our fountain I pulled a set of Polaroids from my pocket and fanned them out in front of my friend.

'Pick a card,' I said to her.

'How exciting,' she said, choosing a picture and examining it, head tilted, before showing it to me. It was a shot of Raymond and Véronique at the Sorbonne – they all were. 'You keep it,' she said, jumping down and kissing me. 'Something to remember us by –'

I had thought we were done, but suddenly Véronique reached for the camera hanging asleep from my shoulder and wound it on and raised it to her eye and fired off one frame, just one, of me with the fountain in the Jardin Marco-Polo. I couldn't bring myself to say it. I couldn't bring myself to tell Véronique that, for once, there was no film in my camera. How could I tell her that her ultimate act of kinship with me would have no meaning? Instead I smiled for her, and she released the shutter and laid the camera on the wall of our fountain and backed off with a wave. For a moment I sat alone and considered the Nikon in my hands. Were we still a team, the camera and I? I wasn't certain, so I separated lens from body and strap and pushed them into different pockets as far as they would go.

After that I went directly to see Madame Georges, last person on my list of goodbye girls and boys. I didn't have to explain why I had come. There was the half-full bottle of sherry waiting on a tray along with two exquisite glasses and a bowl of sugared almonds, the sweets softly luminous in the dark salon. Was I expected? Were my motives this obvious? That my friends seemed ready and willing to watch me leave Paris was a defining characteristic of my final hours there. My time must be up. This inevitable quality I sought to turn to psychological advantage. I was doing the right thing. There was rightness, I swore, in what I did.

'What became of Herr Zwimmer?' I asked Madame Georges early because the big German too had been an important part of my Paris story.

'He shut up shop, didn't he? They shut him down, poor man, for offending public decency. I thought you knew that.'

'I can't believe he's gone,' I said. 'For a few days back there I saw him as an uncle figure.'

We stood with our backs to the street. We always stood in this room. Although it was furnished with chairs of several different eras and styles it was a room for standing in. It was above all a shuttered room. Again and for the last time I had an urge to open the slats to let the city in. Yet Paris was already inside. The room *was* Paris.

'To London —' Madame Georges said in a way that suggested she was happy to toast the city for my sake or in my name only, as an urgent concession to a unique friendship, its meaning undefined or undisclosed, before raising the tiny glass to her lips without quite kissing the rim there. She smiled secretly then, mistress of our rite. 'My, how you've grown here, Billy,' she finished archly, discarding her fragile goblet with a sigh.

As ever in the company of Madame Georges I deemed it fitting to say as little as I decently could. In many ways our friendship had flourished, like a strange flower, in near darkness. On the one hand we didn't need to converse, such was the particularity of our mutual sympathy. On the other we had agreed tacitly not to put whatever it was we shared at risk from strong opinion. These had been our terms of engagement – I saw no reason to alter them now. At low volume from the vast gramophone in the corner of the room came Ravel or Debussy or Fauré or Saint-Saëns. I couldn't tell which it was – when I told myself it didn't matter I felt a stab of guilt as after a betrayal. A few moments passed with only the music to console us. It was inevitable I should come to think of T-L and Lafcadio in this subtle interval. I saw T-L in a coffin, of course, in the guise of Marcel Proust. Looking back, there was already a hint of madness on display then, with worse to come. My sense of Lafcadio was less clear. That was only right – I had never really known him. It was all with me in this room. Everyone, or everything, that mattered at that moment was right there beside me. I am speaking now of T-L and Lafcadio and, yes, Lafcadio's morphine – it was only a matter of time, surely, before they conspired to undo me. As the music rose to a climax in a place far away, one or two key sentences leapt out from the few that were spoken, then hung in the air forever.

'A change has come over the boy in the days since you knew him best,' Madame Georges advised me with a little shudder. 'He's been breaking his own golden rule –'

'His golden rule?' I said in keeping with my practice of neither raising nor lowering the conversational temperature in this salon.

'Such a shame,' Madame Georges suggested pointedly for my exclusive benefit, 'that Lafcadio has begun taking his own medicine after all this time. Do you understand what I'm saying?'

'Have you seen something? Is there something you know?'

'Clever Billy – how quick you are to learn. Shall we call it our special quality? Some people see further than others, don't they? If only I could decide whether it's a blessing or a curse –'

Was it a warning? It was a flare exploding in the sky. I didn't hesitate. I took my cue to leave and went straight to T-L's place on rue de Rennes. I wasn't sure what I expected to find or do there. As I drew closer I had a desperate idea in the form of a wild promise I would be forced to honour if I wasn't already too late. Yes, I would ask Lafcadio to come with me to London. With every footstep this unlikely proposition buoyed me up and spurred me on. Now I ran. When I rang the bell the massive door swung open immediately. It was as if T-L had been waiting on the other side for me to come, to witness, to judge. He was pale, unnaturally so, and his hands, when he took mine, were cold and damp. Right away I understood what had happened in the rooms above.

'Where is he?' I asked, pushing past T-L on the stairs.

'On the bed,' he told me calmly. 'First left – I think you'll find the door is open.'

On a grey sheet in the stinking bedroom Lafcadio was laid out like a prince slain in battle. Had he been arranged or composed? It was dark in there, but not too dark to discern the dispensing toolkit gleaming low on the bare floorboards beside the mattress. My first instinct, prudish and unworthy, was to open a window. Although I looked and looked I could find no window to open.

'He's only gone and stopped breathing,' T-L announced, with a carefully calibrated resentment, from the doorway behind me.

'That can't be,' I said. 'Don't you know Lafcadio never takes his own medicine?'

'Oh, really?' T-L said. 'What the devil are we supposed to do now? The stupid bugger's walked out on us for good.'

MRS CHARLES DE GAULLE

Photographers, did you say? I make it a rule to have no truck with *soi-disant* lensmen and women of any stripe. I have no particular beef with them, on the other hand, either. How is my idiomatic English coming along, by the way? No, my focus, as ever, is on my husband and his legacy. I've said it before, my little presidential cabbage, and I'll say it again here so that *bien pensant* commentators, historians and hagiographers might know – the darkest hour is just before dawn. That's *our* dawn. Let there be press bods, lashings of them, *then*.

Oh – and for the record, since you haven't asked me yet, I still believe I was right to insist privately on the segregation of boys and girls in our dormitories of disciplined scholastic enquiry. Youthful cohabitation can only give rise to things unhelpful, including moral minefields, slippery slopes, the thin ends of various wedges, the tips of manifold icebergs, and – my favourite, this – assorted buns in the oven. He was ready to up sticks, or to down tools, or, like Churchill, to take up whisky and watercolours. He had gone beyond sulking – he no longer even cared. But for me, and a few obscure generals, he would have thrown in the towel – the towel of destiny – in the hour of maximum darkness. As it is, I shall have my place in the history books. In front of every great Frenchwoman stands a man.

CHAPTER SEVENTEEN
Montparnasse

WHY WOULD I CHOOSE TO HELP HIM? WHY WOULD I help T-L get rid of the body? That's the question anyone would ask, isn't it? If I told you there were no obvious answers at the time would you believe me? Nothing was straightforward – why would it be? What was clear was T-L's determination to rope me in from the word go. Right from the start it was a case of what *we* might or might not do with Lafcadio's body. Not that T-L saw precisely how I could be, or why I should be, implicated – not yet. His impulse was the reflex action of an innate cunning roused, a defensive by-product of the calculating intelligence I had worshipped like a novice. How clever of T-L to spread the guilt my way in a stinking bedroom above the busy rue de Rennes as night fell for the last time on the city of love.

'What are we going to do with the body, Billy?'

'I don't know, T-L. I'm not actually convinced it has much to do with me.'

'Oh? I don't believe anyone has been closer to poor Lafcadio than you these past few weeks.'

A couple of options emerged rapidly. One or two possibilities presented themselves early for discussion. In spite of the challenging circumstances, I saw right away I had to be clear about my motives for acting as I did. Pity, then, I failed to find the requisite clarity.

The first option put forward by T-L wasn't, in my opinion, a realistic proposition in any meaningful sense. Motivationally it was a non-starter. It certainly couldn't be described as a plan of action. According to this half-baked scenario we would abandon Lafcadio where he lay and simply vanish into the Paris night.

'And go our separate ways?' I said, speculating as hard and as fast as I could.

'Only until the coast is clear,' T-L said. 'I'm sorry, Billy – soon we'll be together.'

'What about your junkie actor friend?' I said without dwelling on the implications of what I had just heard about *being together*.

'Armand?' He would just have to explain it as best he could.'

'They'd still have to come looking for you. You see that, don't you?'

'But not for you, Billy – is that what you're thinking?'

'No, that's not what I'm thinking as a matter of fact.'

Do you see my difficulty? I could have taken up T-L's opening offer and run with it as far and as fast as possible. In all likelihood such investigative efforts as were made would be directed at T-L. I couldn't do it. In my heart I felt only one course of action was open to me, or to us. It involved repatriating Lafcadio's corpse. It meant returning his body to his two older brothers in the Goutte d'Or.

'What – you're planning to pitch up there with Lafcadio in a taxi?' T-L suggested witheringly.

It meant surrendering to the gendarmerie, of course. For T-L the game would be up. Or would it? As the seconds ticked away in a Paris apartment I tried to work out what T-L stood to lose. Why not summon the cops right now and call it a tragic accident? Sure, there would be consequences. It wouldn't be the end of the world, though, would it? Except for Lafcadio, that is.

'Did you kill him, T-L?' It just came out at that point. Call it self-regard. It went to the nub of what I felt. Deep down there must have been a part of me that believed T-L would kill Lafcadio *to get at me*. 'I mean – are you responsible for his death?'

'Dear Billy –' T-L shot back. 'Might that perhaps be a question to ask yourself at this time?'

It was almost dark. Although we could barely see the whites of each other's eyes neither of us chose to switch on the light. To T-L's further strategy I acquiesced reluctantly. He said we should remove the body from these rooms immediately. He meant we should take it elsewhere before Armand returned. That way we would keep our options open. That way we would buy time to work out a plan. All this happened quickly. I swear when I said yes to T-L's proposal I saw it as a temporary measure only. It wasn't a solution. For that I needed time to think. I shouldn't have tried to think. I should have followed my instincts. Then I would have done right by Lafcadio. What T-L said last was the thing that went on to curse him utterly.

'No one will miss him anyway,' he said. 'Isn't that the crucial thing to bear in mind?'

We dragged the body head first down the communal stairs. In death, as in life, Lafcadio was light. No one came out from this or that apartment. It was perfect – as perfect as it could be.

'Did you see any spyholes?' I said, panting a little at the foot of the stairs. 'Do you think anyone saw us?'

'I didn't see any spyholes,' T-L said, out of breath himself. 'Are you ready for this, Billy?'

'What about the scooter?' I said, scanning in my head a list of worrying variables.

'Forget it,' T-L replied in a way that suggested he had already considered the scooter, currently standing beside us in the hall. On the floor at our feet was the scorched jerrycan (with a painful pang I watched them all parade before me – the petrol can, the shattered wing mirrors, Lafcadio's grin, and Nana's knapsack rescued from a recent riot), which T-L kicked negligently as if to check whether it had anything in it. 'I'll come back for the scooter later.'

'You don't think we should use it to carry the body?'

'I don't think we should draw attention to ourselves.'

We stood behind the door to the street with Lafcadio's corpse propped up between us. We had an arm each around his back. His own limp arms were draped over our shoulders, his hands clamped there on either side in ours. T-L adjusted the heavy head so that it lolled forward like a drunkard's. The head hung very low.

'The crash helmet –' I said. 'We should have brought it down.'

'Too bad,' T-L said. 'We could have done with three of them.'

Then we heard a key in the lock. We shuffled backwards. The door swung open from the street. It was Armand, I decided, coming home. He invited us, smiling indulgently, to step outside first, but we stuck, silent and motionless, to the wall while he squeezed past, tossing some remarks over his shoulder before he reached the stairs. The big door was open to the street. We edged through it sideways, awkwardly. To me the nighttime city looked lovelier and more vital than ever. The air – it was fresher than I had expected. We were in the clear now. On rue de Rennes we made our way south, moving slowly and steadily, towards Montparnasse station.

'Was that Armand?' I said. 'What did he say?'

'Nothing. He asked about the scooter.'

'We'll have to get rid of it.'

'I told him it was mine now.'

'We shouldn't have bumped into him like that.'

'Forget it. We're doing fine.'

'Is that boulevard Raspail? We should avoid the main streets.'

'We're doing fine.'

'Maybe we should hail a taxi.'

'No taxis, Billy –'

'Then tell me where we're going.'

'You'll see when we get there.'

'Jesus. What did I say? There's a police checkpoint there.'

'Don't shout, please. We're going to cross the road now. And when we get to boulevard du Montparnasse I want you to sing.'

'What? You know I can't sing.'

'I'll lead and you follow – in French, of course.'

'Crazy fucker, T-L –'

There was no moon. We approached Montparnasse cemetery by way of rue Émile-Richard. In the shadow of the perimeter wall a deeper darkness was our ally. T-L scaled the wall and hauled the body up by the arms while I pushed up from below until Lafcadio straddled the parapet like a dead rustler on a bounty hunter's mule. When I looked up I glimpsed T-L's outstretched hand, but I shook my head and pulled myself up and slid down the other side before lowering Lafcadio to the dirt as gently as I could. My arms ached and my throat was on fire. I decided it must be exactly the same for T-L, and that satisfied me – I didn't want there to be any question between us of relative weakness of will. I knew what I was doing. I knew what T-L had done. If he hadn't killed my friend he had, in my eyes, let him die. It was the same thing, wasn't it? Now he was planning to get away with it. And I, Billy Morton, was going to help him. I had to do what I did. Having started out, I had to go through with it. I had the rest of my life to pay for it.

We stood Lafcadio upright for the last time, draped his arms around our shoulders, and frog-marched him the final thirty paces along the gravel path. It wasn't as if we had earmarked a particular location sympathetic to his nature or outlook. We had no intention of digging a hole for him next to Baudelaire or Huysmans or any of that set. We chose the first available hiding place among the crypts and monuments, laying Lafcadio to rest in a natural gutter next to the chapel of the family Saint-Saëns. With no digging implement at our disposal it was the best we could hope to do.

'He'll always have the music,' T-L said, searching Lafcadio's pockets.

'What are you doing there, please?'

'I'm looking for the scooter key, slow-coach.'

T-L held the key aloft, together with a few grubby banknotes, which he then offered to me.

'Put them back, please,' I said, sinking to the ground with my back to the nearest tombstone.

'You're a fool, Billy Morton.'

'Tell me something I don't know,' I said. 'What happens now?'

'The rest of your life,' T-L said, 'if you're unlucky.' He must have read my mind. He was smart enough to see inside my head – all the time he was one step ahead, with the world playing catch-up. 'Don't worry, Billy,' he went on, pocketing Lafcadio's money and then tossing the scooter keys in the air repeatedly. 'It's just the two of us from now on. Lafcadio was only getting in the way, wasn't he? From tomorrow we'll start over. We'll look up Véronique – I ought to get the low-down on the baby, right? Everything will be different from tomorrow. We're in this together, aren't we? Especially after bumping into Armand so carelessly back there. Never mind. Come and fetch me first thing and we'll make our plan. Come now if you want to. No, I know you want to be alone with Lafcadio to say your goodbyes. That's awfully nice, Billy. That's terribly sweet –'

After T-L split I cried alone beside my late friend's body as it stiffened quietly under a blanket of leaves. As a matter of fact I was stiffening too – it was getting cold and I hadn't eaten. I wasn't sure what I was waiting for, unless it was to be released, or absolved, by the dawn. Yes, I had to be there for Lafcadio – nothing else would do. In truth, the hours passed quickly, the way they must do for the condemned man in his cell. I must have dropped off at some point because when I next looked up the sky was blacker than ever, and I could no longer read the names on the nearest tombs. At this time, or soon after, I made my biggest mistake in respect of Lafcadio. By abandoning him before the night was over I did my late friend one last unscripted disservice. I say unscripted – deep down I must have wanted it to happen this way. I made it happen this way because I was lost and scared (I offer this as explanation rather than excuse). But first there was something more trivial I needed to do at dead of night in Montparnasse cemetery, if only I could recall what it was.

I heard a noise, as of a twig snapping underfoot – I took this as my cue to leave. I got up and forced myself to look in the trench. For an instant I nurtured a wild hope my friend's body might have vanished, but it was still there, ghastly now. And there had been an unhappy development. Lafcadio's eyes had sprung open during the night, and now he glared fiercely at me as if to accuse me of some private betrayal. Well, I knew all about that one already. I tried my best to close my friend's eyes again, but they popped open time after time, like a doll's eyes, with a persistence that was touching. Then I recalled what it was I had intended to do. It was a modest enough thing, goodness knows, and I didn't understand quite why I did it. I pulled the few, by now somewhat crumpled, photographs from my pocket and leafed through them until I found the particular image, disregarded by Véronique only hours ago, of Raymond with her at

the Sorbonne. Then it came to me – we were all family. There was
nothing we wouldn't do for each other. After I had torn the image
in two I installed the fragment featuring the cat-killing Nazi under
Lafcadio's hand where I imagined (yes, I have been a major league
fool) it might serve to throw this or that investigating gendarme off
the scent – my scent. Then I quit Montparnasse cemetery. Yes – I
left early, not knowing where I should go or what I should do. On
the other hand I knew what I had done. I couldn't acknowledge it,
but I knew. By leaving early I was allowing T-L time to empty the
petrol can over Lafcadio's corpse before setting it alight. Why else
abandon my post before my watch was over? Why, you ask, leave a
photographic calling card on a corpse that might be torched at any
time? I don't know. I can't explain it. As I walked I tried not to let
my panic show. I tried hard not to feel anything – to *feel* would have
been disrespectful to the memory of my dead friend. Soon I began
to question what I had actually done to betray him. I meant in life.
What had I done that was so wrong? Page by page I reworked the
notes of my relationship with Lafcadio. I had to do that. On the big
streets a new day was beginning like any other. How could that be?
An early delivery of meats was well underway at Closerie des Lilas.
I went in and asked for a glass of water, and when they gave me one
without demur I had the comical idea everything might be all right.

Rebecca

These authorial interventions must have a function if they are not
to be viewed as unwarranted interference or, worse, an indulgence.
My intention in presenting a multi-faceted version of events, using
historical commentary by the principals, is to give the sense of a life
seen in the round, in close up as well as from longer range, the rival
perspectives acting finally to complement or corroborate each other.

(Is it a twin-lens reflex camera that offers this type of parallax view? Billy would know, and Dad would have known.) The experience is of the documentary truth – it's as if you had come across a diary in a locked drawer and sat down to reread it after many years. Above all, I want my protagonist, using footnotes and parenthetical asides as necessary, to own his story as completely as possible – then, now, forever. For my part, I don't even want to be in it, except where I have a duty to bear witness to certain details *because I was there too.*

CHAPTER EIGHTEEN
After the Fact

I HAD TO LEAVE PARIS AS SOON AS I COULD – this much was clear. I also had to act as naturally as possible so that Nana, my hostess of several fascinating weeks here, suspected nothing of the night's fatal doings. Acting naturally – did it mean trying harder or less hard? I wasn't sure. In taking up my camera again I was doing my utmost to say – look at me, the snapper who came and went as if nothing had shifted decisively in the landscape of human affairs. The Nikon I wielded would help me by insisting on action pure if not simple, on the instinctual deed untrammelled by thought and the corrosive influence of other people's ideas. I saw this plainly in a manner that was redemptive. The relief occasioned by the camera's heft, when I experienced it anew, was almost sexual. To be making a last portrait of Daniel Cohn-Bendit on my final day in Paris felt very right, and for this I thanked Nana freely, once I had got used to the changed working conditions revealed late. For a few perfect moments given over to considerations of film speed, shutter speed and aperture (in so far as these impacted on camera shake, depth of field, grain and granularity), not to mention the disposition of the subject and other factors beyond my control, everything felt morally just.

We gathered in the imposing amphitheatre at the Sorbonne, a suitably sober environment of wood panels and gilded inscriptions, as the revolution drew to a close. We were all here – the journalists, the student spokespersons, their front bench team, the groupies, the assorted hangers-on (I include this final ironic classification in order to give myself the opportunity, at this eleventh hour, to belong) – as history lurched forward disappointed, losing interest in local events with every second. Me, I faced inevitably a choice between 1/30th at f/4 and 1/60th at f/2.8, these options located fairly and squarely within the high-risk zone for hand-held exposure, as we awaited the arrival in our midst of the activist-in-chief. The relationship between shutter speed and aperture – it had its own beauty, persuasive and practical. It offered a sound basis for understanding. I could go up a notch on one scale and down a notch on the other. I might go up two notches here and down two notches there, accepting a smaller measure of light for longer, or sanctioning a larger ingress over less time. Although the exposure, its quantitative effect, stayed the same, my ability to freeze motion, say, or to limit the zone of interest, was made negotiable in ways that argued dominion over life. As for the leading student – he didn't appear. Not there, not then. After Nana ushered me discreetly through a small door into an antechamber I found myself in the presence of various handpicked newsmen with notepads at the ready. From behind a desk bristling needlessly with microphones, the now *former* student champion, exiled cynically by the march of events and since smuggled back into town by factional forces, fielded questions alone and for the last time.

'The communists insist on the need to engage with the state in order to prevent a repressive backlash. To have pressed home your tactical advantage when you could have done so – would it merely have given the army an excuse to intervene more harshly or more punitively on the streets of Paris?'

And again, still in English –

'The Communist Party's Mr Marchais has described certain students as fascist provocateurs who in private despise the working class. Would you care to comment on that assessment?'

And again –

'Are you, in point of fact, just a German anarchist?'

Then Danny the Red selected a microphone, which proved to be dead, and cleared his throat carefully with a view to telling us a revolution – any revolution – was bound to be hijacked before long by vested interests, so that those who began by leading it went on to be betrayed by it. At the emotional high water mark of this short but impassioned speech I released the shutter, with the result that the former student spokesman was captured, mouth open, microphone in hand, at the centre of a landscape format composition in black and white and for all time. He wasn't one of those (this is informed speculation on my part) who thrilled to de Gaulle's radio address at half past four that same afternoon. Nor was he one of half a million loyal citizens who reclaimed the streets, shortly after the president's rousing broadcast, in the name of France's Fifth Republic.

'I expect we can all go home happy now, Billy,' Nana suggested with an editor's eye as the private press briefing broke up. 'See how in tune you are finally with the mood of the age?'

It was over. The joy, the wonder, and the angry love I had felt in respect of the city – these were a savage memory as, sad pack on my shoulder, I headed north towards the Gare du Nord for the last time. I didn't go by way of rue de Rennes – of course not. I had no intention of hooking up with T-L again as discussed in a bad dream in a city cemetery. To feel so alone, so bereft, in Paris after all I had been through was hard to take. Goodbye, Lafcadio! Are you there now in your rude trench, eyes wide open, staring at the sky? I still didn't know the truth about how Lafcadio had died – whether T-L could be said to be actively responsible for his death. He was much too savvy, surely, to let Lafcadio OD like that unless he wanted it to happen. This disturbing notion I couldn't shake off. The shocking inconclusiveness of it made me feel sick, but not quite as sick as the idea, painful legacy of last night, that I had allowed Lafcadio's body to be burned beyond recognition. Again I saw the petrol can below the scooter in the hall. I saw T-L kick the can, and heard its silky slosh. As I left the Latin Quarter behind I clung to the wreckage I had earmarked for my exclusive use thirteen hours ago and more. *It wasn't my fault.* I couldn't be blamed for Lafcadio's passing. What happened later was *after the fact*. The sense of looming disaster I had harboured for so long – how could I have guessed it would come to this? Still I had to live. If I didn't manage to draw certain lines in the sand, Paris would haunt me until the end of time.

There was one final twist, too desperate to dwell on at length. I have said I had no intention of meeting him that day. I had almost convinced myself he had no intention of tracking me down either. As for his obsessive protestations of attachment – these were, I told myself, the regrettable side effects of a finely tuned instability. They would depart as readily as they had come. I shouldn't have thought about any of it. T-L sped past me somewhere between the Sorbonne and the first bridge (all the pride I had taken in knowing the names of the city's streets had evaporated). I swear to God it was T-L. He was joyriding Lafcadio's scooter. That was how I saw the thing. He was riding the bike conspicuously – no, *provocatively*. He was riding it the way Lafcadio had ridden it. He was doing it to shame me. Even before I reached the river I understood I could never be free again.

Part Three

The Seer's Inkling

Chapter Nineteen
A Map for Heroes

IN THE GROUND FLOOR RECEPTION ZONE, bristling as usual with helmeted couriers, of Miss Laurie's newspaper offices I asked for a large envelope and sat down to wait. As I dropped my thirteen rolls of exposed but undeveloped film, of Kodak Tri-X and Ilford HP4 rated variously from 400ASA to 1600ASA and marked accordingly with scratches for the benefit of the processor, into the envelope one after the other I experienced each transaction as a dagger thrust to the heart. Every film cassette was a curse. Every image, latent now but waiting to ripen poisonously in the dark, was a verdict on me, and an indictment of what I'd done. I had done it for Miss Laurie. Hadn't she more or less commissioned me in these very offices just a month or so ago? Now she would welcome me home, the Nikon slung proudly across my chest, from the front line, and scatter the film cassettes with her one sound arm like gems or bullets across the desk and raise a mug of tea to me, the veteran. How I hated myself in London that day. The Nikon was a boulder around my neck. Its weight was unbearable. Where once it had lobbied self-righteously on behalf of the truth, now it was silent. There was no light left in the world because I had killed it. There was only darkness for me, and a sense of shame so palpable it reeked. The camera had turned against me. Who could blame it? That I had stolen the Nikon from under Jacobson's nose, from a college storeroom under conditions of trust, only made the whole thing worse. Total eclipse – there was no daylight left anywhere, or not for me.

'Miss Laurie will see you now,' announced a young intern, an Aussie or a Kiwi, from the halfway point on the stairs.

Because I couldn't go though with it I was obliged to flee. Into the London darkness (it was nearly lunchtime on a sunny Saturday in early June) I dived, leaving behind my bulky envelope with wild instructions entrusting its contents to the one-armed picture editor whose brutal integrity of vision I couldn't possibly face – not today, not tomorrow. Back then Miss Laurie had seen something in me. Now she would have seen right through me. The penetrating gaze that had settled at the drop of a hat on human promise would, with the same forensic facility, have registered the taint or spot. Already the mark I bore inside me threatened to make itself known outside, on my body, on my skin. Was it there now – a small but growing blemish on my forehead that alerted the world to the moral tenor, if not the active detail, of what I had done? I didn't know. The only mirrors I had consulted for three days and nights were attached to the cars parked outside Holland Park. Of course, I hadn't actually done anything, had I? It was what I *hadn't* done that damned me.

Having failed to see Miss Laurie I took myself, without daring to think too much about it, to my old place of work. In visiting the college I understood attraction and repulsion marched side by side in my subconscious mind. Rather than confront the waking reality of what I did or where I went, I preferred to think in these abstract terms. There were no flagstones underfoot for me that day. There were no brick walls enfolding memories. When I gripped the black rail beside the college gates I did so in the hope of receiving a mild electric shock. I felt no such thing. Although I held on tightly, I felt nothing. There was no one on the steps – no one I recognised. Why would there be? It was Saturday. Was it even term time? I couldn't say. Only one idea counted – I had walked out on my job. All the while I wanted to a painful extent to be on the inside of the fence. I would have given anything to be inside it. (In fact, I had nothing to give, except for a camera that belonged rightfully on the far side of the rail anyway). At the same time I had a horror of being anywhere that would choose to have me. It was tragic and pathetic. As I slunk around London like a wounded animal I was reluctant to check my reflection in the windows of shops in case it wasn't there.

Next up was the house that Jacobson and Rebecca, father and daughter, shared lovingly in close proximity to Chalk Farm station. How astonishing to think that, until recently, I had called this place my adopted home. I remembered it fondly as a shrine to lurid wall coverings and stuffed creatures – here common decency flourished like a religion. Jacobson's van was parked outside. How reassuring and unsettling a stationary vehicle could be – in this it stood for the man himself, or for the mixed feelings I had for him based on guilt and dread and a respect close to love. Once again I had the urge to break cover, to rush forward blindly, to abandon the stolen camera on the doorstep like a foundling baby. That would have been silly. Although the day was bright, a light burned fiercely in an upstairs room – I saw that right away from safe distance. In my imagination I saw Becky at a table lit by a desk lamp, her fingers on the keys of her typewriter, not writing quite but poised and ready to unleash a new sentence, a short sentence and a good one. She was describing a map for heroes. She was scattering lies and half-truths like cattle before her. The fact that I had given virtually no thought at all to Becky this past month or so struck me suddenly as a ludicrous lapse in taste, an unpardonable mistake. I had only to cross the road and ring the bell and make everything as it was. I swear I was about to do that. Then I saw a form at the upstairs window, a human figure, no doubt, but one that came and went in the blink of an eye without conforming to my stock notion of what a figure at the window, at this window of this house, might look like today of all days. It wasn't Rebecca. It wasn't her father either. Who, then, or what, if not the ghost of Lafcadio on a day trip to London? Hadn't I been prepared to bring him here myself in return for his life? Instead of taking a step forward in Chalk Farm I took a step back. In my mind I saw a succession of faces at the upstairs window. Briefly I glimpsed them all in turn, the ones closest to me today of all days. Aside from poor Lafcadio there was Raymond, of course, and Lafcadio's brothers, first the older then the younger one, with T-L himself bringing up the rear. It made perfect sense to me that T-L was here. Wouldn't he make his way, by hook or by crook, to this very place in order to track me down? He certainly would. For perhaps a minute I forced myself to regard the upstairs window. No further ghosts presented themselves there during that interval. Then I turned away from the house and tramped north towards darling Hampstead.

Remember Hamish, the burly Scot? He had once had his way with me over a kitchen table in return for some hard cash I needed urgently. Now I needed additional cash from Hamish. As I rang his bell again and again I resolved to do whatever was necessary, with or without a kitchen table, to fund my new lifestyle on the streets of the capital. What I really wanted was a hot bath or shower. Sure, I was hungry as hell. Strictly speaking, no one could see that. Strictly speaking, no one could smell that. On the scale of personal vanity it barely registered. A hot bath, on the other hand, was all that stood between reason and where I currently languished (along with clean underwear, perhaps, if push came to shove). No luck. I knocked and rang, rang and knocked. Hamish was in Scotland, at a castle with a moat and drawbridge. Even Hamish, he of the expansive appetites, found it in him to resist me assiduously on this day. It was official – I was out of step with the march of life.

I had already walked for miles. There was nothing else for it but to walk a few more. As I walked, a plan took resentful shape in my head. It had to do, inevitably, with the camera that had turned against me. Yes, I went unfed. I went unwashed, too. Home these first few days and nights had been a thicket of rhododendrons in Holland Park not far from the tree under which I had scattered my father's ashes. That was OK with me. I had few complaints about these arrangements. My father was under a tree, and I was below a bush next to him. It was June. It was mild enough. I slept with all my clothes on – all of them. Such cold as threatened I saw off with a hot rage stoked by my folly. I was twice a fool. Hadn't I run out on my home as well as my job? No night was black enough to hide me from myself. At midnight I woke up in response to a recurring vision of Lafcadio. First his eyes opened wide and met mine. Then he sat up in his graveyard ditch and smiled, teeth sickeningly white, with petrol can, so light and empty, in hand. All the while the flames conspired to consume him, without quite nailing that grisly task.

I sold the Nikon cheaply to a secondhand photographic dealer in Portobello Road. First I forced myself to confront the idea that Jacobson's stall was located just around the corner. This was part of my penance – I had at least to view the stall, to glimpse Jacobson, before I disposed of the item that hung around my neck like a rock. Guess what? The stall wasn't there. There was no sign of Jacobson. I searched high and low for the trestle table strewn with wondrous things, with optical knick-knacks, with pages torn from history – my history. The table was gone. It was a further blow. (This verdict on how I reacted to the stall's absence is largely tendentious – in fact I probably experienced a measure of relief.) To one betrayal I added another. Immediately I had sold the camera I felt better – I worked hard to convince myself of this. First I had stolen the Nikon, now I had cast it off. For a moment I stood shoulder to shoulder with the underworld movers and shakers, the rogues and the cheats. Then I felt sick at myself. The funniest thing was I couldn't bring myself to spend the money I had got for the camera. That's how screwed up I was. There was real heartbreak in my casual denial, expressed in the sale I had just made, of my beloved photography. Photography was the law. It offered a design for life, its regime harsh but fair. All my adult days I had used its knobs and dials to navigate experience, to hold the world to account and myself with it. Basically, I didn't want to go on. After I had sat on a park bench for an hour, fighting back angry tears and generally feeling sorry for myself, everything fell into place and I knew what to do.

When the man approached me at Piccadilly Circus at around dusk I was ready, stomach full now, to make it work. Two coppers loitered at the bottom of Shaftesbury Avenue. They were my age, give or take – too young to acknowledge the possibility of forbidden love. The policemen were distracted. Everyone was distracted by a delegation of Buddhist monks gathering for a snapshot on the steps below the statue of Eros. As I watched them assemble, my back to a railing under the neon cliffs, some of the monks smiled in a beatific way and others called raucously to the picture taker to get a move on. Then their flashbulb went off, and it caused my man to change his mind. He had been sauntering towards the statue from the top of Haymarket, but now he discarded his cigarette and appeared to change his mind about something important, glancing at his watch and then striding past me as if he had just remembered it was his wife's birthday. Still, he gave himself away. As he passed by me his eyes dipped involuntarily below my belt for the smallest fraction of a second. I don't think he could help it. When I caught up with him minutes later in Trafalgar Square he was leaning against a parapet on the north side glaring down at the lions and the fountains.

'Got a light?' I asked him, recalling sadly the time we had all demonstrated right here against a distant, dirty war.

'I have at that,' he came back unsmiling, extending his cheap lighter towards me and sparking it up after a few attempts.

'Got a snout and all?' I went on with what I judged to be the right amount of local colour.

Once we were puffing away side by side, the National Gallery behind us, and the river, sensed but not seen, in front, he asked me how much it was for oral. It was a good question. Apart from the matter of who might do what to whom under those circumstances there were a number of economic factors to review, a thing's worth residing not only in itself but also in its perceived value to this party or that. Supply and demand – these were key players, lurching here towards a negotiated outcome.

'Five quid,' I said, considering the cost of a bottle of gin before doubling it and rounding the total down in a concession to modesty.

'That's a bit steep, isn't it?'

'Not when you shift your focus from price towards value.'

'Cocky one, aren't you? Budding comedian, if you ask me.'

'There's some would give plenty to see my comedy bud –'

'Got any tattoos on you, son? On your upper bod, that is?'

'Sorry. You don't possess a bath, do you, by any chance?'

Adrian was a kind man who had lived quietly with his mother beside the railway in Parsons Green until she passed away suddenly but peacefully, leaving Adrian the terraced house in Novello Street.

There was a yellow bird in a cage on the upright piano. There was a bunch of flowers in an enormous vase – artificial flowers, Adrian told me proudly. The piano stool was crammed, beneath its hinged lid, with sheet music. What else? There was a squat, deep television in one corner of the front room – a portable, Adrian informed me, fiddling determinedly with the vertical hold.

'It'll take your mind off it,' he said. 'The picture will, I mean.'

I didn't want to take my mind off it. I didn't tell Adrian that, but he probably sensed it, using a special type of insight honed over a lonely lifetime. He found various novel ways to humiliate me, the flickering television interrupting us every now and again to report the fatal wounding at a US hotel of Robert Kennedy, once a hero of mine. Although Adrian exceeded by a wide margin the terms of our agreement, I waived any additional fees in the interests of fairness.

'What do you want to be, Billy?' my host enquired generously, perching on the toilet seat as a train clattered past outside and I slid below the surface of the water in the bath.

'I don't know,' I said honestly, even as the idea of something new took up provisional residence in a remote part of my heart. 'A paperback writer, most probably.'

'That's nice,' Adrian said with an exile's eye for what had been left behind in the long, slow flight from joy. 'I hope all your books have a happy ending.'

I liked Adrian, and I think he came to like me a little. He gave me what I needed in order to carry on, and for that I was grateful. When I left him early the next morning after my second hot bath he wished me all the luck in the world. Then he told me earnestly I wouldn't need any of it. I knew very well he was wrong about that, but I couldn't know how wrong. When I got to Earl's Court I tried to buy myself pen and paper, but everywhere was shut. The urge to *write it all out* – I was obliged to make it wait. Church bells ringing in the region of South Kensington sounded an ambiguous note – ding for good, dong for bad. The troubling business of existence could go hang until later – Sunday, at least, was safe. That was how it felt to me beside the Serpentine with all the couples messing about in hired boats. Everything was exactly as it should be. Swans swam in a stately way. Wet oars flashed as in a dream. In certain respects my low point in the city represented a kind of calm before the storm.

ADRIAN

He was a dirty little bugger, and no mistake. It took a lot to warm him up, but once you got the lad going there was no stopping him. As a young man he seemed to have plenty to offer – why then did I get the feeling he was running away from something? He was out to punish himself as best he could. That's how it looked. What else? He was very respectful about my mother's passing. Funny thing, as in funny peculiar – he cried when Bobby Kennedy took a bullet.

CHAPTER TWENTY
Bloomsbury

PERCY GIFTED ME A KISS, VERY TENDER, which I acknowledged, eyes shut, with a smile. I heard the kisser pad across the bedroom floor in bare feet. Or were his feet clothed? It was difficult to tell. As I pictured in turn the socks held high on the calf by suspenders, the shoehorn and the shoes, I took in the aromas, fused by the rhythms of the hour, the quick hour before work, into an olfactory cocktail, Sahara dry, as it were, on the tongue and reassuringly masculine in tone, of Vaseline hair tonic and Cherry Blossom shoe polish with a carefully judged top note of aftershave, plus Percy's first cigarette, French *sans* filter, of the day. There was no work for me. That was number one. Two – there was nowhere I needed to be. There was nothing I had to do – not if you excluded the everyday business of playing hide and seek with myself in a room full of mirrors. In fact, there *was* something I badly wanted to do today. How could I have overlooked it? The scents strongly present – had they temporarily scotched my bitter sense of it on their astringent mission to please? The whole notion of it had barely left my thoughts for a fortnight. Nothing could be more important to my cause or more relevant to my case. Now, suddenly, there was real urgency about what I must do if I wasn't to be too late altogether. It meant asking dear Percy, a gentle literary editor and my newest friend, for yet more money.

208

'Don't forget to meet me at six, will you?' he said, knotting his tie at the window while, above and behind him, the breakfast clouds parted ecstatically over Eccleston Square and Victoria.

Oh, I was content enough as I raised myself up on one elbow in bed. For three happy weeks with Percy I had really had no sense of time passing. I lived strictly in the here and now. For me there was no past and no future, which was an ideal state of affairs given my overwhelming desire to forget *everything*.

'What would you do if I said I didn't want to go?'

Percy hesitated, edged with morning fire, at the window before bending down slowly, his white shirt going bang, bang, bang in the triple mirror of the dressing table, to open a low drawer.

'I don't know,' he said, unfazed, turning away from the tallboy and hitching up his elasticated braces, a hardback copy of *The Quiet American* tucked under his chin. 'I thought you wanted to, that's all.'

'Did I give you that impression?'

'You gave me to believe you were intent on becoming what is commonly known as a scribbler.'

'I have my diary, it's true.'

'Your journal.'

'Journal, diary – what's the difference?'

'See what I mean? Meet me at six o'clock if you want to get it from the horse's mouth –'

'I prefer my horses in the landscape – galloping, for example, on a moonlit beach at midnight.'

'By which I mean our society of novelists, short story wallahs, budding Eliots and bearded Ezras, plus a veritable Lady Ottoline in the shape of our hostess, not to mention the writers of film scenarios and, yes, *journals*. Oh, and the odd debonair publisher, too.'

'Not you, surely, Percy?'

'You'd be amazed at how attractive I can appear to someone looking for a three-book deal.'

'Aren't you concerned about what people will think when you show up with a younger man, as in me, on your arm?'

'Why should I be? Are you not my exciting literary discovery, precociously talented but woefully unschooled? In any case – times and attitudes are changing, don't you think?'

'Not so you'd notice down the boozer.'

'Confront the bastards, Billy, but always with a glass of fizz to hand. And now I must go earn what is widely referred to as a crust in order to keep you in the manner to which, et cetera, et cetera –'

'Ah,' I said. This was the moment. I hadn't tried to engineer it particularly, which was good. It came straight at me, as if from the pages of a novel. 'Can I borrow some more money, please?'

There was a short delay here, the most likely reason for which was that Percy was cramming his books into the battered brief case he kept in the hall beside the door to the landing.

'Of course,' he called out warily. 'What's it for?'

'You know what it's for,' I said. 'The whole world knows.'

'The camera?' Percy said, leaning back into the bedroom. 'As in Portobello Road?'

'I have to do this,' I reminded him, striking the pillow because I sensed I had already waited too long to act.

'My dear old thing,' Percy said, frowning from the doorway with maximum understanding.

'I'll pay you back,' I said, 'when I have a job. Provided I don't walk out on it, of course.'

'Now, now – you only did that to help a French lady friend who was in trouble, remember?'

'I'll pay you back, Percy – cross my heart and hope to die.'

'Look – I thought we'd discussed this. Forget the money. This isn't about money. I thought you agreed it's time to bid farewell to photography. Lovely, lovely photography – it isn't hard enough to do, is it? It isn't difficult enough. There has to be a tougher way to speak the truth, if that's what you want to do. Is it what you want to do, Billy? Isn't now the time to become the writer you are?'

'And what would you know about that?'

'Gee, thanks – I've seen what you write. I know who you are.'

'I'm sorry I said that. I still have to buy the Nikon back. Don't you see? It isn't about photography. It's about personal integrity.'

'Ah, integrity – I think we might have done something on that in the debating society at prep school. How much do you need?'

I felt wretched. As I made my way on foot towards the camera shop in Portobello Road I thought myself the worst of men. I had to find a way to leave Percy – funny Percy. It wasn't right. He was too decent. He made me happy, asking little of happiness himself. He was content to support me. He didn't care whether I got a job or not. It wasn't as if he set out to own me in any sense, or to control me in any way. He was no obsessive, unlike T-L. He was brave and kind and good, and when I looked around his flat with me in it I asked myself – is this all there is? Then I added – *you wanker, Billy Morton*. Percy was wrong about one thing – he didn't know me. Yet he was right in a roundabout way when it came to my relationship with photography. Could be I wouldn't shoot another frame in my life. What better way to hurt myself? From today only the simplest pleasures would move me. Hello, sky. Hello, trees. For the first time it occurred to me I ought to spend more time beside the sea. Before that I had to buy the Nikon back and press the reset button on my miserable life. It didn't matter what I did with the camera. I might donate it to the deserving poor. I didn't get the chance. The Nikon was gone – snapped up, so they told me, not long after I flogged it. I didn't ask who had bought it. I elected not to find out. In a way I was happy to let it go. It meant a new start. It meant lowering the curtain on this whole sorry camera redemption episode knowing I had *tried my best*. That was the position as I made to quit the shop on the path to sunnier days. I thought I was home and dry then. How could I have thought such a foolish thing?

It was darker. It was suddenly very dark, as before a hailstorm in summer. There was a man in the doorway of the shop. He had to step aside to let me pass. This man was tall and smooth of cheek, with head shaved like a skinhead's. The last time I saw Raymond he had a beard, didn't he? Why would he be here in London, if not to track down the father of Véronique's baby, or to learn who had attached a photograph of a Nazi to a blazing corpse in a cemetery in Paris? If Lafcadio had burned so brightly wouldn't the Polaroid have gone up in smoke too, your honour? And, yes, I'll say it again – I had nothing to do with Véronique's baby. That was T-L. That was T-L's work. It was hallucinatory, wasn't it, all this? Raymond was an illusion, a trippy flashback. It was absurd to suggest I might bump into him like that in a photographic dealership in Portobello Road. Raymond no longer existed for all practical purposes. None of them existed now, except in my conscience. I had to believe that, otherwise I wouldn't be able to sleep at night.

'Well, would you Adam and Eve it? He actually came at six sharp.'

'Punctuality costs nothing, I think you'll find – handy enough when you're flat broke.'

'Want me to fill you in on our Henry?'

'Who's Henry and why does he matter?'

'Oh, dear – I expect you'll get the hang of it.'

There was nothing more to be said. It was all in the moment. Percy grinned, delighted, and wiggled the bell pull, and we made our way, hand in hand to start with, then laughing for no apparent reason, up the worn stone stairs one house away from the junction of Bedford Square with Gower Street. We didn't so much approach the voices filtering down from above – rather the cigarette smoke, increasingly present as we climbed, set the compass for our ascent.

'Welcome to Bloomsbury, Mr Bond,' Percy said when we got to the shiny black door stationed slightly ajar.

'You have interfered for the last time,' I told him, toying with the massive knot of my tie.

'Is that *my* suede tie, or an exact replica?' he asked me as the door swung open poetically with a creak to reveal a tall woman got up simply but expensively in an unfashionably long dress.

Henrietta, our hostess, had an 'at home' on Wednesdays from six until eight, except during August when she holidayed on Capri. She was, Percy warned me in a whisper, of a certain type. It was no secret (at least not as far as she was concerned) that her sentimental education had been at the practised hand of Ford Madox Ford in the wake of an epic picnic at Glyndebourne. In her feeling eye she wore the dark history of the twentieth century to date, while on her head, underwritten by a complicated infrastructure of jewelled pins and brooches, a bird's nest of blue and grey hair aspired fearlessly to the condition of modern art.

'My dear Percy –' Henrietta began now, holding her cigarette aloft while offering up her cheek.

'Henry, dearest,' Percy murmured, kissing all available surfaces three times according to an established formula.

'Pimm's, darling?' Henry proposed, unruly eyebrows vaulting generously to include me in the offer.

'Rather,' Percy said, winking at me as if to suggest affectation under these particular terms and conditions was nothing more or less than a proper respect for the past.

We were in a high ceilinged room that looked over the square. Here and there the large space boasted interruptions in the form of lacquered screens depicting flamingoes, peacocks, humming birds and other exotic species not native to Gower Street. Immediately I felt at home in Henry's world.

'Oh, but do tell me *all*, Percy,' our hostess demanded, waving a ladle above an enormous punch bowl and appraising me candidly through the glossy fronds, impossibly luxuriant in the Bloomsbury half light, of an aspidistra. 'You must have ransacked *le tout Soho* to find such a sympathetic looking plus one, darling. Are you lovers, or have you come together in a professional capacity? Or is it both? Of course it is. One senses as much right away and approves. Mix business with pleasure if you can, I say. Why not the moon *and* the stars? I put it to you frankly. As for that remarkable tie, young man – I think the knot may merit a Nobel or an Oscar or something. Is that your sartorial handiwork, Percival?'

'Henry, Billy – Billy, Henry.'

'And what is it you *pen*, dear boy?'

'Just film scripts at the minute,' I said, improvising madly and blushing in a similar vein.

'Oh, bad luck – we all have to begin somewhere,' Henry said, squeezing my elbow to indicate she was merely being humorous in line with her function and role. Now she steered us towards the first decorative screen and a sprawling group of vocal guests, and as we went she took my arm like an intimate aunt and leaned closer and whispered it at the top of her voice for anyone to hear. 'You will look after dear Percy for us, won't you, Billy? You must.'

'Don't let Henry fool you,' Percy interposed happily. 'She sees everything and knows everyone.'

'Wait till you hear this evening's reader,' Henry said, as if to remind us finally of the matter at hand, before moving to withdraw discreetly. 'I should make her a three-book offer PDQ, Percy.'

'Ah, Percival, my dear fellow − chin-chin. It's Percival, chaps. Backs to the wall and all that −'

'Gentlemen − I want you to meet Billy, an exciting new talent, and one to watch out for.'

'And how is life at Heinemann? I still haven't got my hands on the new Burgess.'

'Oh, that awful man − his ego must be at least twice the size of what was once Bechuanaland.'

'Is it terribly funny, Percy? My wife's a big fan, you know.'

'Laughs easily, I suppose − your wife.'

'Pity us − we've been trying to pay someone to ghost the new 007, but no one will take it on.'

'And what is it *you* write, Billy?'

'Screenplays, mostly.'

'Ah, rotten luck.'

'Oh, I don't know − we all have to start somewhere.'

'Look − there's Henry. I think we're going through now.'

We took our places, Percy and I, in the back row of a seated audience of some twenty people on the other side of the gorgeous screen. I couldn't really see. I hadn't really looked. Then Henry was saying some fine words of introduction − something about quality of voice or confidence of tone. When I looked up at last I saw Becky at the right hand of our hostess. She looked different to me. Why wouldn't she? She wore a sheer red dress like a cocktail party dress and matching lipstick and drop earrings, and in her hands, pressed to her stomach, she carried her sheaf of typed pages. The effect was just right. It was true – she looked like someone ready to make an accommodation with success. I didn't hear what Becky read. I had no idea what her story was about, or whether it was set in the past, the present or the future. Instead of listening I spent roughly twenty minutes wondering how so much could alter in such a short space of time. It was about perception. It was about image, or self-image – I saw that, of course. In her new guise or with an alternative look Becky struck me as an advanced version of herself. Whereas I had gone backwards, surely, so that any gap in understanding between us was likely to be wider than it ought to be. And I thought about the abandoned Nikon, naturally enough. It was tied in forever and a day with Becky's father. It would never let me go. That was OK, because I deserved everything that was coming my way. After the warm applause Henry called for questions. I was thinking about a time way back in the past when I had risen to speak and Véronique had slapped me down. Or, rather, she had slapped me and then I had stood up to speak. How I wished I could return to a time when I was different. Soon I began to fight back. It was something Percy had said. He said you had to find the toughest way to do a thing, or words to that effect. Perhaps he was right. Was this the hardest way to be me? I was the sum total, no more and no less, of all that had gone before. Everything I had said or thought or done had brought me to this perfect pitch. From out of nowhere it came back to me – my one true reason for being. Yes, there was nothing I wouldn't do to be more like myself. Then I was on my feet, and shaking.

'Have you still got my painting of the moonlit horses stashed under a bed?' I enquired of Becky to evident amusement locally, my naked impulse departing wildly from social convention in response to a tidal surge, deep within my blood, of authenticity.

There was no shame. Wasn't it merely the most characteristic thing on my mind? For a moment two tendencies prevailed among our number, these being a shuffling of feet and a clearing of throats. No one in the salon knew when normal business might be resumed.

'Why *Cornwall* out of the blue like that?' Henrietta asked finally from the front row in an attempt, subtly supportive in its scope and reach, to hold Becky editorially to account.

'Because I wanted to convey the sense of a flight from reason towards madness,' Becky explained without hesitating. 'So, to me, Cornwall stands here for the very limit of the knowable world.'

After Percy had congratulated Becky on her reading and asked her if she had representation yet (not as such, she told him, although there were a number of literary agents in the room) it was my turn to make polite noises of an untutored kind on the theme of narrative voice. Then it was time to drag the difficult past, beating its chest and pulling faces and making a terrific song and dance about the whole thing, into the even more awkward present. We were alone together, the novelist and I, at an open sash window looking south across the square with a rogue streetlight coming on below us and the night clouds rehearsing for later in a pink sky above.

'Where have you been?' Becky asked me, as if to confront first things first.

'I went to Paris,' I said. 'You already knew about that –'

'Yes, but where have you *been*, Billy?'

I didn't come back to her on that one. How much spare time had she got? There was a queue of interested people waiting to talk knowledgeably to her about dialogue and description and point of view and character. After a moment she took up again.

'I know you're in some kind of trouble.'

'What makes you think that?' I asked.

'T-L told me. Isn't that what we're meant to call him?'

'T-L?' I said, pulse accelerating, pores flooding.

'He's been living with me,' Becky said, 'while he waits for you to show your face. He had the strange idea you would show up first at my place. He's probably waiting for you there now.'

'What kind of trouble?' I said, impossibly thirsty suddenly.

'Isn't that the question I'm supposed to ask you?' Becky said. 'Something serious, T-L said. He said he wanted to help you – no, to *protect* you. That's what he told me when I took him in.'

'T-L's living with you now?' I said, working hard still to picture the alarming scene. 'What about your father?'

'Dad's dead,' Becky said, nodding resolutely beside me. 'The funeral was yesterday.'

'Dead?' I said. 'What do you mean dead?'

'As in deceased,' Becky said. 'He hanged himself from a tree on Hampstead Heath.'

'On Hampstead Heath?' I mumbled like the blood relation of a village idiot.

'Either that or someone else hanged him,' Becky said. 'He left no message. He didn't leave a note.'

It was my fault – everything was. Now Henry led Becky away from the open window with its nagging draught. Percy put his hand on my shoulder and asked Becky to send him something to read – three short stories, he said. Becky was a few feet away now. She was backing off with her successful pages in her hand. She might as well have been light years away. Then she smiled bravely or maturely or something and raised her hand as if to confirm what we already knew – yes, she was a big girl now.

'When are you going to come and fetch them?' she asked me.

'Come and fetch what?' I asked her in mechanical way.

'Your horses,' she said. 'They're still under the bed where you left them.'

'What kind of tree?' I asked, taking a step closer.

'A copper beech,' she said, turning away.

Although it was early, and Percy wanted to slip off to a little place with live music he knew on Frith, I resisted the idea of having fun. I didn't mention Jacobson's death to Percy. I wasn't sure if, or how, it fitted in to what we had going. Could be my reticence here had to do with a sense I carried inside me that what we had going would, despite Henry's interest and investment in it, end shortly. It turned out Percy already knew about Jacobson.

'Next week it could be you reading,' he said, not quite joking, in the taxi heading south.

'I'm not sure about that,' I said blandly without really thinking about it. I was thinking about something else. I needed to get a job right away – that was the main thing. With the money from a job I would be able to pay Percy back what I owed him. Decent Percy – he didn't ask me about the camera, as if it was a point of principle with him to avoid the subject of money owed. It wasn't just about money. Finding a job was bound up with an urgent need to act like a man. In a matter of a few seconds it became the only viable way to save my life. If I could have jumped out and landed a role, any role, in that moment I would have stopped the taxi there and then. 'Actually, I think I should probably forget about writing just now and find myself a proper job –'

'Ah,' Percy said. 'What you're saying is you're leaving me.'

'I didn't say that,' I protested.

'But that's what you meant.'

There was no rancour – of course there wasn't. There was only a thoroughly decent resignation and a silence into which all Percy's fine feeling dropped like a stone. I said nothing. I made no apology. It was the right thing to do, wasn't it? It was the right thing to do, under the circumstances – to show Percy a quiet respect. For most of the way we sat side by side without speaking. The swollen river itself wasn't nearly diverting enough to break the spell.

'Tragic about poor Rebecca's father,' Percy said at last. 'She showed real spunk tonight.'

'Yes,' I said, taken aback and momentarily wrong footed. How could Percy know? It was a conspiracy – everyone knew more than I did. Then it came to me – Henrietta would have known, and she must have told Percy. 'She's a real trooper is our Becky,' I added in a voice quite unlike my own.

'Amazing coincidence you knowing each other,' Percy said.

'Do you think so?' I said. 'Yes, I suppose it is.'

'It's an omen, obviously. It's a sign of something.'

'Something good or something bad?' I said, winding down the window and breathing in hard.

'Don't be silly – *good*, of course. People get what they deserve in this world, Billy.'

'Do you think so?' I asked for a second time. This time I really meant it. This time I really wanted to know. There was something gnawing at my insides like a beast trying to get out. What was it? It was what Becky had said about her father. *Either that or someone else hanged him* – hadn't she used those terrible words? In my heart was a mushrooming malaise. In my head was a dire vision, which featured Raymond, skull shorn like a Nazi's, and a rope, and a copper beech tree on Hampstead Heath. It was a shocking image to conjure up in a taxi. Its import was frightening and sickening. I know, I know – there was no earthly reason to link Raymond with Jacobson at that time, or any time. One was a neo-Nazi studying in Paris while the other was a Jew living until recently here in London. Except that there *was* a link, wasn't there? That link – it was me. The panic and confusion I had worked so hard to banish returned redoubled – this time they were informed by a desperate sense that I had wronged, or would duly set about wronging, my newest friend. 'You really are a special person, Percy,' I blurted out with the white cliffs of Pimlico my witness. 'I hope you get what you deserve in this world.'

Henrietta

He was far too young to write anything useful – that instinct usually arrives later in a man. What I got from him nonetheless was a type of moral seriousness that boded well for his art and for his relations with Percy. I will not have any harm come to Percival. I won't have any whippersnapper or upstart, regardless of brains or looks, play fast and loose with dear Percy's feelings. As it turned out, I needn't have worried about Billy. He had an angel at his side and the devil at his heels like a snarling dog. How else to account for the almost physical intimacy he appeared to enjoy at any given moment with what was right and what was wrong?

CHAPTER TWENTY-ONE

Cry Foul

THERE WAS TOM AND THERE WAS BERTIE too. Add to them Acker and his sidekick Jock. These four I knew already. These four were proper porters in the sense that their job was to transfer this or that patient in a wheelchair or on a trolley from the medical or surgical wards to the operating theatre in the new wing. No doubt they had other duties and made other sorties from one day, or one shift, to another. Mostly they ferried patients from A to B – that was their principal task. This was in the big hospital at Archway on the slope running up towards Waterlow Park and Highgate village.

For me the routine was different. As the stationery (but rarely stationary) porter my role was to distribute basic supplies like paper towels and toilet rolls and rubber gloves to every corner or outpost of the sprawling estate. So, in the pecking order of porters I was at the bottom, which suited me perfectly. It was what I wanted. It was where I deserved to be. Strange to tell – I was back in a store man's coat. My entire working life was to be spent, I concluded proudly, in such a garment and station. Meanwhile, my trolley was my loyal ally. My barrow was my confidant, the only friend I could count on one hundred per cent in a parallel universe of passages and tunnels, labyrinthine in its physical arrangement and its esoteric schedule of rules, regulations, protocols and procedures covering every aspect of conduct and engagement. Such order was profoundly welcome to me. To be told what to do a hundred times by a hundred people, all expert in the internal supply of goods and services, struck me as proof of heaven. It meant I didn't have to think for myself. For the first two weeks it worked well. Then people stopped telling me what to do and I was at sea. All the while I had failed to take up Becky's invitation to rescue my painting, my horses. Don't get me wrong – scarcely a moment went by without Becky, the whole notion of her, banging on the door to my thoughts and fixing to burst in. It didn't matter whether I was stalking the linoleum corridors of the hospital by day, or tossing and turning by night on the lumpy sofa in Percy's living room – Becky was there, knocking. Somehow I hadn't made it over to her place yet. That was set to change.

'Did you visit that thieving bookie yet, Billy?'

'Not yet, Tom – but I will.'

'Did I give you the spondulicks, son?'

'You did, Bertie. You did.'

This was an unofficial aspect of my role. Because my delivery duties took me further afield than any other porter's I was ideally placed to carry the various bets to the nearest bookmaker a stone's throw from the hospital precincts. In the morning I put the money down and brought back the chits with the odds and stakes written up in my own hand on behalf of my colleagues. In the afternoon I returned to the betting shop at the furthermost reach of my rounds to collect any takings, distributing these discreetly in one of several busy lifts, going up or going down.

'Will you fetch me my winnings later, Billy?'

'I can't today, Acker. Saturday is my half day.'

'Right you are, son. Right you are.'

The copper beech is a hanging tree –

Regarding Becky there were any number of things weighing on my mind. What must she be feeling? That was the first item on my list. Tied in with my sympathy for Becky was a sense of my own failure to grieve adequately for my father, for Dad, when I had the chance. *The copper beech is a hanging tree*. And now Jacobson was dead, strung up at his own hand, or the hand of another. How could any confusion or doubt attach to an action of such brutal finality? That was what I struggled to comprehend in the bright and lonely strait between Maternity and Gynaecology on the first floor of the main building's annex, gifted to the hospital in more philanthropic times by what the plaque described as a grateful mother of seven. Could Raymond have hung, or hanged, Jacobson? That was the question I had to confront if I wanted to live my life from here on. Could he physically have managed it, acting alone to eradicate one more Jew on behalf of some dark sect? No, no – he must have entered into a diabolical pact with Lafcadio's brothers, his own sworn enemies, in order to boost the manpower quotient beneath a spreading tree on Hampstead Heath one night. These black musings were obviously the workings of a damaged psyche. Around and around they went inside my head. So, Jacobson was no more. And now I would never be able to atone for having stolen a Nikon camera from the college store all those days ago. It was a lucky let-off, wasn't it? Who could possibly have predicted the cards would fall in that way? The other thing that exercised me increasingly was the question of what T-L had told Becky about Paris. How much did she know, and how was I to find out *usefully*? There was much dread in my head as I pushed my barrow from ward to ward. Only my trolley was true. Oh, no – Percy was true too. I still hadn't worked out how best to leave him. Having migrated from his bedroom to his living room I had at least reached some kind of staging post on the road to elsewhere.

In the lift going up were Jock (his personal style suited canny each-way bets) from Glasgow, and a kid with serious acne who was strapped into his wheelchair. It was impossible not to view the kid's wheelchair as a travelling version of the electric chair.

'Going up?' I said, hitting the button to close the doors.

'Top floor,' Jock intimated, jaunty as a Pools winner.

'Penthouse suite?' I enquired as brightly as I could manage.'

'That's the one,' Jock confirmed, cheerful as you like.

Penthouse suite was code for the electric shock department on the roof of the main building. I had never called there on my daily rounds. Perhaps they had no use for rubber gloves or paper towels within their therapeutic regime. Suddenly the kid in the wheelchair gripped my sleeve and buried his face in my coat and began to wail like a stricken animal, like a beached whale or something tragic. It should never have happened. Those little straps were there to retain the lad's wrists. Then the doors opened just as they always did, as though nothing was amiss in the world, and Jock peeled the youth's fingers from my arm and wheeled him away to the penthouse suite. This kind of event occurred every day at the hospital. What started out as affecting quickly became mundane in the scrubbed light. I got to thinking maybe Jock had deliberately left the wheelchair's straps undone as a concession to the kid. That's how it was for me in those days. I couldn't discern the true meaning and value of things.

After clocking off I went directly to Chalk Farm using a mix of bus and train. I didn't want to give myself a chance to change my mind. T-L answered the door, which was ideal. It was imperative I speak to him first, on his own, without Becky. There was no other way to do this. We didn't talk to begin with. T-L grabbed his sports jacket and a flat cap, and we made straight for Belsize Park, forking right at Pond Street for South End Green and the open spaces beyond. I had so many questions for T-L I didn't know where to start.

'Will you show me the tree?' I said once we reached the grassy scrubland and the ponds on the near side of Hampstead Heath.

'No camera?' T-L said. 'I would have thought you would have wanted to take a few pictures *in memoriam.*'

The copper beech stood alone, without the company of other trees, on a rise above the pond favoured by model boat enthusiasts. The solitary tree was an automatic choice for a hanging – its lowest branches were the right girth and height from the ground. To one side of the tree, half in and half out of its poignant shade, a group of six children, escapees from a nearby party or picnic, blew soapy bubbles into the afternoon air. It was a pretty scene. At least it was prettier than the one I had in my head. There was no easy way of sharing what was on my mind with T-L. How could I begin to tell him the story behind the story of what happened in Paris? He was well out of it. He didn't even know what Raymond, or Lafcadio's brothers, looked like. There was something else – a nagging feeling I had which had started over there in Paris and which strengthened now in the probing London light. To feed T-L facts from this point onwards was plain dangerous. Best keep your powder dry, boy. To share my hopes and fears with T-L was manifestly a risk. Might he not, at the drop of a hat, use them against me?

'How much does Becky know?' I asked once the children had run away. 'What did you tell her?' I said, leaning back, with a small internal cry of pain, against the trunk of Jacobson's tree.

'I told her you were in trouble,' T-L said in a voice that set out to suggest and then confirm there had been no other feasible way to behave under the circumstances.

'You didn't tell her *you* were in trouble?'

'What does Becky care about me? When she suggested I wait for you to show up at her place I felt I had no option but to take up her invitation.'

'That's not quite how she put it to me.'

'She's been overwrought, hasn't she? Not quite herself. Hardly surprising when you consider what happened to her old man.'

'What did happen?'

'I don't know. A suicide without a note – that's how the cops seem to see it. They found his van parked on a double yellow over there beyond the lake. The keys were on him. The whole thing has devastated Becky. I've been doing my best to comfort her.'

'I bet.' There was nothing for it but to let that one pass. There were too many other things to worry about on a shady slope above the water. Below, the model boats came to rest all at once, a partial peace descending on the sparkling scene. Above, a summer breeze whispered in the leaves, darkly purple like oil on mud, of Jacobson's tree. 'So what exactly *did* you tell her about Paris?' I said, returning carefully to my central theme.

'Nothing,' T-L said with a measure, impossible to countenance reasonably, of amusement in his voice. 'You don't think I would tell her what really happened, do you?'

'I don't know,' I said, gathering up my strength. Here we had come to the nub of it. It wasn't just that I couldn't believe what T-L told me any more. It was worse than that. It was worse because I couldn't actually ask him anything either. The petrol of Paris was a fine example of this. It wasn't just any old example. It was the most significant example by a long chalk. What I needed to know before all else was whether T-L had made graveyard use of the petrol that sloshed so seductively within Lafcadio's can. It was all in my head, wasn't it? It was all in my heated imagination. How could I possibly mention it without giving T-L another stick to beat me with? What if he hadn't used the petrol, but said he had? How would I uncover the truth of it? I wouldn't. Why, then, give him a further means to undermine me? No, the only option available was to trap T-L into citing the use of Lafcadio's petrol *unprompted*. As a plan it sucked. As a strategy it had no merit, matching perfectly in this way my current model of existence. 'What did really happen over there, T-L?'

'I don't know, Billy,' he said, and for a careless second or two I thought he sounded all right, the way he always used to sound. 'I'm still trying to make sense of it myself –'

'So what do you want with me?' I said. We had moved on in our game of cat and mouse. It was a new phase, as important and necessary as any other. This last of my questions might just as easily have been the first. Above the pond four young gulls, homesick for the English Channel or the North Sea, vied noisily for a morsel of bread thrown down by a child. The first gull rose up with the prize, the others protesting furiously at the unfairness of life and wheeling hostilely around. Soon the first seagull couldn't stand it any more, opening its beak to cry foul and letting fall the soft, white bounty. 'I don't understand what you want,' I told T-L.

'I don't want anything,' he said, summoning all the reason in the world as if it were his to deploy at will, 'except to keep an eye on you. My job is to help you – you know –'

'No, I don't know, as a matter of fact. So kindly enlighten me because I'm dying to find out.'

'I mean – you wouldn't want to let anything slip that might be better left unsaid, would you?'

All the way back my heart protested at T-L's sinister gall. On the one hand his declared interest in watching over me was a new development. On the other it was a natural extension of what had gone before in the obsession and possession stakes. By the time we got to Becky's place I had it all figured out. Taken to its limit, T-L's desire to silence me would mean killing me now. If you developed that scenario and gave it a reciprocal twist I would have to slay him first. Thus a happy balance was struck in our affairs. The thing that troubled me most about these paranoid ravings was the sense I had that, while I was clearly not made of the right stuff for murder, the jury – as in the jury inside my head – was very much out on T-L.

I didn't tell Becky I was sorry about her father. It would have seemed like too little too late. At least that's what I told myself, as if to say nothing was nobler or more ennobling than the alternative. In fact, my reticence was bound up with the idea I had that there was something about Jacobson's death that was *all my doing*. I knew I would have to talk to Becky about it eventually. By not dragging the whole thing up now I was doing her a service, wasn't I? And she didn't press me on what kind of trouble I was in. She was pleased to see me, and that made me glad in the way a man who has stumbled across a desert is glad to hear voices singing finally outside his own head. When she handed me my painting I felt something that might easily be called love. It was unclear who or what my emotion was targeting *precisely*, but I didn't care about that. I dived right in. Then I surfaced and shook the glittering water from my ears.

'Why don't you keep it?' I said, flipping the painting so that it faced Becky. 'I mean why don't you keep it for me?'

'OK,' she said, 'if that's what you want. Back it goes under the bed until further notice.'

It was settled. Now the picture would be a token of something enduring between us. If only everything in the minefield of human affairs was as safe and as sound as that, I was thinking. No doubt Becky too had a hankering for solid ground. Then T-L was with us in the room (a crimson room lined with stuffed birds in glass cases), and I began to think about something else. It had to do with what T-L had said back there under Jacobson's tree. *I've been doing my best to comfort her* – that was it. Oh, my. He had done his best to comfort Véronique, too, hadn't he, in his time?

'Will you stay and have something to eat with us later?' Becky asked me, her unexpected warmth catching me off guard. 'There's at least one thing we've been wanting to discuss with you.'

'We?' I said, my pinball thoughts ricocheting madly from one possibility to another.

'We're launching a literary review,' Becky said. 'We'd like you and Percy to be part of it.'

'You and T-L are launching a magazine?' I said with an acute sense suddenly I was living my life backwards.

'This time it's going to be different,' T-L interjected, taking a humorous swipe at recent publishing history. 'Of course, we hope you'll contribute pictures, Billy. What about your shots of Paris?'

I made no further comment on their review. I gave no insight into my disaffected status with regard to photography. 'Sorry I can't join you for something to eat,' I said instead, thrusting my horses at Becky awkwardly. 'You haven't seen anything, or anyone, unusual in these parts, have you?' It was a dumb question, but I had to ask it. It was on my list, like all the others. 'No, I suppose not.'

'There's something else, Billy,' Becky said in a newly solicitous way that struck me as a verdict on my hangdog bearing. *How much did she know?* 'I hope this won't come as too much of a shock,' she went on, 'but Dad left you some money in his will. I had planned to tell you as soon as I could. I would have told you over supper –'

'Are you sure?' I asked numbly after a short delay. I didn't set out to be impertinent or rude. Naturally, I didn't. In fact, a reflex instinct – the urge to modesty or diffidence – guided my intention. Very simply, I had never thought of Jacobson as having any money of his own, far less any to give me. 'There must be some mistake.'

'Nope –' Becky said, smiling sweetly and shrugging. 'There's no mistake. When are you free to see the bank manager with me?'

Outside it was a perfect English summer's day. Cirrus clouds loafed in an ice blue sky. Soon the mercury would fall far enough for linen jackets or pink cardigans. At Chalk Farm station I was sick on the tiled floor – if you hate yourself enough you've probably got it coming to you. In the lift going down I began to think about Jock and the lad with acne and the penthouse suite all over again. The more I thought about it the more certain I was – the Scottish porter had deliberately left those straps off as an act of kindness. Having convinced myself about the motivational framework for the episode I felt better about it. Now only its true meaning eluded me. As for Jacobson's will – it might have been funny in a comedy skit in hell. The whole thing was a bad joke. The more I tried to punish myself over Jacobson the more he contrived to absolve me. On the train someone asked if I knew God, then started yapping as if we were old mates. That's what happens in this city. Drop your guard for a second and all the crazies are lining up to be your best friend. Had I imagined for one moment it might rescue my cause I would have signed up there and then for any old cult in the deserts of America or the wilds of Cornwall. Events, forces – they were closing in. The truth – it had my number. Cornwall – it would have been far too small to get safely lost in anyway. The limit of the knowable world, Becky had called it. Still, it was way too close for my taste. Pulses of unrest went out from me to all points of the compass on that fine day. Soon there would be nowhere to run to and nowhere to hide.

Chapter Twenty-Two
The Guilty Typewriter

WHEN THE SECOND LETTER ARRIVED I WAS ALMOST ready for it, which is not to suggest I had made a psychological accommodation with what was taking place. What I mean is I was better prepared, much of my initial shock having been replaced by anger. While the letter lay downstairs on the doormat, transfixed by a notional shaft of sunlight and awaiting discovery alongside various utility bills and circulars, I washed the last of Percy's shaving cream from my face and hurried to complete my ablutions. This was on a Friday – we were getting ready to go to work as usual. Percy, because that was the type of man he was, had given me first use of the bathroom in the knowledge that my wages would be docked if I ran late.

'There's another missive for you,' he announced, squinting at the envelope with feigned suspicion before tossing it at the sofa and shrugging off his dressing gown in one timesaving motion.

'Another?' I countered with mock surprise, eyeing the typed envelope from distance with a studied indifference. My key weapon was banter. Only banter with Percy could disguise how I really felt. 'I don't recall taking up with any pen friends over there in France.'

'To receive one unsolicited French letter is unfortunate – two looks like carelessness. Some students of statistics might be tempted to conclude there was a postal pattern developing here.'

'It looks like I may after all have to start a fan club. Can I help it if I'm more popular on the other side of the Channel?'

'France must be ruled out, I'm afraid. The second stamp, like the first, bears the head of our gracious Queen.'

'There's a feeble joke in there somewhere involving you and – well, *you*, Percy.'

'Fly now, sweet bird of youth. Age must to the pitiless glass –'

'Shall we meet again later today, Biggles? I take it you have the drop-off coordinates?'

'I know where Becky lives, yes. She's in touch with the office –'

That was it. That was the explanation for the letters. No, not an explanation for the letters as such, but an explanation at least for how they had reached me. *She's in touch with the office.* Yes, why not? If Percy knew where Becky lived why wouldn't Becky know where Percy lived? And, by extension, where I lived? All the way to work I carried the second letter in a sensitive spot next to my heart. I didn't want to open it. At the same time I was unwilling to give it undue weight in the overall scheme of things. It would have been a mistake to lend it too much credence.

By mid-morning I was approaching the furthest reaches of my round, my trolley light, my coat heavy with the betting monies, most of these in loose change, of my colleagues. In the draughty subway linking Haematology to Radiology it struck me in the shape of an unlikely boost to the ego – these modest betting stakes grew larger from day to day. There was no question about this. The proof was there for all to see in the heft and hue of the coinage I transported. Although the ratio of silver to copper in my coat pockets burgeoned from shift to shift, the returns on any associated investments failed to climb in a proportionate way. It meant sadness for the boys. But I took it as a sign of their growing faith in me as a courier that they continued to lay their cash, more and more of it, down. Thus they made of me a kind of mascot or pet. There was something different about me in their eyes, but they hadn't worked out what it was. All that would change soon enough. It was inevitable they would put two and two together on the basis of something I said or did. It was only a matter of time before something – the too fastidious action campaigning hard on behalf of sensibility – betrayed me. Then the fun would begin. It was what I wanted. To fight the same fight in a thousand ways every minute of my life – what else was there for me except the pull of the tides and the motion of the planets? It had to start somewhere. Why not here, with these excellent fellows, today, as soon as possible? Meanwhile they invited me, during a tea break confab conducted in a series of whispers, to take up a position on the inside of their longstanding hospital goods smuggling ring.

'The previous stationery porter, Steve – he was in on the act too,' Jock explained.

'It has to be you what carries the items in question from here to there,' Acker elaborated.

'No surgical instruments, no pharmaceuticals –' Bertie added like a referee confirming the rules.

'A little at a time,' Tom said. 'Slowly, slowly, catchy monkey – that's us, son.'

By not signing up right away for their entrepreneurial scheme I did a bad thing in the eyes of my colleagues. There was no point in explaining I had little need for rubber gloves and sticky tape on an industrial scale. It wasn't about the goods. It was about them. I could hardly tell them I wasn't one of them – not if I valued my life or my health, which I still more or less did, despite all the nonsense going down. Instead of telling Tom, Bertie, Acker and Jock what I really thought of their offer I locked myself in the toilet and opened the second letter speedily, without hesitating. It was no different to the first. From a sheet of plain white paper the seven words jumped out at me once again in starkly typewritten capital letters. I KNOW WHAT YOU DID IN PARIS. I had expected something more of the second letter – a multiplying of the menace factor, or a shift in tone from copper standard towards silver. Nevertheless, the words had the effect of sucking the air from my body. Again, it wasn't so much the content of the letter as its provenance that got me, and in asking who could have sent it I was really asking who knew where I lived, all of which led me straight back to Becky (for this I relied on Percy's morning intimation). Only Becky knew, surely – Becky and, by association, T-L. Yes, T-L again. No one else could be expected to know or care where I hung my hat, could they? As for Becky – I couldn't, in all conscience, point the finger of suspicion at her. Or could I? Until recently I had had the luxury of viewing Rebecca as a neutral observer of whatever front I presented to the world. Had T-L turned her? Had she crossed the line of loyalty? Someone was banging on the toilet door now. Was there a note of menace in that act? Intuitively I tried to match a face to the character of the assault on the woodwork, picturing in turn Jock, Acker, Tom and Bertie.

'Come out, come out, wherever you are,' Jock called. 'Don't worry – I just want a wee peck on the cheek.'

At five to three I was hunkered down outside the Midland Bank in Camden High Street, adjusting my borrowed tie in the wing mirror of a parked Jensen and waiting for Becky to show as arranged. She was late, which struck me as out of character, and when she finally turned up at six or seven minutes past the appointed hour she was accompanied by T-L, kitted out like a salesman or an undertaker in a black suit and tie, which I hadn't expected. Also out of character was Becky's manner. She was flustered, or preoccupied, with a high colour in her cheeks. Ordinarily she was calmness itself.

'T-L drove,' she said just inside the bank's doors, as if to head off a range of early enquiries. 'We had an accident in Dad's van.'

'It was no accident,' T-L said. 'Some maniac tried to run us off the road and into a lamp post in Kentish Town.'

'But that's terrible,' I said, turning from one to the other in the hushed banking hall as a stampede of questions got going inside my head. Why wasn't Becky at the wheel? She was such a safe driver. Was T-L insured to drive Jacobson's van? Why was he even here? Or did they operate as a team now? These hysterical considerations had an important role to play – they shut out, temporarily at least, the fact of the accident, or incident, itself. As an orchestra of alarm bells struck up inside me I did my best to dispense comfort. 'Are you OK?' I asked, drawing on emergency reserves of composure.

'We're fine now,' Becky said, breathing in hard and eyeing up the banking hall as if she couldn't decide whether its masculine air, all marble and dark wood and trapped cigar smoke, was reassuring or disquieting. 'Let's just get on with it, shall we?'

Sudden sunlight slanting in steeply from two tall windows had a distorting and disorienting effect. We were bent on identifying the most likely candidate for manager, but in the event he found us.

'Ah, Miss Jacobson and friends,' said a bald man, surprisingly young, with a red moustache who arrived out of nowhere behind us, as if he had been shot through a trapdoor, and who beamed at us as though he had always liked being kept waiting. 'This way, please –'

Moments later we were in a chamber with frosted glass walls rising on three sides towards a decorative ceiling from which a fan descended on its long stalk, rotating slowly but purposefully. From beyond the book-lined wall behind an imposing desk the traffic of

Camden Town failed to penetrate an institutional quiet. There was a flurry of easy muscularity as Mr Harkness, our genial and capable host, swung an extra chair into position on the roomier side of the desk, and during this time I instinctively warmed to his style. Then we sat down together, like church goers or first offenders, opposite the breezy banker, with Becky, very poised now, her chin raised up stiffly, at the centre of our respectful row. After a routine statement, or restatement, of names, roles and relationships we were off and running. Harkness, it turned out, was assistant branch manager in temporary charge today, his senior colleague having been detained unexpectedly in the City by an emergency dental procedure.

'First let me offer my condolences on behalf of the bank, Miss Jacobson. I know this is a difficult time for you, and we want to do everything we can to make things easier.'

'Thank you,' Becky said, smoothing the hem of her skirt.

'In respect of your father's will −' Harkness went on, opening the loose-leaf binder on the desk at a marked page. 'Some aspects of what he leaves are uncertain as of today.'

'You mean the insurances,' Becky said.

'Exactly so,' Harkness said. 'Some doubt remains at this time as to the exact status for insurance purposes of your father's death.' He broke off there as if to uncouple one idea from another, to swap this thinking cap for that one. 'I understand he left no note.'

'No, he didn't.'

'I'm awfully sorry.'

'You're very kind.'

'In terms of what your father leaves to Mr Morton −' Harkness said, consulting his papers with arching eyebrows before looking up at me with his friendliest, most fiduciary smile. 'Could this be the moment to upgrade that Post Office savings account, I wonder?'

I didn't hear the next few conversational exchanges inside the Midland Bank. After the assistant manager briefed me on my good fortune I gawped for a while at an area just below his eyes, taking in his bushy moustache and, in a more peripheral way, a polka dot bow tie, then switched my focus to the backlog of urgent enquiries building up inside my head. I was thinking about Jacobson's van. The incident barely touched on by Becky and T-L was my primary concern as the fan turned above and the voices swirled around me. There was something I needed to know. One thing mattered more than all the money in the world at that moment. Becky and T-L – did they see who tried to run them off the road in Kentish Town? Was it three women? Was it five women bearing earthenware pots on their heads? Was it one man, a lone gun? Was it, by any chance, two men of (let us imagine for the sake of racial completeness) Arab extraction? Now Harkness was shutting down his big black binder. What had I missed? What kind of message did my silence give out about my character or my class? In the impressive office in Camden Town the fan still turned, but we were entering a new phase.

'Ah, Exeter –' Harkness was saying with a lively enthusiasm. 'To read what, may I ask?'

'Oh, English,' Becky said negligently. 'I'm really not good for much else, I'm afraid.'

'Lovely part of the country,' T-L chipped in using his easiest charm and lightest touch (I had all but forgotten in the space of a few short months how easy and light these could be).

'Exceptionally lovely,' Harkness confirmed, getting up behind the big desk. 'The whole of Devon is tough to beat in the summer months, is it not? Cornwall's special, too, of course –'

'Cornwall *compels*,' Becky said, rising now beside T-L and me. 'You do sometimes think you've reached the edge of the world.'

'The last place on earth,' Harkness said, beaming again as he pumped our hands. 'Go too far too fast and you might drop off the end. But not before you launch that magazine, I hope. Vital to sink your energy into something creatively absorbing at a time like this.'

Outside the bank I kissed Becky once on each cheek and T-L shook my hand like a public schoolboy before we made straight, at my insistence, for the street in which the van was parked. It looked OK from the front – I saw no broken headlights, and no crumpled bumper flecked with paint from the street lamps of Kentish Town. The damage was to one side of the vehicle – along the entire length of the driver's side ran an ugly welt about six inches wide and deep enough in places to puncture the metal. There was something else that disturbed me. As it dangled grotesquely from a ruptured stump the broken wing mirror took me back to riotous Paris, to Lafcadio's scooter, to everything I didn't want to recall. The front tyre on the passenger side of the van was flat.

'Doesn't look too bad,' T-L said with his Englishman's gift for understatement and emotional camouflage. As an actor, he seemed to say, I do any part.

'What exactly happened?' I said.

'They drew level,' Becky said, 'then rammed us from the side.'

'Twice,' T-L said. 'I know maths was never my strong point.'

'They?' I said casually, running my finger along the damaged paintwork. 'How many of them were there?'

'Pick a number between one and three,' T-L said.

'Let me do the sums for you,' Becky said. 'Two –'

'Two men?' I said.

'What do you think?' Becky said.

'Are we going to report them?' T-L said.

'Did you get their registration number?' I asked him.

'No. I was trying to avoid mowing down assorted pedestrians, many of them taxpayers going about their lawful business.'

'I'm not sure about reporting it anyway,' Becky said. 'I'm not convinced I trust the police to do their job any more.'

'Did either of you get a look at the two men?' I said, bringing matters to a head after a suitable pause in honour of Jacobson.

'Not really,' Becky said. 'One of them had a scarf of some sort wrapped around his face.'

That was it. That was the clincher – a throwaway observation that had the effect of seizing my heart and twisting it clockwise and then anticlockwise as far as the organ's bindings would allow.

'Better fix that front wheel and get out of here,' I said.

'Have you changed a tyre before, Billy?' T-L asked.

'There's always a first time, T-L,' I said.

'Not this time,' T-L said. 'I'm afraid we don't appear to have a spare tyre as such. Or am I missing something obvious, Becky?'

'Sod the tyre,' Becky said, collapsing tearfully into a chair on the pavement outside a Portuguese coffee shop. 'Would someone kindly explain why two complete strangers tried to kill me today?'

'It's a mystery.' T-L said. 'One can only put it down to a case of dangerously mistaken identity.'

We polished off Percy's sherry shortly before Becky served up the macaroni. This was later the same day after a frustrating afternoon and early evening spent getting Jacobson's van back on the road. I was trying gamely to dwell on the issues at hand, but it was hard to concentrate one hundred per cent on a publishing adventure when the world was busy falling apart. We had gathered at the big house in Chalk Farm to discuss the new magazine. All the while I carried the second letter, with its seven ugly words, close to my skin. Bit by bit I made a plan to expose the letter's origins. It was my typewriter plot. I would at least achieve this much tonight, so help me God.

'Shall we get down to post-prandial business?' Percy said, thus inaugurating the first editorial meeting of a literary review yet to be devised or designed, let alone financed or launched. 'Do we need,' he went on, 'a mission statement – as in some kind of declaration of aesthetic objectives or governing principles around which we rally?'

'Let good writing be our sole *raison d'être*,' T-L put in quickly.

'Good writing or new writing?' Percy asked.

'The new,' Becky insisted quietly.

'Any writing,' T-L came back emphatically. 'Any writing on any subject, I mean. It could be fiction that asks how we might live. It could be reportage – the events in Paris, say, or the Derry scene. Or it might be criticism. Yes, it might be film criticism –'

'No criticism,' Becky said.

'None at all?' Percy asked.

'I don't think so,' Becky said. 'Didn't we say this review would be devoted to imaginative writing – to prose fiction, and to poetry, of course, which we agreed was the higher form?'

'Why not criticism?' T-L said. 'Didn't we also say we needed higher standards with which to challenge the market? If a book sells today it's hailed as a work of genius. The word is applied left, right and centre to novels and movies of widely differing quality. What we need as much as anything is a set of objective criteria for judging books and films. That's why we champion criticism.'

No one spoke. Percy nodded thoughtfully before scribbling a note in the end papers of his paperback copy of *The Glass Bead Game* in translation. 'What does Billy think, I wonder?' he asked loyally.

'No photography,' I said.

'No photography?' T-L and Becky repeated in unison.

'Just put a line drawing on the cover,' I said, 'and save us all a lot of production grief.'

'But how else are you going to contribute?' T-L asked.

'What about the pictures you took in Paris?' Becky said.

'Billy can write for us,' Percy said. 'Billy's a writer now.'

'Are you kidding?' T-L said. 'You can't be serious, old boy.'

'I've rarely been more serious in my life.'

'All right, all right −' Becky said. 'We owe it to ourselves to be clear about who's in charge here. I mean editorially speaking.'

'A ship needs a helm,' Percy noted democratically.

'Had you imagined yourself in that role?' T-L asked him.

'As a matter of fact I had always assumed Rebecca was our de facto editor-in-chief.'

'You don't think editing a literary review would be ruinous to the imaginative life?' T-L said. 'I don't think Becky would get much writing done, would she? She would simply make a lot of enemies.'

'You don't think it's necessary to make enemies,' Percy said, 'as a condition of good editing?'

'I'll be going up to Exeter soon enough,' Becky said. 'Isn't that the point of this conversation?'

'Not quite,' T-L said. 'The point of the conversation is this − how are we going to get Graham Greene for the first number of our as yet untitled review?'

'Leave that one to me,' Percy said. 'I'm sure I can pull a few strings at the office. He *is* one of our authors, isn't he? Better hurry, though − he's probably packing his bags for Cuba or the Congo.'

Dissolve to later the same evening in the big house. It had been a long day already, and Percy had gone home. For me, intent still on examining Becky's typewriter in order to establish the source of my unwanted letters, the business of the day was not yet done. Becky's Remington, I knew, awaited my attention on a desk in an upstairs room at the front of the house. After I had dried and put away the dishes I went up there to locate the typewriter. On the way I passed a bedroom whose door was ajar. The only light in the room came from a candle on the floor, so that the shadows of T-L and Becky sitting cross-legged at a low table danced across the ceiling as they moved. It was obvious after a few moments they were summoning up the voices or spirits of the dead by tracing the passage of a glass, to which they attached one finger each in turn, from letter to letter or from number to number as described on the surface of the table. All this came as a shock to me. It was fascinating and horrifying at the same time. To see the individuals I knew or loved best roll their heads like that, to hear them moan, was disconcerting. As to whom they were trying to contact, it wasn't for me to speculate, but I did so anyway. Becky was trying to contact her father, of course, to find out what really befell him on Hampstead Heath. T-L was trying to reach Lafcadio in a Paris cemetery. Who else could be on his mind at this time? Against the backdrop of these supernatural enquiries I made an important breakthrough. It came to me with new clarity – there was no link, despite my recent efforts to forge one, between Jacobson's death and Lafcadio's brothers. (In assessing any ongoing threat to life and limb I had ruled out the influence of Raymond.) Which was more likely – that a man should commit suicide without leaving a note, or that two men should travel all the way from Paris on a mission to hang him, in the absence of any clear motivational connection, from a copper beech tree above a shallow pond? Which was *less unlikely*? In upholding a verdict of suicide I made a valuable breakthrough in the case. Not that I was off the hook. There was still the question of Jacobson's van, the accident, and the two men with or without scarves. *One can only put it down to a case of dangerously mistaken identity*, T-L had said. Oh, T-L.

I inserted a sheet of paper into the carriage of the typewriter, pressed the shift key, and began to type those seven little words. It was as I had expected. There could be no doubt. What clinched it for me was the damaged impression of the letter 'P'. It was beyond question that this was the guilty typewriter. That still didn't tell me who had typed the letters and sent them. I was about to find out.

'Running a little something up for our first edition?' T-L asked from the doorway.

'Why did you send me those letters, T-L? Did you think that was clever or funny?'

'I really don't know why I sent them, Billy. That's the honest answer. Believe me – I can't offer you an explanation because there isn't one. I didn't choose to do it. It chose me. It was part of a role I was assigned. For are we not pawns in their game?'

'I don't think so, T-L. Not as far as I'm concerned.' There we were. And T-L had reached a sort of tipping point in his delusion. His disassociation from himself was complete. I had been ready to confront him with the truth of the danger he faced from Lafcadio's brothers intent on revenge. He could hardly be said to be in denial about this because he wasn't actually aware of the brothers at that time. What else? I had been ready to ask the questions that could never be asked. Did you return to Montparnasse cemetery with the petrol can that night, and did you set the body alight? I didn't ask those questions. I asked T-L two others. 'Don't you think you need help?' I said. 'I mean – don't you think you should see a doctor?'

'Ha, ha, ha. Very droll, I'm sure. Don't worry, Billy – you'll be rid of me soon. I'll be going on a long journey.'

'Oh? Where to?'

'Who knows? To the last place on earth, I expect.'

'Sounds exclusive,' I said, 'or expensive.'

'We'll always have Paris, though, won't we?' T-L said.

Then Becky was alongside him. Was there something between them? Their bodies were practically touching. Becky too asked me if I was writing something for the magazine. She looked exactly the same as she had looked at supper, or soon after, so that it was hard to know if she had found what she had been seeking since then in a candlelit bedroom animated by unlikely shadows and groans.

Later that night on Percy's sofa I had my strongest feelings to date of impending disaster. I wasn't sure how it would happen, and I didn't know when it would come. I slept soundly enough until just before dawn when a vivid dream, more compelling somehow than your average break-of-day fare, had me wide eyed and gasping for air. I didn't as a rule attach too much weight to dreams in terms of trying to discover their relationship with the future. If pushed I saw them as flashy hand mirrors distorting the past. But in my dream of the jilted bride, a pretty woman wearing a blood-soaked wedding dress and wandering alone on a desert highway, I found enough to make me reconsider the value of the subconscious encounter as a harbinger of what might be. It wasn't the gore – the stray bride told me the blood was the blood of her dead baby. She herself was on fire. That was the key thing for me. She was on well on fire, but she didn't burn. As is the way in dreams, portentous things happened between us before the blazing bride turned, without warning, into Becky. I didn't try to interpret the dream by interrogating its design particulars or its narrative arc. It was a general impression I held to as the curtains billowed ominously above me. Slumping back down with a whimper on Percy's sofa I thought I saw how it would end – with madness and with fire. That morning I was late for my shift.

There *was* a note. There was a short note addressed to Rebecca. At first I aimed to leave this somewhere prominent in the house. The coast was never clear for me to do so on the night in question. Next I debated leaving the note inside the van at the edge of Hampstead Heath. This option I dismissed as too impersonal, too mechanistic. By now I was getting desperate – there is no other way to say it. My principal focus was necessarily elsewhere at this hour. It was on the rope, largely. For a moment I considered concealing the note about my person, in a hip pocket, but here too I baulked, this time in the interests of taste. There is really no good way to leave a note if not in an envelope labelled with a name and propped up on the nearest mantlepiece. History has come down firmly on the side of this way of working. Just before the end I tore the note (handwritten, seven lines, signed with love) into a number of pieces and scattered these on the surface of the ornamental lake directly below my tree. The fragments floated there, face up or face down, for a time, but when I looked back from the slope they had gone. You will make this all right, Billy. I know it. If it takes a hundred years you will make it all right with Rebecca. I ask this as your friend. As for what was in the note – it no longer matters, does it? Picture it if you must – a few platitudes plus a little poetry of the conventional variety designed to explain or excuse the act. In the event it seems the note itself might as well not have existed from the outset, despite my clumsy efforts to do the right thing by it. Absurd, I know. This type of betrayal, a betrayal of *all reasonable faith*, I could no longer accept in life.

CHAPTER TWENTY-THREE

The Long Journey

BY MONDAY MORNING A MORE PRESSING FATALISM coloured my outlook. The ugly tale was entering a dangerous new phase. What assailed me from the moment I woke up had actually been needling me all night – I just hadn't allowed it to rise to the ragged surface of my awareness. It was Percy. He wasn't in the flat. He hadn't come home. There was no need to check the bedroom or the bed. I knew right away something was wrong. Then the telephone rang and for a second or two I felt like I was viewing a *noirish* flick. This must be the matinee screening, very black and white. Then it came to me – I wasn't watching the movie. I was in it. I was starring in it. Still the telephone rang, impossibly loud in the prelude to a London day.

'Hello?' I said, the receiver held at an involuntary remove from my ear.

'Billy? It's Percy.'

There was something odd about the voice. At first I thought it must be someone trying to impersonate Percy – no, to disguise his own voice. Someone was calling me with a handkerchief or a scarf stuffed into his mouth. Why would anyone want to pull a stunt like that before breakfast on a Monday morning? Then I twigged it – it was Percy calling with a mouthful of broken teeth or some such.

'Where are you?' I asked him.

'Can't you tell? I thought you might recognise the background soundtrack.'

'Nope. Give me a clue.'

'I'm in hospital, Billy – *your* hospital. How funny is that? The telephone is sitting on a trolley with little wheels beside my bed.'

'That's hilarious, Percy. What happened to you?'

'Can't really speak, old bean. Not to worry. Just remember – flowers, please, not fruit.'

After I showered, shaved and scrubbed my teeth, discharging all three functions with the maximum attention to detail I reserved for the most challenging of days, I grabbed a slice of toast and ran downstairs to confront the world. On the doormat was an envelope addressed to me in the typewritten style with which I was by now only too familiar. The third letter, its stark and sinister presence in Percy's hall, struck me with the force of a karate chop. It made no sense, given that T-L had already confessed to the epistolary crimes of the hour. What could it mean? It was too much to think about at that time, so I simply snatched up the envelope and bolted.

There was a flower stall at the hospital, but I resisted the urge to buy Percy's flowers until my tea break. Establishing the sequence of events correctly is important. If you're looking for the connection between one thing and another it pays to set your facts down in the right order. I didn't know which flowers to get for Percy. The rules governing flowers were unknown to me in my days as a stationery porter. A nice girl in the shop chose the flowers for me – a fragrant display of something purple with here and there a splash of yellow. In the lift going up to the wards I ran into Jock. It was just the two of us, plus the flowers, in the lift. The scent of the blooms charged the stale air with an idea of beauty that was overwhelmingly sad. It must have been too much for Jock. The sudden beauty packed into such a small space for such a short time was too much for him. He seized my throat with one hand and pinned me to the wall of the lift while with the other hand he gripped my crotch and squeezed as hard as he could for as long as he could before the doors opened in the way they always did, as if everything was for the best in the best of all possible worlds. I didn't know what Jock meant. It was impossible to know if his action was a form of abuse or something else – a type of confession, or affirmation, delivered in a language he couldn't follow. He couldn't understand the lingo, so he just spoke louder. That's why he had left the kid's straps undone. He wanted to go free. Now Percy's flowers were broken, but it didn't count in the big scheme of things. Percy would have understood everything. When I caught up with him five minutes later he was repairing his damaged copy of *Under the Volcano* with sticky tape, wearing hospital issue pyjamas that were several sizes too small for him, below a tall window, open to the mild air, of frosted glass.

'My dear old thing,' he mumbled through a mask of bandages. 'Did you pick those flowers with boxing gloves on?'

'What happened?' I asked for the second time that morning.

'Two handsome thugs took a dislike to me in the woods behind Jack Straw's Castle.'

'You look terrible, Percy.'

'You should have seen the other chaps.'

'What did you do to them?'

'Nothing. I didn't get a chance, did I?'

'What did you say to them?'

'Ah. I think I probably quoted Wilde at them. I usually do.'

'Oh, Percy,' I said, taking his hand and squeezing it. It was my fault. It was my fault that Percy had roamed the woods in search of warmth. My coldness did it. 'What are we to do with you?'

'Do with me what you will. I thought you'd never ask –'

'Seriously – is there something I can do to make it better?'

'There certainly is. Fetch me my brief case without delay.'

'Oh, no – what happened to your brief case?'

'It too fell foul of events last night.'

'My God, Percy – all your books are ruined.'

'Well thumbed, I prefer to think. Is my little tape recorder still there? My dicta-thingy should be in there.'

'Hang on a minute. Yes, it's here.'

'Then your destiny is revealed, sir. It falls to you to interview a certain Graham Greene this day in place of our Rebecca, she being otherwise detained, according to a message she left at the office. I'd do the job myself if I looked less like an Egyptian mummy.'

'Otherwise detained?' I said, my jeopardy antennae twitching wantonly all over again.

'She said something had cropped up,' Percy said. 'She offered a thousand apologies. Notice how everything is connected? Rebecca can't make it, and I'm in no fit state. T-L, did you say? I'm not sure we really want to go there, do we? As for you, Billy Morton – in my famished commissioning editor's heart I know you to be a thousand per cent right for the job.' He paused briefly before concluding in a different tone, his voice faltering just a fraction. 'By which I mean you'll always be the right one for the job as far as I'm concerned.'

I met Graham Greene as per instructions in the smoking room of the Byzantium at the Park Lane end of Piccadilly. It was cool and dark in there – the very model of a gentlemen's club in a corner of Mayfair. First I had to borrow the house tie. Then I rested my tape recorder on the reception desk and announced my business. They gestured silently towards the pillars and two plants on pedestals that delimited the quietude, thickly carpeted and gloomier than ever, of the inner sanctum beyond. The best-selling author of a quantity of books I hadn't sampled raised himself up from a winged armchair, irresponsibly craggy of face in the low lamplight, before dropping his cigarette into the ashtray beside him, folding up his *Times*, and extending his big hand loosely.

'Haven't I seen that tie somewhere before? And you are?'

'Billy Morton.' After we sat down opposite each other I placed the tape machine deliberately between us on a coffee table. 'I think you might have been expecting someone else.'

'No, I don't believe so. Shall I call you Billy? Better call me Mr Greene, I think.'

His blue short-sleeved shirt he wore outside his baggy pants. His look was one of lugubrious vitality. His eyes ran clear, his brow creasing deeply above them as if to shield their gaze from imminent disappointment at something or someone. If he was unhappy about the youth or likely inexperience of his interviewer he didn't show it more pointedly than that. Evidently he had been briefed to expect me rather than Becky or Percy or anyone else. He was attentively at ease. He would have given the same impression anywhere. He had met in one hundred hotel lobbies and airport departure lounges, I understood from Percy's notes, many of them lined with sandbags, their corrugated iron roofs the gathering place of vultures.

'Thank you for seeing us, Mr Greene.'

'Us? It's just you, Billy. Whisky?' The novelist raised his arm and swung his upper body towards a service hatch glowing dimly in the depths. 'I don't belong here, but they tolerate me,' he explained. 'You know – I hardly think I'm the one to consult about libel.'

'Libel?' I said, leaning forward to switch on the tape recorder.

'You wanted to ask me about Shirley Temple.'

'I did?' I said, checking the red light was showing.

The Hollywood studio said my review of their movie accused them of procuring Miss Temple for immoral purposes. We had to close down a perfectly good magazine –'

'I see.' A man appeared and took the order for two whiskies. I took a deep breath and dived in. Although I wasn't sure how to set about interviewing the famous writer I understood I had to steer our little chat. As a man of the world he would get that. What I wanted to do was ask Mr Greene to read my screenplay before giving me his honest opinion. Had I been writing the script of our encounter, events would have unfolded thus. 'I didn't come here to talk about Shirley Temple,' I revealed, calling up in my head the shopping list of questions suggested by Percy from a hospital bed.

'Good. Then fire away.'

'Would you agree there's a crisis in criticism today?'

'Are you talking about movies or books now? Well – it doesn't much matter either way, because there has always been a crisis in criticism. There always will be. And that is because the critic must entertain. His review is more important than what he reviews. The critic must eat, must he not? Week after week he finds nothing to talk up. He has seen, or read, it all before. It offers him no clue as to how to live his life. His head drops. His heart sinks. He loses his readers, but not before he loses his job.'

'As a famous Catholic –' I said, and then broke off. Now the large whiskies were on the table, together with the chit to be signed. 'Do you identify with a Catholic sense of guilt in Hitchcock?'

'Hitchcock? I don't think so. Catholic guilt? No, I don't think so. Do you know The Wrong Man? Henry Fonda plays an innocent man made to feel guilty. So Hitchcock has him pray to the Virgin Mary while the close-up of his face dissolves into the face of the real culprit. There's your guilt – your misplaced guilt. There it is in the pure language of cinema. Do you know Vertigo, Billy?'

As a matter of fact I didn't know Vertigo. On the other hand I was beginning to experience *a sense of* vertigo. This had nothing to do with the gulp of whisky I had just taken in an attempt to keep up with my rangy companion. It was about the newspaper on the table between us. The paper was on the table. On top of the newspaper sat Percy's dictaphone, its twin spools rotating as faithfully as you like. There was a picture peeking out from under the tape recorder – a newsprint image of *me* taken somewhere, I felt certain, in Paris. I found it hard to take my eyes off the picture – rude, I know. My interlocutor was speaking of *The Aspern Papers* now. He said Henry James was probably the first screenwriter in our language. All of a sudden he reached forward and eased the newspaper from beneath the tape recorder and spread the pages on top of the drinks. At this time I was struggling to work out who could have taken the picture of me. It was a tightly cropped shot. Its background was uncertain. Even so, my hunch about Paris was strong. Someone had snapped me using the Nikon in the city of love. One by one I identified the chief suspects, lurching violently from Lafcadio and Nana to Herr Zwimmer and Madame Georges. It was hopeless – I couldn't recall who had tripped the shutter. Then I saw it all with thrilling clarity. I was standing in the Jardin Marco-Polo with the fountain behind me as seen by Véronique at the last. How could that be? The Nikon – I could have sworn it was empty. Could I have been mistaken? It was a type of miracle. I didn't know how else to view it. In front of me was an entire double page spread given over to my photographs of Paris. For some strange reason that shamed me I started to blub – not much, of course – in the smoking lounge of the Byzantium in front of Mr Greene. Blame it on a sudden and ridiculous access of pride that knocked me off balance and made me think I might have got something right for a change. I blamed it on Miss Laurie. The one-armed picture editor had syndicated my best shots of the Paris unrest, together with my name and a miraculous portrait of me, for the whole world to see and judge.

'What does it mean?' asked the celebrated novelist and critic who sat opposite, once I had composed myself. He didn't ask what was wrong. He was a step ahead of me, attributing effects to causes in line with his creative calling.

'I'm not sure,' I told him. 'I'll have to think about it.'

'Was there something else you wanted to ask me?' he said.

'I wanted to ask if you would read my screenplay,' I said.

'Ah,' he said, nodding with interested satisfaction. 'I thought there must be something. Would you rather be a fine photographer or a mediocre screenwriter, I wonder?'

'How can you tell I'd make a mediocre screenwriter?'

'I can't. But I can see you're already a fine photographer. So, drink up and don't be too hard on yourself, Billy Morton. You can probably leave that for the rest of us to take care of, can't you?'

In thanking Graham Greene for the hour he gave over to me I understood our encounter was preordained. It was, as Percy had said, a matter of personal destiny. When the famous novelist invited me in a Mayfair club to choose between one version of myself and another he was opening a door to the future. It goes without saying I was grateful to him for his attention and insight. The problem for me was the future itself. I wasn't sure I wanted to go there.

It had to have meaning – that was my preferred scenario. Where I chose to open the third letter had, if possible, to have relevance or resonance. It was getting dark as I made my way to the Serpentine, and soon Hyde Park itself would close up for the night. Already the boats were roped to their moorings and the shutters were down at the snack bars. It should have been the river. The river would have been ideal. No matter – the big-hearted lake in the bosom of the city would have to do instead. When I opened the third envelope I tried not to think about what it connoted or signified. The whisky was on me still – that was an excellent call, Mr Greene. Inside the envelope I found the usual one-sheet letter designed, as ever, to mythologise its sender. (Why *type* the message, T-L? Why not just scribble a note from now on?) This time the message was different. I quickly came to understand the import of THEY KNOW WHAT WE DID IN PARIS. Enclosed with the letter was a supporting artefact. It was a Polaroid image of Raymond. It was the Polaroid fragment, slightly charred now in a shocking way, which I had last seen on Lafcadio's corpse in Montparnasse cemetery in Paris. It told me I was right to be afraid – afraid of everything.

Before me was the lake, iconic in the twilight. Beyond the lake the lights of Knightsbridge offered no comfort. What did it mean? It meant the game was up. It was up for me. It was up for T-L – he saw that finally. How did it work? Lafcadio's brothers had salvaged a fragment of photograph from the cemetery. By posting it through Becky's front door they served notice they were closing in on T-L. That's how I viewed it. And what about me? The photograph was scorched, wasn't it? That could only mean one thing in my eyes. It meant T-L had returned to the cemetery with the petrol can after I had abandoned my friend's body to its fate. Which was worse – the horror of this apprehension or the fear of what might yet be? Then I saw my get-out. It was coming at me, glowing magically, from the water. T-L hadn't set Lafcadio's body alight that night after all. He had gone back to the cemetery with the petrol, yes, only to change his mind at the last minute, pausing to rescue the photograph I had planted. That's right – he had scorched the image himself just now in a bid to curse me forever. It was humanly possible, wasn't it? It was reasonable, surely, to explore each avenue, to turn each stone, in the search for salvation. At the edge of the water I saw it clearly then – what was happening around me. *I'll be going on a long journey*, T-L had said. *To the last place on earth*, he had said. Had he spoken figuratively? What if he had meant it literally? He meant Cornwall, didn't he, at the end of the line? Of course he did – the clues were everywhere to be found. They were in the utterances we had made and in the lines we had written and in the spaces between the lines. And Becky was going too. She was going along for the ride. There was no need to confirm this. I simply knew it to be true. Something had cropped up, she had said. Indeed it had. Why go there, Becky? Why do that? Look – all the light was away now. Only the ghastly items in my hands were visible. Was I damned, consigned forever to the dark? I still didn't know. I had to find out. Goodbye, Jock – I forgive you. So long, Acker, Bertie and Tom. May your gee-gees all triumph. In my head I was already writing my note to Percy. Dear Percy – please don't worry on my account. As I peered west towards the ends of the earth, London had never looked so lovely or felt so lonely. They were out there tonight – Becky and T-L. They were out there now, jaws set, eyes smarting, on the long journey. Now I too would go on that journey because I had to know everything.

Miss Laurie

It's a simple enough concept, is it not? If your pictures aren't good enough you aren't close enough. He was close enough. Using that 35mm fast wide-angle as his standard lens he had to get close if he wanted to fill the frame. He was brave in that way – fearless but not reckless, I would say. (I once forfeited an arm failing to strike such a balance in the photographic danger zone.) So, I salute you with my good arm, Billy Morton. A payment awaits you here, of course. For me it was natural to move right away to syndicate your Paris shots. In the face of someone better than you at what you do, your duty is clear. You will beggar yourself in order to burnish his or her star.

CHAPTER TWENTY-FOUR
The Last Place on Earth

I DIDN'T GO BACK TO THE HOSPITAL – NOT TO JACK it in, not to say goodbye, not to collect what was owing to me, not even to see Percy. Instead I went to Shepherd's Bush roundabout and joined a queue of hitchhikers journeying west on the motorway towards the last place on earth. In my mind I had the image of T-L and Becky driving hard and in silence along the ever-narrowing peninsula that led to a picturesque harbour besieged by gulls and a special kind of light. This was my take on Cornwall at the time – I kept it in front of me because I had little choice. I didn't know where I was going, except to that furthermost county, wide in the jaw, then tapering to a gullet that swallowed you at the last. If I didn't know where I was heading, I knew one thing – the clues or the answers I sought lay in the journey itself. This important conviction was bound up with the feeling I had that only by *acting* could I make the future right. It had all made perfect sense in the clever books I had read so avidly. To undo I must *do*. On this simple philosophy I staked my being.

Up ahead on the slip road the hitchhikers paraded in couples – here two girls together, there a girl with her big chest in front and a bigger boyfriend behind. It was a beauty contest I couldn't hope to win. There were too many damsels in my path, and such a long road to travel. All the time the same old questions were queuing up to be answered in my head. Take T-L, for instance. How long had he known he was in physical danger? No doubt he had considered the possibility that the tawdry events of Paris might some day catch up with him – but not like this, surely. Hadn't I already told him he needed help? Back then it was all about his subtle madness. It was obvious now – what I had meant was he needed bodily protection from the consequences of his actions. Although I saw bad outcomes everywhere I refused to speculate on what they entailed for me. It was true – I no longer really knew what I had done and whether I was culpable. Because it was pointless to dwell on these debilitating unknowns I switched my focus to another, to Cornwall, to the idea of Cornwall as experienced alongside Becky and T-L these past few days or weeks. Was there a clue in there to what I was looking for? For half the night I had cast my mind back and then forward again across all available Cornish references, taking in, for example, what Becky had said to Henrietta at her literary salon and to an assistant bank manager in Camden Town. It was no good – I failed to reveal any fresh truths. There was only the sense, laughably uncertain and improbable on a motorway verge at around midday, which told me all roads led to Cornwall. Never had I needed help so badly. What I lacked was a signal. It was almost time to knuckle down and pray – the opportunity was unarguably there, and it wasn't beneath me to do the needful. Suddenly a car (it had to be a Morris Oxford, or a Minor, or one of the popular shooting brakes with wood cladding) pulled up right alongside me. There was no debate about this in my mind – the car stopped *for me only*.

'Heading west?' the driver called out, reaching across to lower the window further.

'To the last place on earth,' I said on the basis that if I spoke these six words they must be true.

He was a vicar, a reverend, a prelate, a priest – I didn't know which. That he was a man of the cloth, or the dog collar, was the principal thing to note about him. Could be he thought his station gave him special rights in this world. That's what I would say about him if you asked. All I know is that some time after he invited me to tilt my seat back as far as it would go (from the outset I suspected a sexual motive it seemed only decent to discount) I heard him begin to recite the Lord's Prayer in joyful voice. When I opened my eyes he was masturbating vigorously beside me with a smile on his face and a finger on the wheel. He must have been thinking about it, or working up to it, for some time, because when he reached the part about leading us not into temptation he shot a load over the petrol gauge, the speedometer and the steering column. Then he finished his recitation in the same inspired vein. Although he never took his eyes off the road, or the horizon, I judged it prudent, in the interests of health and safety, not to interrupt his train of thought before the evangelical tide had ebbed. For me it was a false start.

'Stop the car,' I said, reaching behind for my knapsack.

'I can't stop here. Let me take you to the next junction.'

'Stop the car. Unless you want me to puke all over it –'

Once I had scrambled up the steep bank beside the motorway I found myself looking down on a flooded gravel pit. It was a scene of unexpected tranquility, and for a time I lost myself in that. Soon the calm was broken and normal business resumed. A Pan Am 707 was coming in to land, impressively loud and astonishingly close to where I stood. The undercarriage came down with an awful thud – I made this out clearly despite the general noise. As the Americans peered at me from the portholes I fell victim to a crazy impulse to welcome them all unconditionally, arms flailing. I swear I saw their anxious foreheads pressed up against the windows. I guess I wanted to be on that jet plane coming in to land, to have life rise up at me all over again, no questions asked. I wasn't actually *sick*. If I was to any extent discouraged by what I had just experienced in the car I was determined not to let it impede my progress. What I had to do was change tack very slightly. Who could blame me for tearing off in the wrong direction? I was trying too hard. Yes, that was it. My thinking thus far had been about securing the right lift, or the best ride, the one that counted. How else would the answers be offered up or revealed to me? Now I saw it. All I need do was submit to the rhythm, or the will, of the road itself. The road would sustain me. It would deliver me from myself. The road was brave and true. It was a river carrying me to the heart of everything that mattered. I had only to go with the flow in order to get to where I was going.

When the VW Microbus drew up I had a first opportunity to put my new, more laid back, approach into practice. The bus itself was painted in what might best be described as a hippie style, with flowers, rainbows and other motifs drawn from the natural world. That was OK with me. All four Germans inside wore headbands – blue, red, green, yellow – as if they were team captains or seasoned delegates making their way to a bandana convention, and this too was OK with me given my more free-wheeling disposition.

'Going west?' asked a blonde woman, our Miss Yellow, at the open window.

'Why not?' I said, as if I didn't ordinarily bother to delineate in advance my overall direction of travel.

'West is best,' she assured me, offering up the damp stump of a reefer. 'Jump in and let's write a groovy song about it –'

On the road to Stonehenge they asked me for my views on a range of topical issues, including the war in Vietnam, the events in Paris, the bomb, and what they labelled the Russian menace. The strange thing was how little I had to say on these subjects. In terms of both Paris and Vietnam I could reasonably claim to have rubbed shoulders with the ideas of the hour. I made no claims. It was as if there was a wall between where I stood and the deserts of opinion. Perhaps all the smoking, or the smoke, undid me. My priority now was to go with the flow, and this cast me inevitably in a listening, as opposed to a speaking, role. For half an hour or so, in the company of earnest strangers and with England's fields rolling reliably past, I enjoyed a delicious sense of freedom licensed by social consensus.

'We all have to make a stand,' insisted Mr Blue, our current driver, referring to the USSR's global ambitions and proxy wars.

'Not least here in Europe,' Miss Green suggested, putting the finishing touches to a joint.

'We should know,' commented Mr Red. 'We Germans, of all people, should know –'

'Each of us must take a stand against violence, or intolerance, or injustice, or tyranny,' said Mr Blue in the way of someone who was used to having the last word.

'And each of us,' added Miss Yellow conclusively, 'must do it in his or her own way.'

We shared a picnic lunch among the ancient stones, rounding the whole thing off with some chanting in German and the ritual ingestion of certain mushrooms about which I had doubts. An hour later they set me down finally with warm good wishes for the future (if these related more to the fate of the planet than to me personally I forgave my fellow travellers easily), and roared into the evening. That was how I found myself stumbling towards Glastonbury on a lonely road in the final period of the day. There was a fine drizzle, very penetrating, in the sultry air now, and, in the distance beyond the rape fields, the first lights flickered in the town and came on. I sighted a woman up ahead. Up ahead a woman walked in the same direction as me in a wedding dress. There could be no doubt about the dress. The way it conformed so particularly to my memory or recollection of a recent dream was scant comfort. Only the back of the dress was visible – there was no sense at that time of blood, of baby's blood. With mounting dread I quickened my pace in order to close the gap between us. I say dread. In fact, there was relief too in my haste, this latter sensation fed by a compelling awareness of what was at stake. It was *happening*. I had never been more certain of anything in my life. When I caught up with the young bride she told me she had waited all day in vain at the altar for her childhood sweetheart to tie the knot. No extra context was provided here, and I didn't ask for any. Truth is I was feeling decidedly queer by then, and I believe the jilted bride sensed something of my hallucinatory discomfort. She lived in a caravan on the outskirts of town. She was pregnant, she told me, but I saw no blood on her dress.

At the edge of a dense knot of wagons bordering the site of a travelling fun fair was the place she called home. After she removed my damp clothes, starting with my shoes and then working her way down from the top, she peeled off her wedding dress and hung it up carefully on the door of a cupboard. She asked me to make love to her, and when I hesitated, looking down, she lifted my chin up and made love to me as best she could, standing in front of me in a tiny space with the lights of the big wheel coming and going on her skin. When I asked if it mattered that she was pregnant she only smiled – I took that to mean it didn't matter. In her eyes I saw the laughter and cruelty of the travelling show at midnight. Call it the fun of the fair. At a certain point I watched her pupils dilate massively as if to capture the most marginal wavelengths of light, or to broadcast the subtlest expressions of feeling, or to mark the passage – a version of it at least – from this world to the next. After it was over she made tea using the special leaves she had picked in the church graveyard, and we sat facing each other wrapped in blankets (for an awkward instant I experienced these as the pelts of rough beasts) at the fixed table that took up much of the living area in her capsule on wheels.

'Where's your man?' I asked her urgently. 'Where's he gone?'

'I don't know,' she told me. 'I haven't looked there yet.'

'Looked where?' I said. 'Into the tea leaves, you mean?'

'Right now he's just missing,' she said. 'Same as your Ma –'

'Ah,' I said. 'So you know about my mother?'

'Not really,' she said. 'I have an inkling, that's all.'

'What do you see?' I said. This was it. This was it. *Shall we call it our special quality?* They came back to me then as if it was yesterday – the knowing words of Madame Georges. These words she uttered as poor Lafcadio lay dying. *Some people see further than others, don't they?* Oh, they do, Madame Georges – they most certainly do. 'Do you see something?' I asked the seer bride. 'Do you see anything at all?'

'I see fire,' she said.

'So do I,' I told her. 'I see fire all the time.'

'I know,' she said.

'What else do you see?' I asked.

'I see a harbour,' she said, 'with a chapel rising above it. And two boats putting out to sea.'

Then she told me of the huer's pageant, a Cornish celebration of an old fishing tradition that was strictly within the scope of my searches. She saw the boats put out with seine nets trailing behind while, on the sands, the townsfolk linked arms in ranks to sing the song of plenty and, from the cliff top, the huers, their eyes on the pilchard shoals darting densely below, directed the boats this way and that with their practised horns and their cries of *heev'a, heev'a.*

She said she saw all this when she looked into my eyes as we made love just now. She said she would see more if we did it again. She said she could tell me where I was going if I really wanted to know. That was all very well, I told her, but how could I trust the quality and accuracy of her insights and intelligences?

'Ask me a question,' she said. 'Ask me any question you like.'

'What do I like most?' I said. 'What do I like more than life?'

'You like horses,' she said. 'Wild horses on a moonlit beach —'

'That's amazing. You really know your stuff, don't you?' Now it was my turn. There was something I had to tell her. It was about my dream. It was only fair to tell her what I had seen there. 'In my dream,' I said, 'you had blood all over your white dress. You said it was your baby's blood —'

'Did I say that?' she said. 'I don't think it could have been my baby. Much more likely to be the baby of someone you know. It's bad news, I'm afraid. Do you know someone who's pregnant?'

'No,' I said. Even as I denied the possibility I saw the truth of it. Of course I knew someone who was pregnant. I knew Véronique Lamartine. And yet it wasn't the face of my French friend above a bloody wedding dress that confronted me in a steamed-up caravan on the edge of Glastonbury. It was as per my dream. It was Becky's face I saw. 'No, I don't believe I do,' I confirmed blindly.

'In that case you're free to go,' said the seer bride. 'Unless you want to start all over again.'

'It would be good to know where I'm going,' I said with a view to taking up this latest offer. 'Can you at least help me with that?'

The tea had gone cold. The acute anxiety I had experienced on either side of dusk had returned, manifesting itself in a physical form as waves of nausea. It took all my strength to pull on my wet clothes. Outside, the big wheel's lights had faded. At the fair there was no more fun to be had. As I lurched across the glistening rape fields the evening star was my guide. Where to, Billy, where to? So said the grasses and the soft night air. To the west, I said, the west. To the sea, son, they whispered, the sea. When I reached the ditch at the edge of my field I fell into it and slept like a dead man.

I wasn't sure how much of my recent experience was real and how much was illusory. I had been feeling out of sorts – there was no denying it. What I clung to was a simple idea of myself. I existed, despite numerous psychotropic attempts to undermine this view. I was set on doing the right thing only, and this basic impulse would see me through. When the new morning spilled over the rape fields I was sitting on my knapsack beside the main road awaiting my last ride. There it was, rounding a nearby corner – I saw the sun flash on a windscreen as if to issue a final warning. Quickly I did what I had to do. I swallowed the tiny pill my German friends had pressed on me yesterday as a parting gift, assuring me it would stand me in good stead. It was a calculated risk I took here. It was all bound up with the code of the road – the code I wouldn't betray. Had I not promised myself I would go with the flow? To turn back now was as difficult as to go on. Bingo – it was all settled. I got up unsteadily and stuck my thumb out with as much confidence as I could find. This was on the last day of my quest. There was little time left now, and still I didn't know everything. True, I knew where I was going at last. Less welcome was the inkling I had finally of why Becky had travelled there with T-L. This insight or intuition I simply added to my store of trepidation as the car, a sporty red number driven by a rugby type, pulled in with a squeal of tyres. It was an exemplary lift, this one. It sped me all the way to St Ives – yes, the end of the line. At the same time the little pill was cruising importunately around my bloodstream, morning mayhem on its active mind.

The yacht is berthed, as and when, at Port Vauban, largest marina in all Europe and adoptive home of some of the nicest people you could meet. Every day, weather permitting (and it usually permits), we take a tour of the bay, admiring Antibes from the sparkling sea. There is something magical about viewing the land from out there. Ron says it appeals to the most primitive instinct in us – something to do with crawling out of the swamp. Trust Ronnie! He's so down to earth, Billy. I'm sure you'd get on with him were you ever to find yourself in our neck of the woods. For now let me close (running out of space, darling) in time-honoured fashion. Wish you were here!!!

CHAPTER TWENTY-FIVE
The Huer's Pageant

IT WAS TRUE THE LIGHT WAS SPECIAL. I NOTICED that right away. At the same time it occurred to me this perception might be down to how I felt inside. My action plan was rudimentary. The only way forward now was to comb the higgledy-piggledy streets of the town for Jacobson's van. It was a measure of my disorientation that such a basic aspiration should represent so challenging a prospect. In the car I had been struck dumb by a catastrophic claustrophobia. It was all I could do not to open the door and hurl myself out at sixty miles per hour. The solution was to feign fatigue in order to shut my eyes to everything outside my head. Quickly the solution itself became a form of mental torture – the inside of my head had been designated a nightmarish laboratory for sensory experiment, stuffed now with visions of angels, now with alarms of struggle and strife. My driver seemed to know nothing of my situation. Some people have the gift of sailing through life without stopping to ask why we are here.

On arrival I took myself immediately to the sea. There had to be air around me, as much of it as could be found. And no people – this was a principal precondition, a non-negotiable requirement, of my appalling paranoia. The tide was out – out, but on the turn. As I looked back from Smeaton's pier across the exposed sands of the harbour I saw an artist's sky mutinous with clouds. Above the town

268

the hill was coloured every conceivable shade of green. From here a ladder of pink terraces zigzagged down to the shops on the front. On the harbour ramp sat the lifeboat. Below the ramp the working boats were beached, leaning over, on the sand, with dark beards of seaweed trailing from their anchor ropes. Two items in particular I searched for. In spite of all it was vital to focus on the task in hand. There was Jacobson's van, of course. Nothing could offer me a less controvertible assurance I had come to the right place to find T-L and Becky. There was also the chapel above the harbour – just last night it had featured in a seer's inkling. It was uncanny I should hit both targets with a single sweep of the dazzling scene. Such acuity I could only attribute to the visionary material in my bloodstream, or the existence of God. Then a cloud passed in front of the sun – in a changed atmosphere I became aware of two affecting things. First, there was no one to be seen. There was no one visible anywhere in the town. The second thing was the singing. Had it just started? Or had it always been there, rising and swelling across the generations? The harbour was deserted because the townspeople were gathered elsewhere. I knew where they were, and I understood why they had congregated there. They were massing in ranks on a beach beyond the chapel, arms linked, and singing their song of plenty.

The stone chapel of St Nicholas has stood for many years on a low promontory that separates Porthmeor and Porthgwidden beaches in St Ives. As I scrambled up the headland's scree it seemed to me the tiny chapel must play its part. Why else would the seer specify it so particularly? There was an inscription, which I didn't stop to read, set into the wall of the structure on the harbour side. The door was open – that was a key signifier for me, harried as I was by portents and symbols. The singing was much louder here. They were down there on the beach – I could hear them but I couldn't yet see them. The chapel door, already wide open, opened further suddenly as if to draw me inside. In I dived – into the interior's reverent gloom. It was vital I go in there – that's all I knew. There was one more test I had to fail. There was one more chance to be cursed forever. Again I reached for my groin, expecting my trousers to be wet. I couldn't bear to look down there. Bodily functions – were these still mine to control? Of course they were. It was all in my head. It's all in your head, Billy Morton. There were two men in the chapel. Two men sat with their backs to me in the front pew below the altar. In a way it was what I had expected. I even went as far as to imagine the two men spoke, voices raised above a stage whisper, in bastard French. In fact I couldn't hear them at all – the singing of the beach choir was too loud now. Although it would be wrong to say I recognised the two men categorically as Lafcadio's brothers, nevertheless there was a powerful suggestion of that in my interpretation of the scene. It was dark inside the chapel, and they had their backs to me. How could I be sure without asking them to turn around? I couldn't, and I didn't. It was my last error. There was no other trial I might flunk – not today, not tomorrow. Then I heard the horn, the huer's horn. Now there were two horns – two, or perhaps three. They were right outside the chapel, on the ocean side, and twenty times more lyrical than they had a right to be. After the poetic horns came the emotive cry of *heev'a, heev'a*. I decided I had no further business in the chapel of St Nicholas. From the beach below came the townsfolk's roar.

What happened next became the subject locally of idle gossip and lurid newspaper reporting. I threw off my knapsack – that was the first thing. Behind me the huers sounded their horns. Below me the two boats waited on wooden stilts for the incoming tide to raise them up and cast them off. At this point the two sacrificial victims, their ceremonial fish heads glinting in the sun, were being roped to the masts, one in each boat. Stop! Stop! I shouted in vain – no one heard me above the strong singing. As I slid down the bluff towards the sand the townsfolk parted just for me. Yes, for me – it was as if they had been expecting me, and now, in line with proud tradition, their pageant could begin in earnest. The grinning faces I ignored. There was no doubt in my mind as to who stood bound at the masts of the two packed boats that rose up, oars hanging down, from the stocks. Now I was running towards the surf. As I kicked off my shoes I heard from behind the gorgeous cries of *heev'a, heev'a*. Was the sea cold or warm? I couldn't feel the sea – I had no sensation from it. I seized an oar – it was thrust at me in a gesture of welcome. All the hands reached down and drew me in. They set me on the half-deck dripping. They wanted me to do it. They wanted me to say it.

This sacrifice I make freely so that our nets may be full –

They didn't try to stop me. If anything they fell away from the mast as I approached it. At last the ceremonial fish head rose over me. I had only to reach up and rip it off in order to finish this thing finally. Come out, please, Becky! Come out, now, T-L! These pleas had the note of a sob. As the ceremonial fish head parted company with the sacrificial torso I saw the startled face of a perfect stranger at the mast. How else could it be? Oh, Becky. Oh, my. I heard the horns blow – one, two, three. I saw the flash of light from the shore. The end – it had begun. There was a man on fire at the crest of the bluff behind the crowded beach. The burning man was outside the tiny chapel of St Nicholas. Although the sun was shining you could tell the man was on fire by the way he lurched, copying a star, with legs spread out and arms flung wide to catch a cooling breeze. Oh, T-L. Oh, lordy. I saw the burning man slide towards the sand and fall down. A deep silence attended his arrival there. Now he was on his feet again. He made no sound as such – there was only the roar of his flames in the polished light. No one offered him assistance on the beach. It was true – he was in a place all his own now. Better to finish it off, T-L. He could have rolled towards the surf in order to douse the flames. He elected not to do that. I'm coming, T-L, I'm coming. The last thing I saw before I fell into the sea was a special sight. My old friend was taking his final steps towards me. He was waving at me lavishly. Either that or he was waving in general as a warning to passing shipping. He pitched forward finally at the edge of the water. The last thing I heard as I went under was the hiss of the sea as it met his scorched skin. Down and down I went, then up and up again. I admit it – I'm not much of a swimmer at the best of times. Strong arms pulled me up. Strong arms pulled me in. Then it came to me – if I had wet myself it no longer mattered. Salt water ran from my mouth across the thwart of the gig.

One further observation – a surprising idea came to me while I was beneath the surface of the Irish Sea, or the Atlantic Ocean, in those parts. It must have been as I slipped in and out of something akin to unconsciousness on the cusp of something like drowning. In sum I had the conviction I was about to be saved by an American tourist, a strong swimmer no doubt, vacationing here in Cornwall. The twist was this – my rescuer was already, to some extent, known to me. Just yesterday I had glimpsed his anxious face at the window of a Pan Am jet coming in to land at Heathrow. And this made me think all our lives were somehow connected, those noble with those ignoble, the humble with the exalted, or yours with mine. (When I came to with my cheek pressed against the timber of the boat I was unable to confirm this happy proposition.)

There was more. There had to be. It was about my scorched friend. Although I had come to think of T-L as something less than a pal, or a mate, I continued to hold him dear. I do believe he was reaching out to me at the end. At the same time he was working to remove himself from the fraught picture. He was doing it for me – that was my belief. As recently as half an hour ago I had betrayed him in the fateful chapel of St Nicholas. My cowardly silence there did for T-L utterly. I could have intervened to stop the fire before it visited him, before it came to him at the hand of destiny, or, rather, of two avenging brothers of Arabic heritage provisioned with petrol (local opinion, in the absence of witnesses, and without evidence of foul play, viewed T-L's demise as an extravagant cry for help issued by an attention-seeking drug abuser from London).

From the heights the sirens summoned us. Ambulance sirens called us in off the sea. Goodbye, old buddy. Perhaps it's better this way, T-L. It would have been tough to carry on as before. Now we won't have to. As for the questions I never wanted you to answer – the truth probably resides in the facts as I have come to view them. Did I see you *actively* conspire in the squalid death in Paris of poor Lafcadio? I don't believe I did. Did you set his corpse alight after I deserted it in a French graveyard? I must reluctantly conclude you did that. Oh, Lafcadio – if I could turn the clock back I would. So let fire beget fire. This much is equitable and just, T-L. That is why you burned so brightly today. As for me – it seems my damnation, once provisional, is assured. Bring it on, I say. Why call for further candidates when an ideally qualified frontrunner exists for the job?

Marshall T. Marshall

What you don't know can't hurt you, right? So why don't I spill any leftover beans now, Billy, and spoil your day? Only joking – in fact, I come to praise Morton, not to bury him. But let's not dwell on the unfortunate events of Paris here. There's nothing I can usefully add to what you've concluded already. No, I will just say this. Lafcadio was architect of his own downfall. As for the business of the fire in Montparnasse cemetery – I admit it was a costly mistake. Actually, we don't have a great deal of time. They don't cut you much slack here. This is just a note to say I had no idea you were lurking in the doorway of the chapel of St Nicholas. At that time I was probably hunkered down at the altar counting Becky's banknotes into this or that unforgiving hand. I can see the episode weighs heavily on your mind. Don't you think I would have piped up had I seen you? You don't think I would try to save my bacon given half a chance, rather than take what was coming to me? But thanks anyway, Billy. It's so like you to give a rotter like me the benefit of the doubt. Remember this cad loved you from the start. You were hardly perfect yourself. Didn't I have to introduce you to Baudelaire and a few others once upon a time? Incidentally, if you were there in the chapel doorway, why on earth didn't you take it upon *yourself* do something about, or say something to, Lafcadio's darling brothers? I couldn't see you. You couldn't see me. You didn't recognise them, let's imagine. It's a right old mix-up, isn't it? And now I see too much, of course. If it is any consolation, I would have done exactly as you did, or rather didn't do, in the chapel of St Nicholas. The key point is *I don't blame you*. Your brain was a bit scrambled, was it not? Call it madness. Or weakness. Not quite you, Billy, when all is said and done, as it will be shortly. Must dash. Speak soon. Miss you already, kiddo. Don't be a stranger and all that. Ouch – skin still hot to the touch.

CHAPTER TWENTY-SIX
Practically Homer

THEY KEPT ME UNDER OBSERVATION FOR forty-eight hours, until
my lungs had dried out, in a small ward in a hushed sanatorium on
a hill overlooking the sea. To be prescribed a restorative dose of the
ocean hour after hour like that was a true tonic. It was impossible to
tire by day of charting the shifting relationship, in terms of colour,
light and story, between the water and the sky above. With a clear
sky came the bluest sea – you could have dived in, swimmer or not,
and delighted in the medium's dazzling conversation, all aphorisms
and epigrams with here and there an allusion to death or desire. A
grey heaven, on the other hand, meant green water of the kind you
knew not to trust. Searching for an ocean to drown in after the wax
has melted on your hubristic wings? This one is for you. Central to
these pretentious musings was the struggle, still unresolved, between
the verbal cheetahs and visual gazelles at large on the Serengeti of
my imagination. Was I scribbler or snapper? By the first midnight I
was a war poet composing anthems for doomed youth. By lunch on
the second day I was practically Homer. Then it hit me in a hard
but quiet way, as when an oil tanker strikes a dinghy in the middle
of the English Channel at dead of night – I wasn't a writer at all. By
which I meant I had no calling. It wasn't me. That was what they
all thought, wasn't it? In my heart I agreed with them. When Percy

encouraged me to be a writer he was testing me. He didn't want me to forego that chance. If I could be really good at just one thing it would save me. It was enough. It was everything. Mr Greene saw all that in a Mayfair club. Best to leave any scribbling to Becky.

She visited me on the second afternoon, bringing chocolates unsuited to the warmth of the hour. She also had my shoes and my knapsack – these she had salvaged from the cop shop in St Ives. My recent history, I understood, was all over the papers, as was T-L's. Much was made in this coverage of the actions of a lifeguard from Ohio whose selfless intervention had prevented tragedy (drowning of William Morton) from following tragedy (suicide by immolation of Marshall Marshall). Of Becky there was no mention, which was rather odd. When she gave me her version of events I didn't quite believe it, and this was, to put it mildly, unsettling. How to explain that here? For me, one of the enduring constants has been that you might trust Rebecca Jacobson with your life.

'We were on the beach with all the others,' she said, meaning T-L and her. This was after she had opened the melting chocolates, emptied my knapsack of dirty socks and underwear, and stuffed my sad shoes with hospital toilet paper in a bid to rescue them from the effects of salt water.

'You didn't hear me shout?' I asked her.

'Nope,' she said. 'What were you shouting?'

'I don't actually remember,' I said, revisiting in a light-soaked flashback the hallucinatory anguish and horror of those influential moments above the beach.

'There was a serious amount of singing,' Becky said.

'You didn't see me?' I said.

'Not immediately,' she said. 'When I did see you, on the boat, it was as if all the people were deliberately holding me back.'

'Why would they do that?' I asked.

'I don't know,' she said. 'To protect me from T-L, I suppose.'

'What happened to him?' I said, meaning how could he have been safely on the beach one minute and burning up the next. Now we were getting down to brass tacks. Now we were cooking. For the best part of two days I had had to live with the desperate idea that T-L was inside the chapel of St Nicholas when I entered it. Could it really be possible he languished just in front of me, with Lafcadio's vengeful brothers for company, and only a creaking door between us? Oh, T-L – were you aware I was just feet away in the shadow of that deceitful partition? Still you said nothing. You always knew how to hog such limelight as was going. 'One minute he was on the beach with you,' I reminded Becky, 'the next he was on fire.'

'He told me he had to see a man about a dog,' she said. 'The day before he had been on edge – I mean more on edge than usual. After we got here he slipped away twice. He asked me for money. He asked how much cash I could get in one go. Of course, he never wanted me to be here in the first place. But I had to come –'

'Why was that?' I asked as innocently as I could. All the while I saw I had a perfect opportunity to test my theory that Becky was carrying T-L's child. Still I held back. I saw the blood on the bridal dress. I heard the seer sum up. *It's bad news, I'm afraid.* I couldn't do it. I couldn't bring myself to put my theory to the test. I couldn't see what good it would do, given all the blood. 'Why come?' I said.

'I don't know,' Becky said in a way that failed to convince. 'I was concerned about T-L.'

'What happened to him? I repeated, holding to my text. 'You said he had to see a man about a dog –'

'Once the singing got going he left me on the beach. The next time I saw him he was already on fire. All the people held me back.

Was it an act of kindness, Billy? I couldn't tell. When I called out to you on the boat you didn't hear me.'

I didn't believe her. I didn't believe Becky's version of events. It was as if she had made it all up from what she had heard or read in the last thirty-six hours. Why lie to me? Why lie to the rest of the world? Truth or lie, there was one more question I had to ask. On it rested any hopes I still harboured of laying the ghosts of Paris.

'Did you tell the police what T-L said? I mean about seeing a man about a dog?'

'I haven't told anyone. I wasn't sure what good it would do.'

'Did you tell them you knew me?'

'Of course I did. How do you think I got hold of your things?'

We had been talking very quietly in our sun-splashed confine. We had practically been whispering in deference to the few others in the ward. There was a local silence now, a guilty silence. Where did it leave us, Becky and Billy? It was a funny thing, sad but true. In our silence was a tacit understanding. When T-L said he had to see a man about a dog he meant he was about to set himself on fire in order to depart this life. That was how I left it between us, Becky and I, on the understanding it was better this way. I don't accept I actively encouraged a deception. This was a white lie I entered into because I didn't know what else to do. And perhaps I was right for once in my lousy existence. Perhaps it really was better this way.

The remainder of our talk had to do mostly with the practical consequences of T-L's death. For instance, there was the matter of his next of kin to consider. It was all in hand, Becky assured me. I didn't know what she meant by that. They know where to find us, she added in a cryptic reference, presumably, to her new friends at the local police station. It was all about tying up loose ends now. It was about moving on with our lives. We both saw that.

'How did they discover his name was Marshall?' I asked idly, although no thought could really be said to be *idle* at that time.

'He had his passport on him,' Becky said. 'In case he needed to leave the country, one imagines.'

'That's incredible,' I said. It was a slip-up, wasn't it? It was the only stumble in her story. Why would a suicide be planning to use his passport to quit this place for that? (No poor taste jokes, if you please, T-L, about gaining access to a better world.) No, I thought I knew what it meant. It meant Becky was deliberately provoking me by saying she understood very well that T-L's death was no suicide. His death was about something else, she was saying – something I didn't care to share. After all, she knew about suicide, didn't she? It was in her family outlook, some would have said. 'What else did he have on him when he died?' I asked finally.

'Just these,' Becky said, rummaging briefly before holding up the keys to Jacobson's van.

I didn't sleep that night, my last in Cornwall. Instead I asked God in my awkward way to take T-L in, with or without his charred passport and a yellow fever jab. What got to me in the small hours was the thought of T-L beyond the chapel door. The idea that he failed to ask for help in that position was shocking. It rendered me worthless. And this would be the final verdict on me of my friend. I wasn't worth asking for help. Trust T-L to have the last word. As for Becky – she bore the scars of all this. She was paying for our errors. If she had lied to me earlier she must have had her reasons. Hadn't I lied to, or at least withheld the truth from, her in my time? That night I vowed to tell Rebecca Jacobson everything. One day soon I would tell her the whole damn thing – as in Paris, Lafcadio, and Lafcadio's brothers too. I owed it to her and to myself. Most of all, I told myself at around first light, I owed it to her unborn child.

I wasn't on the beach. That's the first thing to say. When I gave you my version of events I could see you didn't believe me. I don't want to lie to you. I never intended to tell fibs. The truth is I was having an abortion about half an hour from the shore when T-L died. You could probably write a poem about the concatenation of these two events from the point of view of the father and the unborn child. I won't do that. I'll stick to my novel, which is really *your* novel. Yes, I only discovered what had happened on the beach when I read it in a newspaper. Then I found out a bit more from the local police. T-L's passport photograph was a shock – he looked like someone's kid brother. It strikes me as crazy that a suicide would be carrying his passport. It's one more reason why I don't believe T-L planned to take his own life. I don't believe he intended to kill himself on a Cornish beach any more than my father planned to kill himself on Hampstead Heath. Someone else killed T-L, didn't they? Of course, I didn't tell him I was pregnant by him – that wouldn't have been helpful. Had I known he was going to die I might just have kept the baby. See – something cold and dark inside me that only we know. And you would have made the perfect substitute father, Billy. You would have done the job manfully. One day you'll tell me it all, and I will finish writing this story and *fix it for you* because you deserve it. If you haven't quite learned to love the world, you surely will. If you haven't yet found a way to live with yourself, you will. And one day you'll thank me. This summer, which is really two summers – one good, one bad – is our prime season, isn't it? I do so want to write it truthfully, Billy. I do so want it to be true – if not to life, then to us.

CHAPTER TWENTY-SEVEN
A Measure of the Day

WE DROVE BACK TO LONDON MOSTLY IN SILENCE and without benefit of scenic detours. Becky is, as I have allowed, a fine driver. I think it pleased her to take the wheel at this time in order to deliver our shared project – the project of our return to life – as soundly as possible. Any lingering suspicion that existed between us was most obviously at work in our reluctance to cite the past, the present and the future, despite the intrusive currency of all three estates.

As Cornwall's gaping mouth spat us out I told myself I had a set amount of time to put my house in order. With Glastonbury, or the idea of it, receding at last I made an unscheduled concession to wonder. I refer here to my acceptance, after three sceptical days, of the seer's inkling, of the *fact* of it. When I tried to make sense of this episode I couldn't. It was inexplicable – no, unexplained. I put it in the same category as Jacobson's suicide. If there could be beautiful mysteries in life – including Véronique's photograph of me beside a fountain in Paris – no doubt there could be enigmas less pretty or less happy. It was only fair to take the long view here. Some things were known while others weren't. One day, perhaps, the unknown would reveal its hand. Meanwhile we sped along nicely as the radio signal came and went. If I fail to speak up on behalf of the English countryside, or the quality of British road signage, forgive me. The fact is I had neither eye for nor interest in these things as we ate up the miles. We wanted to love each other, Becky and I. That is what I would say about our journey home if you asked me to sum it up.

The only other factor was the sense I had, legacy of Cornwall, that T-L had bested me somehow by spurning my assistance in the chapel of St Nicholas mere moments before he went out in a blaze of glory. This feeling was, I saw, likely to embitter me for the rest of time unless I found a way to face it down. As the highway unwound beneath us I sought consolation where I could. There was the idea, for example, that my late friend must have wanted me to track him to Cornwall having taken up all available clues. Otherwise he might just as easily have fled to Scotland. Then I thought perhaps he only wanted me to follow him to the last place on earth in order to reject me at the end. Thinking is no good – it leads mostly to unhappiness in a young man. Finally I came full circle, insisting on the value of my life. T-L was dead, while I was alive. *It wasn't my fault.* Yes, I had made mistakes. Now I was free to live my life faithfully.

With the big city on the horizon I still hadn't broached them – the two subjects or frames of reference most present in the silence between the passenger and his driver. Hadn't I vowed to tell Becky everything? That was last night. Today the view, like the weather, was different. The right time would come, an ideal time, or a better time. I got this instinctively. I wasn't copping out here. I genuinely imagined a better time waited just around the corner for Becky and for me – for all of us – if we could only hold the line until then.

The final consideration was Becky's pregnancy, if such a thing existed outside my head. Once again I failed to grasp the nettle. It was the blood on the wedding dress that gave me pause. As the seer had said, it didn't bode well. What I wanted to do was warn Becky. Regarding what, exactly? In any case it was wrong, surely, to issue a warning so drenched in blood. How could it be useful to someone already with child? For ducking my duty here I accept every ounce of blame. My best excuse is tied in with my confusion over T-L. At the time I couldn't find the right perspective on Becky's pregnancy. What I'm admitting to – no doubt it was unworthy of me. Holding me back from speaking out was an unfamiliar prejudice that asked why Becky would want to have T-L's baby in the first place.

From the radio we had news. Czechoslovakia and the USSR were to hold talks aimed at slowing the pace of reform in Prague in return for a withdrawal of tanks currently on manoeuvres. All of a sudden we were home. Lit up below the red sky the city swallowed us without a murmur. There was the question of where I wanted to be dropped off, if indeed I knew where such a location might lie. It was understood between Becky and I that we would see each other very soon. I didn't say anything. I got out at Percy's place with my knapsack and rang the bell without looking back. There was a light on at the upstairs window. I saw that as a positive sign. I had a key somewhere about me, of course. I just wasn't sure I had the right to use it any more. As I opened the door I kept before me the idea of the Percy I held dear. He didn't want to lecture me, to give me the benefit or otherwise of his years and his experience. He didn't want to tell me what to do, or how to be. Now, finally, it was me that was ready to give. Yes, I was ready for that. But was I already too late?

'Don't forget I still have your painting,' Becky called out from behind me. 'Of the horses –'

'Sure,' I said, raising my hand in the doorway. 'I won't forget.'

Everything was the same and yet nothing was the same. If that sounds corny or trite, I have no plans to apologise. The smells were the same. The piles of unread books were the same. At least Percy's face looked better. His bruises were fading and the few stitches had gone from his cheek. He didn't ask me where I had been. He asked me if I had decided whether I was a writer or a photographer, and I told him I had. Then he fished my old Nikon from a drawer with a flourish like a magician – yes, I mean the same camera stolen by me from under Jacobson's nose and sold to a secondhand dealer in Portobello Road – and pronounced himself mightily pleased I had made up my mind at long last. I didn't ask Percy how he had pulled off that business with the Nikon. He must have rescued the camera right after I first told him about it, feeling sorry for myself the way I did back then – no, loathing myself, or behaving like a big kid or an even bigger fool. Now the whole upshot or outcome made Percy so happy I thought he would cry. For my part, I didn't dare dwell on exactly how much that old camera meant to me – I left all that for later. Then Percy asked me if I was here to stay this time, and I told him I was. It was high summer. We were at that lovely stage of the evening when the lights are on but the sky retains a measure of the day just ended, and in the long, unguarded moment between one world and another I thought I saw how it could be.

LAFCADIO

Tout est pardonné, Billy. Can you hear me? All is forgiven. It's not your fault. *Ce n'est pas de ta faute*. Look – blue sky above and below me, two fish in hand, and you on a bank of the river not far from town. *Bon courage, mon ami*. I will always love you. *Je t'aime jusqu'à la mort* –

<u>1968</u>
Chronology

8 JANUARY: As he visits a new swimming pool at Paris Nanterre University France's Minister for Youth and Sport, François Missoffe, is challenged by Daniel Cohn-Bendit and supporters demanding an end to segregation of male and female student accommodation.

30 JANUARY: Tet Offensive begins, Vietnam; 4,000 communist commandos infiltrate Saigon, attacking multiple targets including the US embassy.

2 FEBRUARY: Paul Simon and Art Garfunkel record Mrs Robinson for 45rpm single and Bookends LP release, Columbia Studios, New York City.

17 MARCH: Tariq Ali and Vanessa Redgrave lead anti-Vietnam War protest march on US embassy, London; mounted police confront demonstrators.

22 MARCH: Daniel Cohn-Bendit and supporters occupy administrative site at Nanterre faculty outside Paris, inaugurating ongoing campus unrest.

4 APRIL: Dr Martin Luther King Jr. is assassinated in Memphis, Tennessee.

27 APRIL: Abortion Act 1967 comes into effect, Great Britain.

1 MAY: *Enderby Outside*, by Anthony Burgess, published by Heinemann.

3 MAY: French Interior Minister Christian Fouchet closes Nanterre campus; protesting students march on central Paris and occupy the Sorbonne.

10/11 MAY: Responding to all-night running battles in the Latin Quarter of Paris, France's acting premier Louis Joxe orders riot police to storm the student barricades; at 5.30am students disperse following an appeal by their principal spokesman and *de facto* leader Daniel Cohn-Bendit.

13 MAY: France's Confédération Générale du Travail calls one-day general strike in support of student actions.

24 MAY: Students attempt to burn down Paris stock exchange building.

30 MAY: Following defiant radio broadcast by President Charles de Gaulle, 500,000 loyal Parisians rally in defence of France's Fifth Republic.

5 JUNE: Senator Robert F. Kennedy is fatally wounded at the Ambassador Hotel, Los Angeles, California.

20 AUGUST: Warsaw Pact troops invade Czechoslovakia to halt the reforms, dubbed 'communism with a human face', of Alexander Dubček.

16 OCTOBER: African-American athletes Tommie Smith and John Carlos give black power salutes after winning Olympic gold and bronze respectively in the men's 200m track event, Mexico City.

7 DECEMBER: Beatles' ninth studio LP, The White Album (double), enters the UK chart at No. 1, occupying the top spot for the next eight weeks.